RAVE REVIEWS FOR PENELOPE NERI!

"Penelope Neri always brings fascinating characters and a lively story to readers. You'll find all that and a colorful backdrop, sensuality and quite a bit of interesting historical detail in this memorable, fast-paced tale."

—*Romantic Times* on *Keeper of My Heart*

"This entertaining, sensual story . . . [will] satisfy readers."

—*Romantic Times* on *Stolen*

"Ms. Neri's romance with Gothic overtones is fast-paced and sprinkled with wonderful characters . . . a really good read."

—*Romantic Times* on *Scandals*

"Neri is a genius at creating characters that readers will love, and for spinning a magical tale that will leave readers longing for more."

—*Writers Write* on *Scandals*

"Penelope Neri proves again that she is a splendid writer of historical romances."

—Phoebe Conn on *Enchanted Bride*

UNDER THE COVER OF NIGHT

Madeleine gasped, her eyes wide with terror as the last shreds of sleep were torn away like rotted curtains.

A powerful man loomed over her, broad shoulders framed by the ruddy flames that licked at the logs on the hearth. His arms were wrapped around her, holding her helpless, unable to move. Unable to flee.

She drew a shuddering sob and tore one arm free of his embrace.

"No, milord de Harcourt!" she hissed, still tangled in the dream, convinced that it was Giles who held her, not Justin. "You shall not do this! Let me go, for I am promised to another!"

"Madeleine?" Justin said. Then again, more sharply, shaking her very gently, "Madeleine! What is it, *cherie?* Wake up! You are still dreaming."

Moonshadow

PENELOPE NERI

LOVE SPELL ✦ NEW YORK CITY

For P. Jane Kacher,
A special lady and a dear friend,
With love and thanks.

A LOVE SPELL BOOK®

May 2001

Published by

Dorchester Publishing Co., Inc.
276 Fifth Avenue
New York, NY 10001

ISBN 0-505-52416-3

The name "Love Spell" and its logo are trademarks of Dorchester Publishing Co., Inc.

Printed in the United States of America.

Visit us on the web at www.dorchesterpub.com.

Moonshadow

"There she sees a damsel bright,
Drest in a silken robe of white,
That shadowy in the moonlight shone:
The neck that made that white robe wan,
Her stately neck, and arms were bare;
Her blue-veined feet unsandl'd were,
And wildly glittered here and there
The gems entangled in her hair."

–"Christabel"
by Samuel Taylor Coleridge

Prologue

To her surprise, the gate that opened into the priory gardens swung wide before she touched the top rung, shedding rusty flakes as it skimmed silently over the grass.

As she stepped through the narrow opening, into the priory's once-hallowed grounds, the thought crossed her mind that one of the gardeners had oiled the groaning hinges. A chill wind and a handful of autumn leaves followed her inside the tangled gardens.

Above her, in the indigo sky, a gibbous moon scudded, high and free. 'Twas a full Halloween moon. A moon for goblins and phantoms. The light it shed rimmed everything with silver. Frost sparkled on blades of coarse grass, forming a crust of rime beneath her bare feet, which were turning blue with cold, she realized. She shiv-

11

ered. What had she been thinking of, to come out here, barefooted? She should have donned shoes and shawl before venturing outside.

By moonlight, the priory's grounds seemed sinister, very different from how they looked by day. Being here at this hour was like stepping back into the past, she thought with a shudder. She could hear nothing, not the hoot of an owl, nor the yip or snuffle of a fox, a badger, or any other creature. Even the night seemed to be holding its breath. Perhaps the Hall *was* waiting for someone, as Justin had once said, in a rare fanciful turn of mind, though for whom it waited, she did not know—and would rather not find out.

Caught up in the eerie spell of moonlight and mystery, Madeleine was breathing shallowly as she made her way down the path of worn flagstones. Each step carried her ever closer to the flicker of light she had seen from her casement window. And, God willing, closer to Justin.

Her long hair drifted on the night wind like the curling mist that rose from the ground as she glided over the frosty grass. Her eyes ached, heavy with exhaustion. The dark smudges beneath them were the result of sleepless nights and uneasy dreams, vividly remembered come the morning. Was she really awake now, she wondered, her nightgown billowing behind her like diaphanous fairy wings? Or still asleep, and dreaming?

The flagstones were uneven, worn down beneath the feet of ages. In the eleventh century, devout Norman knights and pious nuns had trod this same path to take matins and vespers in St. Mary's Lady Chapel. She had seen them in her dreams. Had heard the sweet melancholy of their plainchant in her sleep, as well as the plangent tolling of the bell that divided the nuns' days. She shivered. In truth, since coming to Steyning Hall, the eleventh century had grown more real to her than her own!

In 1067, thick yew hedges had lined the path she trod, forming a gloomy allée, or tunnel. The deep shadows they cast had hid Lord Giles de Harcourt, the brutal Norman knight who was obsessed by the beauty of the Saxon maid, Lenore. Giles had caused Lenore's betrothed to vanish without a trace, like some ghoulish magician, conveniently freeing her to marry him. Lenore had gone to her grave, Madeleine believed, never knowing what befell her beloved Eydmond.

"Come, Madeleine . . . leine!"

The voice calling her name was high, clear and oddly sexless, like the neutral chimes of a glass bell. It scattered her thoughts like beads from a broken rosary.

She halted, violet eyes wide, a metallic taste on her tongue. Her imagination, she wondered? Or Eydmund's voice, echoing down through the ages, warning her that her life—and with it, her unborn babe's—was in jeopardy, as his had once been?

Impossible, logic insisted.

Yet her heart slammed painfully against her ribs in response. Placing a protective hand on her hard belly, she slowly turned around.

"Who's there?" Her voice cracked as she called out in the frigid hush. "Justin? Is that you? Where are you?"

"you . . . you!"

Laughter prickled the fine hairs on Madeleine's neck, one by one.

"Justin? Say something! Is that you?" She ran toward the ruined cloisters, her wrapper floating out behind her.

But although she searched the crumbling nave with its rose-mullioned window, the cloisters, the stone rubble—all that was left of St. Mary's Priory and its church now—she could not find the owner of that bell–like voice.

Because there is no one to find! she scolded herself. *The voice—like the face in the mirror— is only in your mind! If you believe otherwise, you are surely mad! What other explanation is there, unless one believes in . . .*

. . . ghosts?

Perhaps she really was losing her mind? She must be. Sane women did not hear voices. Sane women did not imagine a baby's cries, or reflections, or anything else.

Was she a victim of some ancient curse, she wondered? Destined—like the lady Lenore all those centuries ago—to become the bride of shadows, just as she ha—

"Chérie."

Her heart leaped with joy in her chest. The child stirred, a flutter of wings in her belly.

"Justin! Oh, thank God!" She whirled about, relieved and concerned at one and the same time as she saw him.

He was leaning against a pile of crumbling stone blocks. The tricorn he wore and the lantern he held aloft cast his features in heavy shadow. The folds of his cape flapped about him in the night wind. *Like ugly dark wings*, she thought with a shudder of foreboding. A bat's leathery wings . . .

"What's wrong? What is it?"

She frowned. Justin's voice sounded hoarse and strained. It sounded . . . *wrong*.

She took another uncertain step closer, frowning as she tried to make out his features. "Justin? Is that really you?"

"Of course, *chérie*."

"Could you . . . could you come a little closer?

15

Penelope Neri

I need your strong arm to . . . to lean on. To help
me get back to the house."

Go to him, like a lamb to the slaughter, when
all her senses screamed at her to run?

Never!

Chapter One

The mud-splattered carriage, drawn by a flagging team, rumbled to a halt before towering wrought-iron gates.

Justin, Lord de Harcourt, twelfth earl of Steyning, instructed the coachman to halt before driving on, up the sweeping driveway, to their final destination.

"Hold them here for a moment, Tom. Madeleine? Wake up, my dear. We are here," Lord Justin murmured as the coachman clambered down to open the gates. "Madeleine? We've arrived at Steyning Hall."

Steyning Hall. The name of her new home penetrated the fog. She came awake, embarrassed to find her head resting upon her bridegroom's lap. A gaudy sunset filled the carriage window behind him. It made a fiery nimbus about his ebony head and cast his already stern features in shadow and mystery. He looked, she decided with a shiver, like a fallen angel.

"I thought your first glimpse of the Hall should be from the gates," Justin was saying as he looked down at her. His striking features were, she fancied, softened now with affection. "Come along. Sit up."

At their wedding breakfast just that morning, Justin had turned all the women's heads, she recalled, still stunned that this devilishly handsome earl had made her, a commoner, his bride and lady. "My new home!" she said aloud, stroking his cheek. "I still cannot believe we are married!"

"Madeleine," Justin repeated sternly, shaking his head. He tried to sound exasperated, but could not hide his amusement. "Sit up, do!"

Hastily, she sat up and craned her head out of the window.

Her expectant smile congealed on her lips. Try as she might, she could not stifle a gasp of dismay.

At the end of a sweeping gravel driveway, half hidden by ancient woods, stood Steyning Hall, Justin's ancestral manor.

Far from being the charming country estate she had expected, it was a forbidding heap of stone, carved like a threat from the frivolous sky beyond. The dying sun stained its mullioned windows ruby red. *The color of old blood.*

Moonshadow

Madeleine swallowed uneasily. From where had such a chilling comparison come—and on her wedding-day, no less?

"Are you cold, my dear?"

"A little. Yes," she admitted, though chilly was hardly the proper word for the sudden sense of dread she felt. She was icy all over, both hands numb within her cotton gloves. Numb—in June! What on earth was wrong with her?

Justin draped a shawl about her shoulders and took both hands in his. "Tell me honestly. What do you think of the old place?"

His dark gaze searched her lovely, delicate face, plumbing eyes the velvety violet of pansies for his answer. "Is it really so awful?"

Madeleine bit her lip. Should she tell him the truth? That her first glimpse of Steyning filled her with the urge to bolt, and a sudden irrational fear for her future, although she loved him with all her heart? Better not. A little white lie was preferable here. Steyning was, after all, Justin's home, as well as that of his ancestors.

"Awful? Of course not. But it is . . . *imposing* . . . is it not?" she murmured tactfully.

"Very imposing," he agreed. "And not exactly what anyone would call . . . cozy."

She hesitated, then shook her head. "No, I'm afraid it isn't." She placed her gloved hand over his knee. "Still, looks are not important, are

19

they? Steyning Hall is our home. We shall be happy together here. I know it!"

Her words rang false in the silence. Did she sound a little *too* hearty, as if trying to convince herself, she wondered as her eyes met his deep-blue ones.

He laughed, drawing her to him in a fond embrace. "Bless you, Madeleine. The Hall is a wretched old heap! I know it, my father knew it, centuries of de Harcourts before us have known it! Yet your opinions are always kind, your every word carefully chosen and considerate, your outlook always sunny and optimistic! My dear, sweet girl, I know that with you, I shall be happy beyond my wildest dreams."

"You will?" she murmured, embarrassed by his lavish praise, and the ease with which he had seen through her lies.

"Yes. You are like a . . . a radiant light! You shed happiness and sunshine wherever you go, Madeleine. That is what drew me to you from the very first, my love. Your joy of life. Your goodness. Steyning, I'm afraid, is much like its master . . . distant and often melancholy," he warned. "At times, it seems to me as if the old place is . . . Oh, I don't know . . . waiting for someone."

"Waiting?"

He nodded. "Perhaps that someone is you? It could be wishful thinking on my part, but I believe your arrival is going to change Steyning. The shadows will be banished. You'll see. Together, we will make the Hall a happy home. For us, and for our children."

Our children. Oh, how she longed for Justin's child!

When she had chosen to remain a spinster for the rest of her life and keep house for her father, a country physician, her one regret had been that she would never become a mother. Meeting Justin had changed her life in so many wonderful ways! From the very moment she set eyes upon him, her entire life had changed. Neither it, nor she, would ever be the same again.

"Children? Oh, Justin, yes!" she whispered. Her face shone with love, glowed with happiness. *She loved him so much.* What did it matter if Steyning was an ugly heap of stone, or its master prone to brooding silences? If they were happy together, the lowliest hovel would be a castle, his silences no more than happy contemplations of the wonderful days ahead of them. "I love you with all my heart."

"As I love you, my dear." Justin rapped on the wall of the borrowed carriage. "Drive on, Tom!" he instructed his cousin's coachman, adding for her ears alone, "I am most eager to be home."

Tilting her lovely face up to his, he pressed a lingering kiss upon her lips. One that reached deep inside her, spreading the warmth of love through every part.

"Welcome to Steyning Hall, Lady de Harcourt. Welcome to your new home!"

Welcome, lady fair. I have been awaiting thee, another voice whispered in her mind.

Chapter Two

". . . ninety-eight . . . ninety-nine . . . one hundred."

Madeleine ran the silver-backed brush through her fair hair for the last time, then rose from her chair before the dressing table.

She wore an enormous Turkish bath-sheet, wrapped toga-style around her, as she padded about the huge bedchamber.

Trimming a single lamp, so that the room was lit with only a puddle of golden light, she blew out the other lamps. The fire's flickering glow would provide the only additional lighting they would need tonight.

"Perfect!" she murmured. The romantic mood of soft lighting and flickering firelight was charming. Thank God, the interior of Steyning had proven more welcoming than the outside.

Despite its cavernous size, the chamber was almost cozy now. The crackling log fire gave off considerable heat. The heavy velvet draperies, now snugly drawn across all three huge windows, effectively kept out the drafts. It might well be balmy June, but the old house would be chilly without them.

Skirting the inky shadows that lingered in the farthest corners, Madeleine went over to the tester.

Her nightgown lay across it in readiness, along with her matching wrapper. She unfastened the bath sheet and let it fall to her feet.

The nightgown was of a sheer gauzy fabric. Its dainty yoke, trimmed with lace and narrow blue ribbons, fell into diaphanous skirts. Both gown and matching wrapper were a wedding gift from her younger sister, Felicity.

She had presented it to Madeleine just that morning with the smug, knowing look of a happily married woman, soon to deliver her first child.

"Look, Madeleine, darling. Isn't it heavenly? And so deliciously *virginal*. 'Tis a gift for your honeymoon! Promise you'll burn those wretched flannel tents you wear to bed?" her sister had pleaded, before dissolving into giggles. "Your handsome Lord Justin deserves that much! Why, I fancy this bit of gossamer will bring a smile even to *his* face!"

Blushing, Madeleine had promised—and would keep that promise, she thought, slipping the billowing gown on over her head. It was like a gossamer cloud, so very sheer, she still felt naked as she quickly drew the wrapper on after it.

Mrs. Fox, she'd discovered, was a sensible West–country soul. The housekeeper's kindness and brisk efficiency more than made up for Steyning Hall's ugly and unwelcoming appearance.

"Run along with Fox, my dear," Justin had urged her soon after their arrival. "She'll see you to our chamber and make sure that you are comfortably settled in," he promised, giving Madeleine a chaste kiss upon the brow. "There is nothing to worry your pretty head about. If you need anything, just ring for her."

"You're not coming up?" She frowned. He'd seemed preoccupied, a little distant ever since they entered the Hall. She could not help wondering what urgent matter he had discussed with his butler, Digby, in such fierce whispers, while the housekeeper took her bonnet and gloves.

"Not quite yet, I'm afraid," he answered her question. "I . . . er . . . I have some important papers to go over before I join you. After all, I'm a married man now. I have certain obligations," he murmured huskily. "Run along, my dear. I shall be up before you know it."

"Very well. But . . . do try not to be too long,"

she pleaded softly, mindful that the housekeeper and the butler could not help overhearing their intimate exchange.

"I shan't be." Justin's lips brushed her hair. His warm breath fanned her cheek and made her shiver. For her ears alone, he whispered, "After all, it is our wedding night, is it not?"

His husky reminder, the lambent fire in his sapphire eyes, made her tremble in anticipation.

Mrs. Fox immediately led the new mistress of Steyning upstairs to the master's bedchamber, lifting a candlestick aloft to light their way as they climbed the staircase to the second floor gallery. Their giant shadows partnered them to a chamber in the east wing. Here, Mrs. Fox flung open one of a set of double doors and bobbed a curtsey.

"The master's chamber, madam."

"Thank you," she murmured, going inside and looking around her.

It was a very comfortable bedchamber, if somewhat masculine in its furnishings, which were heavily carved and dark, and its hangings, which were predominantly blue in color.

While Madeleine undressed, Fox sent the bevy of maids that had traipsed after them running in all directions. They were dispatched to fetch fresh logs for the fire, and jugs of water, soap and fresh linens, so that her ladyship could wash before retiring for the night.

Another serving girl was briskly dispatched to take her ladyship's wrinkled traveling ensemble away, with instructions to have it thoroughly steamed and brushed before it was hung up.

Fox also instructed Tabitha, the little chambermaid who scuttled in and out like a frightened rabbit, to warm some brandy with milk for Her Ladyship, and bring it up.

"Nothing like brandy and milk for relaxing a body, there isn't, madam," the housekeeper declared.

Madeleine had not realized at first that Fox was referring to her when she spoke of "her ladyship!"

"The girl I sent for your milk is called Tabitha," Mrs. Fox declared. "Or Tabby, if you prefer. Her mother, Mrs. Lee, lives in the village. I'm hoping Tabby will do for you, Your Ladyship, until a proper lady's maid may be engaged?"

"Of course," Madeleine agreed.

"Now, there's some what cannot abide the girl," Fox continued. "But I always say, there's none of us can help what we are born with, can we now? Our Tabitha has clever hands, and is a deal more willing than many I could name. She'll help you with your hair, your wardrobe and such, my lady, until you find someone better."

"I'm sure Tabitha will do very nicely," Madeleine murmured, wondering, though it was none of her business, what on earth could be wrong with the girl? She had not appeared handicapped in any way. Nor did she have the vacant stare of someone who was 'tetched' in the head.

"Now, then, my lady," Fox finished, drawing Madeleine's thoughts back to the moment at hand. "I won't keep you from your bed a moment longer. Be sure t' drink every drop o' that posset, aye? Ye look worn out, you do, poor lamb," Her plump face was concerned.

"I am a little tired, yes. It was such a long way to travel without putting up at an inn for the night. But, we had no choice."

"My poor lady. Of course you didn't, bless you. Ah, well. Sleep will do you a power o' good. Time enough in the morning to be worrying about the servants and other such nonsense."

After turning down the bed, Fox offered Madeleine a hearty welcome to Steyning, and her best wishes for a good night's sleep.

"We'll do right well together, you and me, I'm thinking, my lady."

"I'm sure we shall, Mrs. Fox. Thank you," Madeleine said warmly. "You've been very kind."

"Think nothing of it, my lady. That's what I'm here for, aye? We're right happy to have you at Steyning, me and the others. Miserable old heap of stones, it is—beggin' your pardon, mum!— but we stay because of Lord Justin, and before

28

him, there was the old master, God rest his soul. Now we have you to take care of, too."

Madeleine smiled. "I'm sure my husband appreciates your hard work. I know I do."

Fox nodded. "I've been saying, what this gloomy old place needs is a new mistress, and some babies toddling about, bless their little hearts. 'Twould seem his lordship felt the same." The woman smiled knowingly.

"The master's found himself a lovely bride in you, my lady, and no mistake! The rest will come, I'm thinking. All in good time, aye?"

"All in good time. Yes." Madeleine's cheeks grew pink as Mrs. Fox stared long and hard—and, or so she fancied—*hopefully*—at her flat belly, before leaving her alone.

Refreshed by a leisurely toilette, her glowing skin dusted with fragrant lilies-of-the-valley *poudre-de toilette*, she carried the small tray that held the warm milk posset, laced liberally with brandy, to an upholstered wing chair by the fire.

Legs curled under her, she sat there, gazing into the fire, lost in dreamy thought as she sipped it.

It was Tabitha who had unpacked her bags and carefully set out her silver brush, her hand mirror, her hairpin and powder bowls while she was still downstairs.

What few gowns she owned now hung neatly in the tiny dressing room that adjoined the bedchamber, while her undergarments and other personal possessions had been stowed in the drawers of the dresser and armoire.

Madeleine yawned sleepily and arched her back to rid it of kinks. The warm milk and brandy had drawn most of the stiffness from her body. She felt relaxed and deliciously lazy as she replaced the empty glass on the tray.

Looking down at the enormous bed, she realized she was most eager for Justin to join her there. Was desire a side effect of the brandy, she wondered with a sigh, or was love the only aphrodisiac she needed? Whatever the cause, her heart raced with excitement. She imagined the night to come, as she had imagined it every night since Justin had proposed to her.

She had known him only six weeks. Six weeks of her one-and-twenty years of life! Yet every time she looked at him, it was like the first time she'd seen him all over again—as if she'd been caught in the blast of a roaring furnace, and a gust of heat had stolen her breath away. She could not help staring at him now, sometimes, as she had stared at him that first time, over a bush that was covered in heavenly cream-colored roses with the most delicate pink tinge to their edges.

Something about the way he returned her look always made her breasts very tender and sensitive, her belly hot and heavy, her legs too weak to carry her.

She had known even then that she would remember that moment forever; the smell of the roses and the honeysuckle on the dewy languid heat of that afternoon, the lazy droning of the bees, for it was in that precise moment that she had known she loved him. That nothing in her life would ever be the same again.

And tonight, in this bed, they would at last become man and wife, she thought, running her hand across the cool slippery brocade coverlet.

Tonight was their wedding night.

Her stomach gave a tiny quiver. Not of apprehension, she quickly told herself, for apprehension was the result of ignorance and she was far from ignorant about what would soon occur between herself and Justin.

She had studied the anatomical and medical works, the models of various organs that her Papa kept in his library. She was, in fact, far better prepared for her wedding night than were most well-brought up young women of her time. Her sister, Felicity, had supplied the sundry little personal details those scholarly works had not seen fit to explain.

So it was not fear that caused the strange quiver in her belly, but desire! She swallowed. Or possibly . . . anticipation!

Its blue brocade folds tied back with tasseled

gold cords, the bed was of truly baronial proportions.

Its headboard was carved with nymphs and centaurs frolicking amongst vines and flower garlands. The four bedposts were actually tall, elongated carvings of the four apostles: Matthew, Mark, Luke and John, their arms raised to support the fringed brocade canopy.

How odd. She would share the most intimate moments of her marriage with these sad-eyed saints of wood looking on! Unless . . . she giggled to herself . . . she blindfolded them all with her handkerchiefs? That would surely put an end to their peeping. . . .

Oh!

As she turned, she caught a furtive movement from the corner of her eye. Dear Lord, she was not alone here! Somebody was hiding in the shadows.

Madeleine held her breath. She could hear the intruder, his low panting like that of a fugitive animal, run to ground. The sound chilled the blood in her veins and dried her mouth. She wanted to turn toward that furtive movement— but dared not.

Help me, lady fair!

The pleading words jangled through her mind.

Whoever it was, he was still there, standing in the shadows. Watching her. She could *feel* his presence, prickling her skin.

"Justin?" she whispered, yet knew in her heart that it was not her husband. "Justin? Is that you?"

There was no answer. "Wh . . . who's there?"

Taking her courage in both hands, Madeleine turned slowly toward the window, where she had last seen the movement. "Answer me!"

The window farthest from both fire and lamp was shrouded in shadows that offered perfect concealment.

She wetted her lips. An intruder—a thief— could easily have hidden up here, before she and Mrs. Fox came upstairs. Perhaps she should have obeyed her first instinct and run home to Whitchurch as fast as her legs could carry her? After all, what did she know about Steyning Hall, or the man she'd married, other than that she loved him to distraction.

What, indeed?

Go! reason whispered. *Get out!* common sense urged.

But she did neither. Instead, she crouched down and grabbed a weighty brass poker from the hearth. And, although her knees knocked, she steeled herself to go and investigate that shadow. She was mistress here now, after all. She would confront the wretch, and send him packing!

But hardly had she made her courageous decision than she discovered her "intruder" was not human at all! The movement, she realized, was what country folk called a moonshadow.

The full moon had back lit the tree outside her casement window. Its bright light had transformed the tree's gnarled and wind-tossed boughs into a human trunk and limbs, and hands that ended in clawlike, witchy fingers!

She shook her head as she returned the poker to its proper place. What a dolt she'd been. What had she expected? The de Harcourt ghost, complete with clanking chains? What a ninny!

Drawing off her wrapper, she quickly climbed into bed, and pulled the covers up to her chin.

Despite the blazing fire, the bedchamber had grown noticeably colder. In fact, the spot over by the window was freezing! She must remember to mention the draft to Mrs. Fox in the morning, so that its source could be found and sealed before next winter. She had little doubt that Steyning would be cold as the proverbial tomb in that season.

Groaning with pleasure, she snuggled under the bedcovers, surrendering to soft bed linens, scented with honeysuckle and wild roses, and to pillows stuffed with goosedown as she stretched blissfully. Steyning might well be a grim, unwelcoming heap of stone from the outside, but Mrs. Fox's beds were as fluffy as clouds!

Telling herself she must stay awake until Justin joined her, she coaxed her heavy eyelids to stay open by watching the play of firelight on the ceiling and walls.

Her thoughts drifted aimlessly as she listened to the creaks and groans of the old house settling around her. Outside, she could hear the wind rising as a summer storm built in fury and magnitude offshore. She fancied she could hear the boom of the Channel as it beat against the white chalk cliffs.

How vast Steyning was, compared to little Rose Arbor, where she was born and raised!

She had followed Fox, her candlestick carried aloft, down seemingly endless flagstone or wooden passageways, lined with mullioned windows and niches that held the busts of captains, playwrights and poets galore, then on, up a long curving staircase, until they reached the master's bedchamber.

She had lost track of how many rooms led off those twisting passageways. The impressions she caught were of lovely paneled walls, of old wooden floors, polished to a high gloss. Of Turkey rugs in exquisite floral patterns, their brilliant jewel colors softened by wear and time. Of heavily carved furniture from bygone days, and crystal chandeliers that held a hundred candles, perhaps more.

Everything was old—some of it very old indeed—and very ornate, but a far cry from ugly.

She thought, with a pang of homesickness, of

her Papa, and of Aunt Bea, their housekeeper and friend, and the simple yet comfortable home she'd left behind.

Everyone from the village and from farms for several miles around called Rose Arbor "Dr. Lewis' House" or simply "the Doctor's." Its walls were of white-washed brick, its front doors painted a deep ox-blood red. Instead of copper gables, turned verdigris by time and weather like Steyning Hall, Rose Arbor's roof was thatched. Wild pink roses and honeysuckle vines rambled over the trellises that flanked the recessed doors. Still more roses bloomed in her Papa's garden; roses her mother, Elizabeth, had planted while she yet lived, which he now tended in her memory.

She sighed. Would she ever learn her way around this sprawling mausoleum? Or would she get lost, as if in a maze? She yawned hugely. *Hurry, Justin, my love!* she urged her husband silently. Despite her best efforts, she was losing her battle to stay awake. . . .

Not five minutes after her head touched the pillow, Madeleine's eyelids drooped as if weighted by lead.

When, moments later, the lean shadow resumed its silent vigil by the casement, Madeleine was deeply asleep.

She did not feel the cool caress of its ghostly fingers upon her wrist. Nor the brush of its chill lips upon her hand . . .

Chapter Three

The Lady Chapel, St. Mary's Priory
Steyning, 1067

"Who is the lady? Tell me what you know of her!" the Norman knight demanded. His harsh whispers echoed through the aisles of the chapel.

Though he put the question to Aelfreda, the prioress, his hot dark eyes devoured the lovely damosel who knelt at the altar rail in prayer, threading her rosary through her fingers. Not the old hag.

"She is the lady Lenore of Rye, monsieur. The only daughter of Godfrey, thane of that place," the prioress revealed grudgingly.

"And is her sire yet living?"

"Alas, no, my lord," the prioress told him, her face hardening. "Thane Godfrey and his sons were all slain at Hastings. They died in battle at Harold Godwinson's side, may God assoil them all." With a pious sniff, she crossed herself.

Giles grunted. The old crone hated him, as her sort hated all Normans! He could see the loathing in her eyes, hear it in her voice. No matter. Let her think what she would. In his native Normandy, such old hags were burned as witches.

Making the horned sign against the Devil beneath the folds of the mantle he wore, he scowled. "And how is it such a beauty is not yet wed?" Was there some flaw in this exquisite creature that was not apparent to the eye? Or had she been widowed by the invasion?

"The lady Lenore was Thane Godfrey's only daughter, my lord. As such, he permitted her many freedoms. One was that she might choose her husband wherever her affections fell. In other words, to marry for love."

Giles snorted his disgust. "For love, you say? Like the lowliest peasant brat? Or the mastiff bitch that mates wheresoever it chooses? Paggh!" He shook his head. "What was her sire thinking of, to squander such a prize! With her beauty and her noble Saxon lineage, she could have married a king, or—the favorite of a king."

"Nevertheless, the lady Lenore is betrothed, sir, and most happily so. She is to be wed at Lammastide. Until that blessed day, she has been placed in our safe–keeping by her betrothed. She is very fair, is she not?" the prioress could not resist adding.

"On this matter, if upon no other, we are in accord, madame prioress. The damosel is as lovely as an angel," Giles said thickly. "To whom is she promised?"

"Why . . . why do you ask, my lord?" The prioress was pale now.

"Because I am persuaded that she would make an excellent wife for me. Her betrothed, woman," he demanded silkily. "What is his name?"

"A-a wife . . . for you, my lord! But . . . that is impossible! The lady has already taken oaths to another. She is already betrothed!"

"It is but the month of June, Reverend Mother," Giles said silkily. "A great many things can happen in the weeks remaining till Lammas. Betrothals can be broken. Hearts—and with them, minds!—may change." *And bridegrooms— particularly inconvenient Saxon ones—could die*, he added silently, an unpleasant smile playing about his fleshy lips.

The prioress shuddered, as if, witchlike, she had read his dark and murderous thoughts, he noted. But she did not tell him the name of the damosel's betrothed, he noted. An honest omission, he wondered? Or was the man's name one that a Norman such as himself might recognize? He smiled. *Oui*, that was it! Unless he missed the mark, the lady Lenore's intended was a Saxon rebel! One of many such fugitives who had taken to the woods in outlaw bands. Outcasts with prices on their heads, they plotted petty insurrections against William, the conquering duke of Normandy, who had been king of England since his crowning and anointing in the city of London last Christmastide.

The Norman knight chuckled. Whoever her betrothed might be, he made a sorry rival for the lady's affections, he thought. Whatever de Harcourts wanted, they got, one way or another. And what Giles de Harcourt wanted was Lenore. . . .

The summer storm that blew inland from the Channel began as the pitter-patter of goblin feet over Steyning's gables, then as the tap-tap-rat-tat-tat of bony fingers on mullioned panes.

A shrieking wind whipped the black sea into a choppy witch's brew. It swirled rain into a stinging fury that lashed the Hall like a nine-tailed whip.

It spat down chimneys and made the roaring flames hiss and yowl like cringing cats. It bent the trees almost double, shaking their ancient limbs so violently, they screamed like prisoners broken on the rack.

But in the master of Steyning's bedchamber, stillness reigned. Her breath misting in the frigid air, Madeleine slept on, lost to dreams. Oblivious to the wild storm outside, and to the presence of her shadowy guardian . . .

Giles hid in the deep shadows of the yews, watching the lovely Lenore as she daydreamed, her face turned up to the warmth of the sun.

She was seated on one of the stone benches that overlooked the fountain, her embroidery frame untouched upon her lap. The same shaft of sunlight that warmed her face made a bright nimbus about her fair head. It gleamed on the filet of gold binding her smooth white brow, and caught the metallic threads in the tablet embroidery that edged her rose-pink surcoat.

Fantailed doves cooed as they fluttered and strutted about Lenore's feet. Others fluffed out their snowy feathers and preened in the spray thrown off by the fountain.

The ceaseless burble of falling water cooled the summer's heat, yet did naught to cool Giles's blood. *He wanted her—and would have her,* he promised himself.

His body was hard with lust for the virginal beauty as he stepped from the shadows, his heart upon his sleeve like a lovesick lad.

"*Ma damosel* Lenore!" he called softly.

She turned, her face bright with joy. "Eydmond!"

* * *

The door to the master's chamber swung inward as Justin stepped inside. Closing the door behind him, he slid the bolt home.

"Madeleine? Are you still awake? Forgive me for taking so long, my dear . . ."

He received no answer, except for the snap of a log upon the hearth.

Going over to the tester bed, he stood there, looking down at his bride. How beautiful she was, like a slumbering angel. His stern face softened as he leaned down to brush her lips with his own. At the first touch of his mouth, she moaned softly in her sleep.

"Eydmond?" Lenore shaded her eyes with her hand. She could not make out her betrothed's features, not with the sun behind him, dazzling her. It cast his face in blackness and shadow.

"Nay, my lady," Giles growled. "It is not your Eydmond, but Lord Giles de Harcourt."

"My lord!" Her embroidery hoop spilled from her fingers to the greensward as she sprang up. Lengths of colored embroidery silks dotted the grass about her feet like fallen flowers as she took an involuntary step backward. De Harcourt was reknowned for both his cruelty and his explosive temper. She would sooner have drawn the attention of a wolf than him!

"For-forgive me, my . . . my lord! In truth, you

startled me!" she murmured, making a deep curtsey and bowing her head.

One hand flew to her breast. 'Twas a slender pale hand, graceful as the wing of a dove, Giles thought. Taking that icy hand in his own, he raised her up. Drew her icy fingers to his lips and kissed them.

"Pleasurably so, I trust, *chere* damosel?" he inquired softly.

Lenore's eyes widened. She flinched as if his touch was not human, but something monstrous. Something repulsive.

"But of . . . of course, my lord. How could you possibly think otherwise?" Lenore murmured, taking the first step in what was to become a dangerous dance of deception. She must never let this . . . this Norman butcher . . . this filthy Norman pig . . . suspect her true feelings, nor guess the depths of her hatred for him and his kind.

Normans had slain her father and brothers, her uncles and cousins in battle at Hastings. Normans had raped and killed her mother and several of her ladies. Normans had razed her father's keep and burned his crops. She had survived rape and death only because of him. Because of Eydmund, the man she loved.

Once he had known the battle at Hastings was lost, and Harold Godwinson—their king!—was dead of an arrow that pierced his eye, his body mutilated by his conquerors, her beloved and a handful of his fellows had fallen back. They had fled the battlefield, not in cowardly retreat, but so that they might defend the keeps and loved ones left at home.

Once the Normans had secured the coastal towns and hamlets of England, Eydmond knew they would forge inland towards the capital, killing, burning and looting as they went. Her father's keep lay squarely upon the direct path to London.

Eydmond had arrived too late to prevent most of the killing and burning. The Normans had slain almost everyone she held dear by the time he appeared out of nowhere, astride his foam-flecked steed. Brandishing his bloodied sword in hand, his golden hair furling on the wind, his blue eyes blazing with love—and terror—he had seemed to her like Woden, the ancient god of war, or an avenging angel.

He had quickly dispatched the drunken Normans who were swilling her father's mead and raping her mother's women, and come in search of her. He had found her hidden down one of the keep's wells. She had been close to losing her tenuous grip upon rope and bucket and falling to her death.

The shock of what she'd seen had left her unable to speak for the time being. Nor had she been able to weep for her dead. Eydmond had

spirited her away to her aunt, the Prioress Aelfreda, at St. Mary's Priory, who had nursed her
back to health. The priory had been her home
now for over a year. And 'twould remain her
home, till she and Eydmond were wed at Lammastide, she thought, forcing a smile for the Norman's benefit. . . .

Madeleine mumbled, stirring sleepily as Justin's
lips brushed her cheek. He pushed strands of her
silky hair aside and pressed his lips to the fragile
flutter of the pulse at her throat.

"Please . . ."

She was dreaming. About him, and of their
wedding night, probably. He smiled as he
straightened up. God knows, he'd dreamed
about her—ached for her, waking and sleeping.
Being close to her each day—her unique tantalizing scent like dew-drenched orchids filling his
nostrils, sharp and devastatingly female; her
sweet pliant curves within easy reach, yet un-
touchable, swaying beneath the soft folds of her
gown—had been an exquisite torture these past
few weeks.

He had channeled his sexual energies into riding his cousin's hunters by day, and spent restless
nights pacing the lawns and watermeadows that
sloped down to the river.

Watching the moonlight cut a glittering trough
across the Thames's oily black surface, the mus-

cles of his belly had clenched, hard with desire for his lovely Madeleine. With hair the creamy blond of moonflowers, and eyes the deep amethyst of twilight, her physical beauty was radiant, her character and her beauty of spirit as incandescent as flame. He could hardly believe his good fortune in finding someone like her, of knowing true happiness again, when just a few months ago, it had seemed happiness was forever lost to him. He had feared that the black cloud that seemed to hang over him these past few years was permanent. She had changed all that. She had changed his life, brought the sunshine and light back into it.

Unfastening his stock, he tossed it onto the dresser. Removing his pale gray frockcoat, he draped it over the back of a chair. The embroidered blue-satin waistcoat followed. . . .

Giles knew he had startled her. The fault was in him, not her, he told himself with a rare gentle turn of mind. She could not help herself, poor frightened little dove. Frightened little *Saxon* dove.

"Forgive me if I startled you, *ma damosel*. I have come here at this same time for several days, hoping to see you and speak with you privately." *Without that dragon of a prioress in attendance*, he added to himself.

"Me, my lord? In truth, I am flattered, sir. But

why? For what possible reason have you done me such honor?"

"Surely you can guess my reason? I wished to speak with you privately, damosel," he began in her language, heavily accented. "On a matter of considerable importance."

His words confirmed her worst fears. Left her almost faint with dread. "Indeed, my lord? And upon what matter would that be?" she whispered, feigning innocence of his intentions, although her aunt, the Prioress Aelfreda, had warned her of the Norman's obsession. Her heart began to race like that of a frightened dove when it sees a black shadow upon the ground below, and knows that the hawk flies above it.

Even now, she was caught in the dark shadow of that hawk, in jeopardy from its tearing beak, its cruel talons. She must be very, very careful.

"Upon the matter of marriage, my lovely damosel. Surely other men have told you that you are beautiful and that they wished to make you their own?

"Melissande, my first wife—a lady of St. Valery—has been dead for many years, may God assoil her. As a consequence, I find myself alone—and lonely—in a new land, in need of a chatelaine for the great keep that the masons are building to honor me, even as we speak. I shall also need a son and heir to inherit all I possess when I am dead and gone.

"There are many Saxon maids who would be honored to become my bride, for I am one of Duke—that is to say, one of *King* William's—most honored knights. And yet—!" He shrugged. "What can I say?" he asked with a smile that made her flesh crawl. "My fickle heart has chosen thee, fair damosel. And so, we shall be wed forthwith." His tone brooked no refusal.

"My lord . . . good sir . . . it cannot be," she began gently. "In truth, you do me greater honor than I deserve with your suit, my lord, but . . . it has come too late! My troth is already plighted, my vows—and heart—given to another."

"Then must you break those vows!" he snapped, his retort so angry and vicious, she flinched as if he had struck her in the face. "Sunder your oaths! For you shall not dishonor my name by taking some . . . some Saxon rebel over me! Here. You will wear this ring as my token for all to know that Lenore, lady of Rye, is to be my bride and lady."

With that, he withdrew a golden ring from the drawstring pouch of soft leather he wore at his belt. It was exquisitely wrought. The band was of plaited gold. The huge *cabuchon* amethyst was a pretty lavender hue, surrounded by pink freshwater pearls.

Smiling, he slid it onto her heart-finger, over the braided ring of her true love's golden hair.

She made no comment. Nor did she look down

at the second ring about her finger. Rather, she continued to stare at him, in shock, unable to believe her eyes.

"Look at it!" he rasped. "For with this ring, you shall be mine."

"Never," she whispered, shaking her fair head from side to side. "It is Thane Eydmond of Lewes that I love. I shall be my lord's bride—or no man's. Not even . . . not even yours, Lord Giles."

Crouched by the hearth, Justin stoked the fire with the poker, frowning as he added another log to the heap of glowing orange embers. Sparks showered like a small comet onto the hearthstone. In her sleep, Madeleine trembled as her dreams unraveled . . .

". . . Eydmond of Lewes?" Giles spat. "Your betrothed is nothing but a common outlaw. A rebel outcast with a price on his head!"

"He is my lord, a Saxon loyal and true, and the man who holds my heart," she whispered, her chin lifting in defiance.

The heat thrown off by the fire warmed Justin's face from several feet away. So why was it so blasted cold over here? he wondered as he climbed into the huge bed and stretched out beside his sleeping bride.

* * *

"Then must you pledge your heart to another!" Giles growled thickly, angrily. "For upon my oath, no man shall take you as his wife but me!"

"Then devil take thee and your token, Norman!" she cried, hurling the ring back in his face. . . .

Madeleine stirred, muttering fitfully in her sleep as Justin stretched out beside her. Gathering her in his arms, he brushed his lips across her silky throat, and drew the covers from her body.

The fabric of her chemise was so sheer he could make out the tantalizing lines of her figure through it, the exquisite breasts, the round globes of her bottom, the shadowy triangle where her firm, slender thighs pressed sweetly together. She was lovely, with flawless skin that had the sheen of satin, and fair hair that spilled across the pillow in a riot of cream-colored silk. He buried his face in its mass of soft ringlets and inhaled.

"Mmm. Lilies of the valley," he murmured huskily, tracing the spot where her pulse beat wildly beneath fragrant skin. "The sweet scent of innocence!"

But his kisses were far from innocent as he made love to her.

Chapter Four

Madeleine gasped, her eyes wide with terror as the last shreds of sleep were torn away like rotted curtains.

A powerful man loomed over her, broad shoulders framed by the ruddy flames that licked at the logs on the hearth. His arms were wrapped around her, holding her helpless, unable to move. Unable to flee.

She drew a shuddering sob and tore one arm free of his embrace.

"No, milord de Harcourt!" she hissed, still tangled in the dream, convinced that it was Giles who held her, not Justin. "You shall not do this! Let me go, for I am promised to another!"

Fists clenched, she thrust at his chest with all her might, desperate to escape him.

"Madeleine?" Justin said. Then again, more

sharply, shaking her very gently, "Madeleine! What is it, *chérie?* Wake up! You are still dreaming."

Dreaming?

She ceased her struggles. The fight went out of her. She stared up at him, frowning, before she slumped weakly back to the pillows, ashamed and confused.

How very strange. It had seemed so real! Dream and reality had become one. For an awful, frightening moment, she had truly believed her bridegroom was the hateful Giles de Harcourt— her husband's ancestor, surely?—and that she was fighting for her life, her honor, in imminent danger of being ravished by the Norman lord.

The dream had been so convincing, she was trembling even now, minutes after it had ended. Her heart still skittered in her breast.

"There, there, *chérie,*" Justin soothed, as if comforting a frightened animal. He drew her loosely into his arms to smooth her tangled hair and stroke her shoulders. " 'Twas a bad dream, nothing more. A nightmare! Hardly unexpected, at the end of a long and exhausting day. But you are safe now. Let me help you forget. Let me love you, *chérie.* Let me give you only the sweetest dreams, hmm?"

She told herself it was foolishness on her part. But even so, despite his words—despite knowing that this was Justin, her husband Justin, and not that frightening Giles, nor any other man, real or imagined—she could not bring herself to relax completely. Not at first.

She lay with her back to his chest, her spine rigid as she stared, unblinking, barely breathing, across the bed chamber at the heavy furnishings, half lost in shadow, and at the glowing logs on the fire.

She held herself stiffly, unnaturally, while her bridegroom tenderly caressed her, held her, or feathered kisses over her neck, her hair, her silky shoulders.

She could feel his hands and lips on her, but none of it seemed real. It was if he were a stranger, kissing and caressing someone else. Making love to another woman, a mannequin, while she stood in the shadows and watched their love play.

"Six weeks! I have known you such a little while," he was saying, "and yet it feels as if this moment was a lifetime in the making. Aah, *chérie,* how I ache to love you. To lose myself inside you. To show you all of love's pleasures, great and small."

He did not speak of it to her, but to lie here with her this way, her back to his front, her firm little derriere squirming against his hard member, on this, his wedding night—the night he had imagined more times than he cared to count— was a form of torture, pure and simple.

And yet, he was a man of the world. Experienced enough, where women were concerned, to know that it was vital his bride's first sexual experience was a pleasurable one. If it was distasteful or frightening or painful in any way, she would never come to enjoy what was, between a man and a woman who loved each other, one of life's most pleasurable intimacies.

With that end in mind, he gritted his teeth and curbed his own desire. Drawing her hand to his lips, he pressed a kiss into the well of her palm; an erotic kiss that was more tongue than lips. It elicited a tiny murmur, deep in her throat, and brought a pink glow to her cheeks. Encouraged, he tilted her face up to his and kissed the tip of her nose, then the corner of her soft lips, where her smile began, then her closed eyelids. Dark blond lashes trembled.

"Ever since we met in your mother's rose garden that day," he whispered, "loving you has been the most natural thing in the world for me. As natural as . . . as breathing, say, or waking up in the morning, to find yet another new day has dawned.

"Don't push me away, *chérie*. Don't shut me out. Don't keep me at arm's length—not when I must leave for France first thing in the morning. Anything could happen while I'm gone. So, love me tonight. Love me for always, forever, as I love you. A dream is but a dream, after all, meant to be cast aside or forgotten with the sunrise, so that we may get on with life—with love. I'm here and I'm real, *chérie*. Let me love you."

"Yes," she whispered. "Yes, I love you, too. It is only that the . . . the dream seemed so real. For a little while, I was convinced that you! . . . Well, I thought that you were someone else . . . someone hateful . . . who wanted to hurt me. It . . . the dream . . . it frightened me terribly, Justin. But I did not mean to hurt you with my rejection. Forgive me, my dearest husband."

Her chest ached. Her throat hurt. Tears stung behind her eyes. Justin was, by his own admission, a very private man. One who kept his feelings and his fears to himself. His unexpected and eloquent declarations of love touched something deep inside her, and filled her with quiet joy. It also made her ashamed that she had fought his embraces as if he were some ravaging beast.

"You're the light of my life, Madeleine. I want you to know that. Your sweetness and laughter have dispelled the shadows that have governed my life for so long."

Some somber memory flickered across his striking face, filling his dark blue eyes with tragedy and pain. But he did not share those memories with her, nor explain what he meant by "shadows." Why? she wondered. Because he did not wish to burden her with his problems? Because he did not trust her enough, as yet, to share his deepest confidences? Or because the pain was too new, too recent to speak of?

Either way, his bleak expression tugged at her heartstrings. With a glad little cry, she turned and went into his arms, her dreams of Giles de Harcourt forgotten. Why should she remember them, or him? Except for their dark coloring and their shared surname, Justin and the fictional Giles were nothing alike.

Her fingers threaded through hair as black as night, and crisp as China silk, as he lowered his dark head to her breasts.

She gasped as his mouth closed over a taut nipple and tugged. A long drawnout sigh began, deep in her belly. A honeyed warmth, an answering flutter, filled her lower belly and the place between her legs.

"Oh, yes!" she murmured with a little frisson of delight. She wanted to press against him. To keep him close, always. To take him inside her.

Justin eased the lacy straps of her nightgown down, off her shoulders, baring her breasts and trapping both arms at her sides.

Sapphire eyes dark with desire, he watched the play of emotions cross her face as he trailed his fingers down her throat, past the scented hollows at its base, to her bare breasts. He cupped a perfect pink globe, supporting its luscious weight upon the balls of his fingertips.

Goosebumps made the invisible hairs on her

arms stand up in the wake of his caresses. Her nipples tightened. A nerve danced in the sleek thigh beneath his other palm. God, she was exquisitely sensitive, his little bride. As finely tuned as a virtuoso's violin. Her angelic beauty and coloring were excitingly at odds with the carnal ripeness of her mouth, the sensual curves of her body.

It took every ounce of his self-control to make love to her slowly. Had his lust not been tempered by love, he doubted he could have stopped himself.

Lowering his dark head, he feasted upon her breasts. She gasped, stunned by the answering heat and pleasure that flickered between her thighs, as if breasts and quim were joined in some mysterious way.

His tongue teased the deep-rose aureoles until the tender flesh ruched like crumpled velvet, and the nipples grew red and swollen as raspberries. Damp skin glistened from his kisses, flushed rosy pink, like Italian marble. Erotic. Exciting.

"Ahh, *ma chérie*, look at you," he breathed, his hot dark gaze feasting upon her bosom. "Your breast is like a little dove," he cupped a soft swell in his palm, the ball of his thumb gently stroking its plump curve, "nestled sweetly in my hand. I want to kiss you everywhere, *chérie*. Come. Undress for me, *ma petite*."

Her hands trembling, she pushed the nightgown down, wriggling her hips to slide it off her body. She was aroused as much by the act of baring herself for her lover as Justin was aroused by watching her undress for him.

When she was nude, he lifted himself over her. His weight on his elbows, he tenderly kissed and caressed every inch of her, until she wore the memory of his lips on every part of her lovely body.

Her nightgown lost in the rumpled linens at the foot of the bed, she lay before him, breathing shallowly with desire, aching, yearning, needing, wanting—though for what, she scarcely knew.

One hand resting on her warm, flat belly, he ran his tongue around the rim of her navel, then moved his mouth lower.

"My beautiful Madeleine," he whispered, tousling the downy curls that crowned the joining of her thighs. "Open for me, *ma belle chérie.*"

Kneeling between her thighs, he lowered his dark head and delicately tasted her sweetness, as if she were a luscious passion fruit, with ruby flesh as sweet as wine.

Her breath caught on a scream of pleasure at his intimate kisses. Grasping fistfuls of the linens, she arched up, off the bed. Yet his maddening lips and tongue curled, nipped, lapped, licked until she felt she might go mad unless she had some release from the exquisite torture.

But his hands, clamped over her hips, held her

fast, that he might take his pleasure, and give her hers. This time, their first time, he doubted he would last long, once he was inside her, sheathed to the hilt in that heavenly heat. His desire, his lust for her, was too great. And so, he was determined to bring her to pleasure first, and only afterwards seek his own.

She was moaning and whimpering now. Her hands broke their fierce hold upon his hair to skim feverishly over the breadth of his shoulders. He was, she realized with a start, quite naked.

"Oh, love, love, yes, oh, *yes!*" she cried, shuddering as the dam that had built within her broke at last. Dazzling colors swam in her vision. Comets collided. *"Justin!"*

Pleasure arced through her, driving the air from her lungs in a voluptuous, exultant cry that made the wooden Apostles blanch in shock.

"Yes, darling. Yes, *chérie,* that is the way. Surrender to it. Don't fight it, *chérie,*" Justin commanded thickly, sliding up the length of her body to nuzzle her ear. "Let pleasure take you. I'm here. Nothing can hurt you."

"Justin, oh, Justin . . ." she whimpered, tossing her head from side to side.

"I know, *ma petite.* I know." He kissed the ivory throat she offered up to him in sacrifice. "Ah, *chérie,* do you know what you do to me, my sweet lily of the valley? Say it, *chérie!* I want to hear you say it. Tell me you want me inside you."

There was a thick savage edge to his husky voice. "Deep inside you."

"I want you in . . . inside me," Madeleine echoed. Just saying the shocking words sent another current of excitement sizzling through her. She shuddered, drowning in his deep blue eyes, as if they were an ocean. Losing herself in the erotic spell of pleasure, danger and mystery his lovemaking wove about her.

Her body hummed with fresh longing, renewed desire. Her blood throbbed with an aching need, a roaring dark hunger, that he alone could feed. "Now. I want you inside me. I want you to . . . to make love me. To take me. Oh, Justin, I need you so much. I need you so."

He opened her with his knees. His eyes were the blue of a midnight storm, dark, electric, fiercely possessive. Her nails dug half-moons in the corded swells of his upper arms as lifted himself onto her. She caught her lower lip between her teeth. A spring was coiled in her belly. A tightly wound spring. If Justin touched her in a certain place, the spring would uncoil, and she would be hurled into the wild blue yonder.

She shivered as she looked up at him. In the shadowy light, he looked scarcely civilized. A male wolf, jealously claiming its mate.

For a fleeting moment, she was reminded of the Norman wolf in her dream. What had his name been? *Giles*. Like Giles's, Justin's face was filled with lust now.

She tensed as the head of his blunt shaft nudged her tender flesh. He claimed her mouth in a savage kiss, and entered her. There was a moment's sharp pain as he deepened the forward thrust, then he sheathed himself in her as snugly as any blade, returned to its velvet scabbard.

She moaned, whispering endearments, her pleasure exquisite, her excitement acute, those brief moments of pain forgotten as every driving stroke, every thrust of his hard buttocks and powerful flanks, drove him deeper than ever before. Brought them closer to becoming one.

And then, just when she was convinced she could experience no greater pleasure, he reached between their bodies, and rubbed the tiny bud of her sex with his finger.

"Fly, Madeleine," he whispered, his voice rough with desire. "Fly, *petite ange!*"

Head thrown back, she screamed her pleasure to the rafters as Justin lunged between her thighs, riding her harder, faster, deeper now as his own climax built.

Drops of sweat flew from his brow. It trickled down his throat, losing itself in the black hair that lay like a shadow across his chest. More ran in a narrow line down his hard belly, to where they were joined.

His grip upon her hips tightened as he reached

his own release. The power of it bucked through him like an explosion. Chest heaving, he threw back his dark head and let the lightning take him, roaring his pleasure and triumph as his seed leaped inside her.

Dark head bowed, he fell forward across Madeleine's body, his chest still heaving, before rolling to her side.

Madeleine lay quietly beside him, adrift on a cloud of black velvet. It was as if her very soul had taken flight. The sense of release, of contentment, of utter peace and sweet exhaustion was like nothing she had known before. Even greater was the sheer joy of belonging to this man. Of being his wife, his woman, his lover and his love.

"Justin?" she asked drowsily in the moments before sleep claimed her.

"Hmmm?"

"Did you have an ancestor named Giles?"

"What was that?" he mumbled, his eyes still closed.

"An ancestor named Giles. Did you have one?"

"Um, yes, I believe I did," he answered on a yawn. "Eleventh century. The first earl of Steyning. Why do you want to know?"

"Oh, I was just curious," she murmured.

"Hmm. Well, you know what they say about curiosity, *chérie.*" There was amusement in his sleepy voice. "Now. Come over here, next to me."

"All right. Good night, darling."

Her husband's arms around her, Madeleine slept. And this time, her sleep was sweet and dreamless.

A persistent knocking roused Madeleine from the depths of sleep the following morning.

"No, it is too early to get up, Aunt Bea," Madeleine grumbled, believing herself still at Rose Arbor. "What can you be thinking, to wake me at such an hour?"

"It be me, Tabby, Your Ladyship," a muffled, puzzled voice declared from the other side of the door.

Tabby? Who in the world was Tabby? She forced one gritty eyelid open, grimacing as she looked around groggily, trying to get her bearings.

She was in a tester bed. The four wooden posts had been carved to look like four disapproving old men with long noses and beards. The tester stood in a vast, shadowed bedchamber the size of a small banqueting hall. Its furnishings were of heavily carved dark wood. Blue velvet draperies hung at the mullioned casement windows, one of which boasted a window seat with velvet pillows. Both pillows and hangings were embroidered with golden fleurs-de-lis.

Now she remembered. She was at Steyning Hall—Justin's country home. *Her* home, too, now that they were well and truly married.

Remembering, she smiled dreamily. Last night had been their wedding night. Their very first as man and wife—and what a wonderful night it had been, too, she thought, stretching languorously. But today, Justin would be leaving her alone, summoned abroad on urgent government business. She frowned. Leaving . . . or had he already left?

Still half asleep, she groped about, feeling for him. There was a shallow depression beside her, where he had slept last night. But the rumpled linens were cold.

He was gone to France, she realized, crushed with disappointment. The scrap of sky she could see through a narrow gap between the draperies was blue, not charcoal, as it would have been were it dawn.

She had missed him, and she'd wanted so much to be awake when he left, to give him a loving send-off. After all, who knew when—or even if?—she would ever see him again? She did not know what work he did for the British government, exactly, but it was very dangerous, she was sure. And important, too, if they would send a courier to summon him from his own wedding, as they had yesterday!

For his part, Justin staunchly refused to discuss

his government missions with her, saying the less she knew about his work, the less worrying it would be for her.

In fact, whenever she tried to pry information from him, it was as if a curtain dropped down between them. He retreated, becoming the reserved, mysterious man he was to all but a select handful of friends.

As a result, she'd concluded that her dashing Justin—with his dark, almost foreign good looks and his fluency in the French language, a direct legacy of his Provençal mother, la Comtesse Emilie de Rozier—was probably a British special agent, or a spy. Or if not a spy, then something very like it.

The "urgent government business" to which he had been dispatched was almost certainly connected to the wretched Revolution and the Reign of Terror that had cost so many of the French aristocracy—like Justin's family on his mother's side—their heads. And yet, she had let him go without so much as a kiss in farewell, she thought guiltily.

The brandied milk, combined with several very energetic bouts of lovemaking during the night, had been the perfect recipe for over-sleeping—as had those peculiarly detailed and exhausting dreams! The latter had been of such startling clarity, it was as if they were not dreams at all, but brief forays into the distant past. A journey through time, of sorts.

Did her interest in antiquities and all things ancient account for the dreams' astonishingly detailed nature, she wondered absently as, smothering a yawn, she cuddled up to the feathered bolster once again, and closed her eyes. What could another few minutes hurt?

Immediately, the knocking resumed.

Botheration! "Come in!" she called, stifling another yawn.

The maid, Tabitha, marched in, her starched skirts rustling. She carried a silver tray that held a jug of hot water, a small tea pot, creamer and sugar bowl, and a bone china dish and saucer, delicately painted with pink roses.

The fragrant aroma of tea filled the chamber as Madeleine dragged herself upright, then shoved the bolster behind her back so that she could sit up in bed.

It was Hyson tea. Aunt Bea had always used the cheaper Bohea at Rose Arbor. How deliciously extravagant, to drink only the finest tea!

"Ooops! Beggin' yer pardon, your ladyship!" Tabitha muttered. She was bright red as she pointedly covered her face with her apron.

It was only then that Madeleine remembered she was naked! Hastily, she drew the sheet up, over herself, and rummaged under the bedcovers for her missing nightgown.

She found it rolled up at the very bottom of the bed—exactly where Justin had consigned it, she remembered with a tiny, smug smile.

Shaking out the creases, she pulled it on, over her head.

"Your . . . um . . . morning tea, my lady," Tabitha said quickly. She placed the tray on a small night table next to the tester and bobbed a curtsey, apparently ready to bolt.

"Thank you, Tabitha. Hand me my wrapper and draw the draperies before you leave, would you?"

"Right you are, mum." Another sketchy curtsey.

Moments later, sunshine flooded into the gloomy chamber through diamonds of glass set in wooden mullions.

The light was so bright, Madeleine had to close her eyes briefly, until they adjusted.

"Our Effie will be fetchin' you up your hot water in a bit, mum. When she's done, Mrs. Fox says I'm ter come back and help you dress."

"Thank you, Tabitha. I would like that." She smiled.

Rather than leaving, the serving girl remained where she was, her rough red hands clasped primly before her, gray eyes downcast.

"Yes, Tabitha? Was there something else?"

The maid was very thin, Madeleine noticed. She must have been fifteen of sixteen, but looked closer to twelve, for she was completely without a bosom, poor child—though perhaps for a pretty female in domestic service these days, the lack was a blessing, rather than a curse. Flat-chested, she would be less likely to draw the amorous attention of her master or the sons of the households in which she worked. Even in sleepy Whitchurch, Madeleine had heard stories.

A great many freckles were scattered across Tabitha's complexion, which was almost translucent. Only a few carroty wisps escaped her mobcap, and her white apron had a ruffled bib and strings that were tied in a crisp bow behind her. She was as neat as a pin, yet seemed scared to death. *Of what?* Madeleine wondered. *Surely not of me?*

"Was there something else, Tabitha?" Madeleine nudged the girl gently.

"Er, no, mum . . . er, I mean, my lady."

She was lying. It was there, in her eyes. But what more could Madeleine do? "Very well. Then you may run along now."

"Yes, mum."

With another curtsey, the girl was gone.

Blessedly alone, Madeleine tossed the covers aside, wincing as she padded over to the cheval looking glass.

She was a little stiff and achy, but felt wonderful, even so. Sleek and satisfied, like the cat that got the cream, she thought, tossing off the gauzy nightgown.

Madeleine had never stood before a full-length mirror entirely naked before. Even had she been so inclined, they had not possessed a cheval glass at Rose Arbor, for the Arbor's modest furnishings did not run to such extravagances!

To see herself from head to toe, as Nature intended, was strangely liberating, she decided, mentally comparing herself to the shapely statues of naked nymphs and goddesses she had seen.

The bare wanton who looked back at her from the looking glass had a face with glowing eyes and a radiant bloom to her cheeks that she barely recognized as her own. Her reflection grinned smugly back at her, the eyes faintly shadowed with lavender and somewhat darker in color than usual. Almost indigo, rather than pansy-violet. Her lips were swollen, too, and very red, she noticed, running her fingertip over her pouty mouth.

"Wanton wench," she muttered in a scolding tone, but could not quite banish her smile.

The hair she'd brushed last night until it fell past her shoulders in a sleek mantle of creamy blonde silk now tumbled in a hoydenish mop down her back, like that of a fallen woman's. And yet . . . she had never looked more *alive* than she did right now, nor felt more vibrant.

Plainly, love and marriage—and marital relations—suited her. And it would go on suiting her, she promised herself. She and Justin would be deliriously happy together, exactly as he'd promised. Nothing would stand in the way of that happiness, she promised her reflection. She would not allow it.

She gazed thoughtfully at her reflection in the mirror as details of that odd dream came back to her.

The Norman knight had seemed quite capable of hurting the lady Lenore when she flung his amethyst ring back in his face.

How odd. She frowned as a sudden thought struck her. As Lenore defied the Norman, so had she awakened to find herself struggling in Justin's embrace, convinced he was Lord Giles!

She shrugged off the notion of some sort of connection as utter nonsense. How many times had she dreamed that someone in her dreams was calling to her, only to find, on waking, that she really was being called? It had been a simple dream, no more, no less. The end result of a long, tiring day and an overactive imagination. After all, what else *could* it be?

Snatching her wrapper from the chair back, she hurriedly pulled it on, overwhelmed by the sudden disquieting sensation that she was not alone. That she was being watched. It was foolish, she knew, but even so, the fine hairs prickled down her arms. She told herself that, like the

moonshadow of the evening before, the sensation of being watched was probably the result of
a too-active imagination, once again. Who
wouldn't start imagining things in an old house
like this, which probably had a checkered, perhaps even violent history?

"My darling Madeleine," she could almost hear
her Papa saying. "Your problem is that you are
far too sensitive." It was something he had often
said, she remembered with a pang, missing him
already. "You should get out and about more,
instead of dwelling on things. Breathe the fresh
country air. Take brisk walks along the lanes.
Both will do wonders for your mind, not to mention your constitution."

She smiled. There it was. A country physician's staple prescription for her spinsterish
flights of fancy. Still, her father was right, more
often than not.

"Thank you, Papa. I shall endeavor to keep
that in mind," she told her reflection, aware now
of more persistent rapping at her door. "Come
in!"

It was another maid, this one a bosomy, dark-
haired girl with sloe-black eyes and a sly but
saucy way about her. She was bearing kettles of
hot water for her mistress's morning toilette.
"Good morning . . . Effie, is it?" she guessed.

"Aye, mum, Effie it is." The girl beamed,

pleased that her mistress had remembered her name.

" 'Tis a glorious day, is it not, Effie?" Madeleine added.

Effie giggled. "Aye, mum. Indeed it is. Proper glorious! The master will have a good crossing t'France, I'm thinking."

"Oh, I hope so, Effie. I do hope so," she said with a wistful sigh.

Thus she began her very first day at Steyning Hall, and her second as a married woman. *Alone.*

Chapter Five

A week came and went, without any sign that Justin would soon be home.

Missing him and more worried about his safety than she cared to admit, even to herself, Madeleine decided to walk down to the village. Mrs. Fox, the housekeeper, and Mrs. Beaton, the cook, ran the household like clockwork, as they did when Justin was away on business. They had little need of her, although as their new mistress, they politely deferred to her on matters of the household's affairs and accounts. As a result, Madeleine was left with far more free time on her hands than was healthy—much more than she had been used to at Rose Arbor.

A walk would give her something to do, and something else to think about, as well as draining some of her restless energy. Besides, she had yet to attend church services since coming to Steyning. She was anxious to make the acquaintance of the local rector and his wife, and to visit the village church and churchyard. Making rubbings of medieval effigies was a hobby of which she was particularly fond. She had some fine ones she had made in the churches of Suffolk, where her sister Felicity and her husband David lived.

She would take flowers from the Hall's gardens with her for the village church's altar vases, and perhaps choose some suitable effigies from which to make rubbings for her Papa's collection. He was very fond of such things and she had become quite skilled at making them.

Despite her best intentions, however, it was past luncheon before she managed to escape the sprawling old house and her duties as its lady, eager to explore the world beyond Steyning's sprawling estate.

It was a warm summer's afternoon as Madeleine set out. Great billows of white cloud floated majestically on high like a flotilla of sailing ships with bellying white canvas upon a sea of vivid blue.

Rather than have one of the grooms bring out the dog-cart or harness a pony into the trap for her little outing, she decided to walk.

How the morning had flown, she thought as, carrying a flat basket piled high with roses and irises picked from the Hall's flower gardens, she set off down the driveway.

Steyning's team of gardeners paused in their labors as she passed by, booted feet crunching lightly on the gravel. Although they tipped their caps and nodded politely, they were clearly surprised to see their mistress on foot, like a common country wench.

For the first time, Madeleine had misgivings about her solo outing. Perhaps, given the newness of her title as mistress of Steyning, it would have been wiser to play her part to the hilt, and take a light carriage or a dog-cart into the village, with a servant to accompany her, as everyone clearly expected her to do.

Then again, surely being the lady of the manor gave her the right to do exactly as she pleased, within reason. And what pleased her was to get out in the sunshine and walk, walk very fast indeed, until she could feel her heart pumping and the blood surging through her veins and the wind streaming through her hair and painting roses in her cheeks! So that, she decided, was exactly what she would do. Devil take anyone who suggested otherwise, she thought, kicking a stone with the toe of her boot and sending it spinning away.

"So there!" she exclaimed, drawing the startled look of a speckled thrush in a nearby tree, before it took whirring flight.

Leaving the Hall's gates behind her, she followed lanes hedged with white hawthorn, a flower that in earlier times had been used to garland brides, or to crown the queen of the May. After half a mile, she finally entered the churchyard on the outskirts of Steyning village by way of the old lych gate.

She was wandering amongst centuries of leaning, mossy gravestones, reading their inscriptions, when a chubby man of middle years wearing a clerical collar beneath a black frockcoat hastened toward her. He was rubbing plump paws together.

"Greetings, dear lady! Greetings! You must be the new Lady de Harcourt the village has been buzzing about. May I offer you my heartiest felicitations on your marriage, your ladyship?" the rector exclaimed.

The man was clearly delighted that she had called upon him. Or . . . had he been expecting her to summon him to the Hall, cap in hand? Oh, well, it was too late to worry about proper protocol now. She simply refused to second-guess her every action.

After a few moments of congratulations and polite inquiries after her husband's health, Madeleine explained that she was very fond of old churches and churchyards and would like to explore St. Nicholas's, since it was going to be her parish church. "My father is very taken with rubbings, you see, Rector. I would like to send him some from St. Nicholas."

"How refreshing, if I may say so, my lady. Few young ladies have an interest in such things nowadays. As you will see," he began, clutching the fraying lapels of his worn black frockcoat, "St. Nicholas is a finer medieval church than most. If you will accompany me, my lady, I shall endeavor to show you its best features. . . ."

St. Nicholas, as she had guessed when she spied its Norman tower between the trees, was very old. It appeared to have been built from blocks of the same gray stone as the Hall. No doubt there had once been a stone quarry nearby, hence the village's name. "Steyning" meant "stony place" or "stony cliffs."

Although numerous lords of Steyning had placed their personal stamps upon the building's architecture since its foundations were laid, the bell tower was original, albeit restored in places, according to the Reverend Cargill. One of the foundation stones bore the legend:

"Built in the parish of Steyning by the Grace and Glory of God and His humble servant, Giles de Harcourt, First Earl of Steyning, the Year of Our Lord, 1067."

"You see, my lady? The earls of Steyning have always been generous to their parish church,"

Cargill said with a smile. His plump hands steepled on a generous belly that hinted at the rector's wordly, rather than spiritual, nature. "Most generous."

The charming old reprobate was, she suspected, soliciting a donation from her, even now!

"The font . . . the font cover . . . the rood screen . . . the stained glass windows . . . are just a few of the de Harcourts' generous gifts to the church over the years."

"They're really quite beautiful. You must be very proud, rector," she murmured.

"Oh, indeed, yes. And I consider our parish most fortunate not to have lost such treasures, as did many of its contemporaries."

"Lost? How so?"

"During the 1500s, that puritanical monster, Oliver Cromwell, ordered parish churches across England stripped of ornate trappings," Cargill explained. "In favor of all things plain."

"Ah, yes. Anything of great beauty or value that belonged to the Church of England was destroyed or confiscated, was it not?"

"Precisely. Fortunately for us, St. Nicholas's priest at that time—an enterprising fellow, I've always thought—had the finest pieces taken down to the vaults below the church, and hidden there."

"How exciting!"

Cargill nodded. "Of course, when Cromwell's

agent came, he demanded to be allowed to search the church cellars. He was told he could do so immediately. However, the rector apologized profusely for the somewhat . . . unpleasant conditions the agent would find down in the vaults."

"Naturally, the agent asked the priest what he meant by "unpleasant conditions." Foul odors, the rector explained. They could not be avoided, he added, leading the way down the stairs, since the church had been built too close to the sea. As a result, the burial vaults had fallen victim to terrible seepage, and their contents had been . . . well, um, disturbed." Cargill chuckled. "Needless to say, Cromwell's lackey left Steyning with all possible haste, with not a backward glance, without inspecting the vaults!"

Madeleine laughed. "And the part about the damp and the foul odors, was it true?"

Cargill grinned like a rubicund elf. "Hardly, my dear lady. Hardly! The cellars remain as dry as the proverbial bone to this day."

"Are my husband's ancestors buried down in the vaults?"

"Some, my lady. His lordship's most recent ancestors, including the late earl and dear Lady Emilie, of course. So sad. However, earlier generations of de Harcourts are buried on the grounds of the old priory. The area where you will find their graves was the vestry of the priory church in the eleventh century. Of course, the buildings themselves are gone or in utter ruin now. The graves with their effigies are outdoors, and exposed to the elements. 'Tis most unfortunate."

"The old priory. I see. And where would that be?"

For some reason, her heart was beating very fast, of a sudden. She told herself that imagining both the priory and Giles de Harcourt in her dream was sheer coincidence. Nothing more. During the long coach drive down to Steyning Hall, she had probably seen a milestone somewhere, indicating a certain distance to St. Mary's Priory, forgetting all about it until that wretched dream had recovered the lost memory.

"In it's heyday, St. Mary's was a very large priory, indeed," Cargill continued, unaware of the effect his ramblings were having upon her. The history of his church and the nearby religious houses was clearly the rector's passion. "It was built in the seventh century, to fulfill a promise made by King Wihtred of Kent to the Virgin. A religious house of refuge and hospitality of some kind or another has stood upon that spot ever since. It has withstood the attacks of both Vikings and Norman invaders, as well as Cromwell."

"Really? And where are these ruins, exactly?" she asked, excited.

"Just a stone's throw from the old Hall, my

lady. You can reach them through the side gate off the old herb and spice gardens, if my memory serves. You were unaware of the ruins, then?"

"Yes." She frowned. "Though now I come to think about it, I do seem to remember someone mentioning them in passing." But who? She did not recall Justin mentioning the ruins, but obviously he—or someone else—must have. "To what order did the monks belong? Do you know?"

"Oh, there were never any monks at St. Mary's, my lady. It was run by an order of sisters. *Nuns*," he added for emphasis, turning away from her as a chill danced down her spine. "Madam?"

"Humm?"

"Do come look at the wonderful carving on this end pew. The workmanship is some of the finest you'll find anywhere in England."

"I'm sure it is. . . ."

She did not consciously go looking for the priory ruins that Cargill had mentioned. Or at least, that was what she told herself. She stumbled upon the gateway to them quite by accident, while exploring the Hall's spice and herb gardens.

As the rector had described, the rusted gate was set in a thick hedge of ancient yew that the gardeners had clipped as square as any wall. The six-foot hedge ran along the western perimeter of the Hall's herb gardens, which were fragrant and spicy as they dozed in the warm summer sunshine. Bees buzzed over the crowns of the herbs and the heady scent of mint, rosemary, thyme and tarragon perfumed the sultry air.

To the north of the priory grounds lay what looked like woods. To the south lay meadows, chalk cliffs and the choppy gray Channel—and beyond it, France, its coastline visible on a clear day, everyone assured her. To the west was the ancient city of Dover.

But just beyond the gate palings, weeds reigned. She could see daisies, scarlet poppies and buttercups between coarse grasses and choking creepers. There were also shepherd's purse and other pretty wildflowers common to field and meadow.

She'd rattled the iron palings several times, trying to open the gate by shaking it, before she realized a newer chain and padlock were holding it shut.

"Drat!" she muttered.

" 'Tis best ye stay out of there, lass," a low voice said. She spun around. "Dangerous, them ruins are. Ye can turn an ankle or take a nasty fall, quick as winking. Don't rightly know what's under that grass and rubble."

The man's eyes, as black and bright as two wet stones, met her own. They were full of wicked amusement as he eyed her up and down, and added, "Aah. You'll be the new mistress, I'm thinking."

"Yes. And who might you be?" she demanded.

"Trevor, my lady."

The brows above his black, black eyes were thick, and dark as his curling hair, which he wore pulled back in a raffish queue. His mouth was wide and full-lipped, his nose crooked and blunted, as if it had been broken more than once in his lifetime. His cheekbones were prominent, too, giving his features a savage, unfinished cast.

It was, in all, an oddly disquieting face.

"Very well . . . Trevor, is it?" she ground out, annoyed. "Well, let me assure you, I'm in no danger whatsoever. I grew up exploring places like this, you see. My boots are sturdy, and I'm as sure-footed as any . . . as any goat. I promise you, I won't come to any harm, so tell me. Who has the key to this gate? Do you know?"

"Aye, my lady."

She waited but the exasperating rogue offered no further explanation.

"Well? Who has it?" she demanded, resisting the urge to pinch the wretch or stamp her foot in anger.

"Let me think on it. . . . His lordship has one. Mister Digby, the butler, I recollect has the other . . . but he's away t'London, visiting his—"

"—yes, yes, his sick sister. I know." He looked

as if he might actually be laughing at her, the rogue! "He left this morning."

"And the third—"

"Yes? What about the third?" she asked eagerly.

He indicated the large metal key ring looped to his belt, "—be right here."

"I see," she shot back, furious and quite convinced now that he was making fun of her. "And what is your position in my household, may I ask?"

"Ye might call me the gamekeeper, milady. Trevor Fox, at your service. *Master* Trevor Fox." He made a half bow which, made by any other man, would have seemed perfectly cordial, but which from him was somehow insolent.

Her fair brows shot up in surprise. "Fox, you say?"

"Aye, my lady. T'Hall's housekeeper is my mother, God bless her."

"I see," Madeleine murmured, wondering about the odd alliance that had produced a son so utterly unlike his plump, kindly mother.

This swarthy fellow was more like a . . . a changeling, or a sloe-eyed gypsy child that someone had abandoned on Mrs. Fox's doorstep than her natural offspring.

Trevor, who had been watching her face very closely, chose that moment to laugh, almost as if he had read her thoughts. But before she could comment on it or excuse herself, he stepped in front of her and unlocked the gate.

The lock was rusty. It fought the turning of the key. When it yielded, the ancient hinges squealed in protest. The rungs shed flakes of rust as Trevor swung the gate inward, beating the grass down beneath its bottom rung. "There you go, my lady. Mind your step, now. Even a . . . um . . . a young nanny goat would have to watch its step in here."

He was tall, she realized, a little frightened as she squeezed between him and the hedge, into the priory gardens. Taller even than her husband, who stood six feet. But whereas Justin was lean, the gamekeeper's brawny arms were roped with muscle, like the rigging of a ship.

"Thank you. I certainly shall," Madeleine murmured frostily. Nanny goat, indeed!

The man was an unconventional servant, by anyone's measure, she thought as she waded through tall grasses, much of it higher than her knees. Nor was his attire what one would expect from a proper gamekeeper. A white full-sleeved shirt, worn open, with no stock or cravat covering his wind-browned throat, except for a knotted scarlet kerchief. A seamed black leather jerkin, breeches and scuffed brown boots completed his attire. In one ear, he sported a golden earring, though she doubted he'd ever been to the South China Sea.

Her fascination with Trevor Fox's oddities ran

out at roughly the same time the tangle of weeds and grasses opened out into a large clearing.

Before her, great blocks of stone lay scattered about, some overgrown with trailing vines and mottled green with the mosses and lichens of centuries.

Parts of walls, half-buried by time, jutted from the ground like crooked teeth. A window with stone mullions that had once separated the stained-glass petals of a flower, showed where the chancel of the Lady Chapel had once risen above the nave and the devout nuns who had knelt in prayer there.

It was also here, in the east aisle, that Lord Giles de Harcourt had asked the Prioress Aelfreda to tell him about the Saxon maid, she realized, her heart beginning to race. And over there had been the fountain with the fantailed doves fluttering in its spray, as Lenore daydreamed in the sunshine about her Eydmund. . . .

It was madness, she knew. And yet, standing here, in the ruins, in this place where *they'd* once stood, her dream took on new flesh, new substance, new life—and an odd *immediacy*. She seemed to hear the whispers of the past all around her, like the whirring of the doves' wings, or the rustling of dry leaves. The voices of Lenore. Of Eydmund. Of Giles and even the prioress, Aelfreda.

"If ye're wanting t'see the graves, they're back there, my lady. By the hedge, hidden by brambles."

She had not realized until then that the gamekeeper had followed her through the gate. He gestured vaguely towards the yew hedges.

"Then again, happen ye'd best wait for another time. His lordship's come home, aye?" Trevor nodded his chin toward the sea.

It was only then that she saw Justin. He quietly sat his horse on the head of the cliffs, watching them. How long had he been there? she wondered, feeling unaccountably guilty.

"Justin!" she cried, waving vigorously. "Hallo!"

Picking up her skirts, she ran to meet him, her pale hair flying behind her. Fighting the thick grass and briars that snagged her stockings, she tore up the hill to meet him.

"Oh, Justin! I missed you so much! It was so lonely without you!" she blurted out, panting and out of breath as she clung to his stirrup leathers.

He laughed, his dark blue eyes lighting up. "No more than I've missed you, my sweet. Climb on up here," he urged, pulling her up, before him.

"Oh, I'm so glad you're back! Let's go home!" she sang out. "Let's celebrate!"

Taking the hand he'd hooked around her waist in both of her own, she drew it to her lips and kissed the knuckles. "Mmm." She rubbed her cheek against the back of his hand, like a kitten. "I've missed you so much! Two weeks has been an eternity!"

He slid both arms around her slender waist and kissed her lips. "I've missed you, too, my lady fair. Every moment . . . every second . . . seemed an eternity without you."

"Lady fair? Why do you call me that?"

He shrugged. "I don't know, but it suits you. Does it displease you, my sweet?"

"Not in the least. I like it." She sighed with pleasure. Her husband had come home, safe and sound. He looked tired, saddened, but otherwise unharmed. And, compared to his safety and well-being, all else paled—including her foolish dream and some silly half-forgotten endearment.

"Hmmm. Perhaps we should retire, milord," she murmured under her breath. "I suddenly find myself quite exhausted."

"As do I," he agreed. "But what would our servants think, to find us abed in broad daylight?"

She pressed back against him, heard his sharp intake of breath, and giggled. "Do you care, sir?"

"Not in the least, madam," he admitted hoarsely.

"Then set spurs to your horse, milord, for in truth, I am . . . utterly . . . exhausted."

Rare laughter glinted in his eyes as he touched his boot heels to the black horse's flanks. "Are you, in truth? Get up there, Satan!"

Chapter Six

Steyning Forest
1067

"But the long-haired star foretold Godwinson's death and the Norman victory!" the Saxon argued, his face red with the conviction of his words. "We are but mortals! We cannot alter what is written in the stars!"

"Perhaps not," reasoned Eydmond, formerly thane of Lewes, now self-proclaimed king of the rebels. "But I pray ye, friend Arthur—all of you!—remember this. That which is written in the stars is, at the last, interpreted by *mortals*. And unlike God, men are fallible—as are their predictions."

"Eydmund is right," declared Alan, who sat at Eydmond's right hand. "The fiery comet that blazed across the sky last Easter could as easily have foretold *victory* for the English, and the defeat of the blasted Normans! Mayhap our day has yet to come, when we shall rise up and oust the lot of them from our island, and from our homes and lands. We'll apply the toes of our stout English boots to their Norman arses, and send the bastards packing!"

"How shall that come to pass, eh, tell me that? Last Christ's Mass, Duke William had himself crowned king of England at the great Abbey," Godfrey reasoned. "Then he sailed back to Normandy, and took our captured English nobles with him! The Norman swine he left here have taken over our lands and married our women. Now they're building castles to defend their stolen estates and to bequeath to the children they've fathered on our women! Open your eyes, my lord Lewes! See things as they really are, instead of as you wish them to be! The flower of England's manhood died at Hastings—or has since been taken in chains to France! And Godwinson is dead, too!"

"King Harold is dead, aye, and may God assoil him and all our fallen brothers!" Eydmund agreed softly, his deep blue eyes as calm as a lake and filled with compassion. "But as long as there are men like us—like you and me, Godfrey, Alan, and our good friends gathered about the fire— freedom lives on!"

"Amen, my lord Lewes. We'll drink to that!" roared the young thane's companions. Laughing, their faces ruddy, their eyes bright in the light of the roaring fire, they lifted high their drinking horns, which were brimming with mead or watered beer. "To freedom!"

Watching them from across the clearing, hearing their brave exchanges, tears filled Lenore's eyes. She hastily scrubbed her eyes dry on her knuckles, lest her beloved Eydmund see her tears, then wove between the last of the trees, into the clearing proper.

The shadows hid the gauntness of the rebels' cheeks and bellies; the ragged condition of their clothing.

Coming upon them like this, when they were unaware that they were being watched, she could almost convince herself that all was well. That they were not rebels at all, nor outlaws, in fear of their very lives at the hands of the Normans, but a normal hunting party of English noblemen, passing the night in the forest before continuing their boar chase on the morrow.

Their courage and defiance in the face of enormous odds made a sob catch in her throat.

"Who goes there?" snarled a voice.

A brawny hand closed over her arm. Although she had expected the lookout's challenge long before this, she flinched in surprise.

"It is I, Hal. The lady Lenore." She whispered the password they had agreed upon.

"Your pardon, my lady," came the man's immediate response. At once, he released her. "Pass on."

" 'Tis your lord's good fortune I am friend, not foe," she said, "for I drew dangerously near to your master's camp, before you ever challenged me. Have an ear to the sounds of the forest, henceforth, good Hal—and not to the campfire wit! 'Twill be safer for all of us that way."

Though her words were not overly sharp, considering the severity of his lapse, Hal was stricken that he had failed his lord and lady. Head and eyes downcast, he mumbled, "Forgive me, my lady. It will never happen again."

"It must not, Hal. Their lives depend on it."

Shrugging off Hal's hand, she made her way across the forest clearing, to her lover's side. As he greeted her, and led her away to their bower between the trees, she wondered how he would react to the news she brought him. Or whether, given the circumstances, she should even tell him. They would be wed at Lammas, after all. . . .

"I waited until just after moonrise. 'Twas then that I saw her. She kissed the old woman in farewell, they exchanged a few words, then the lady walked away from the priory. She was carrying

92

a sack, *monsieur*. But I could not see what it was she had inside it."

"And? Did you follow the lady Lenore, as I instructed you?" Giles de Harcourt pressed, slopping red wine into a jewel-encrusted goblet from a golden flagon. He drank deeply. Moodily.

"I did, *sieur*, yes," the servant said.

"And? To what place did the lady lead you?"

"Deep into the forest, sir."

Giles's eyebrows shot up. "The forest, you say?"

"*Oui*, my lord. But alas, I lost her amongst the trees."

"You *lost* her!" Giles's voice cracked like a whip across his newly built great hall. The heads of those seated at trestles below the salt turned apprehensively in his direction. "How so, man?"

"I could not help it, sir! The moon was full and newly risen, yet little of its light fell through the treetops. In truth, sir, the forest was so very dark, I could hardly see my own hand before me. And yet, the lady wove her way between the trees like a—like a pigeon that knows its way home to its cote, my lord!" He shrugged. "What was I to do?"

"And she was on foot, you say?" Giles said thoughtfully, taking another gulp of wine.

His servant nodded.

Giles flung himself down in his carved chair and propped a booted foot on the trestle before him. One of his hounds cringed as he raised his goblet to his lips, as if it expected a blow. "If the lady was on foot, then her destination was close by."

"That was my thought, too, my lord. If it please thee, I could take some beaters and hounds into the forest at first light on the morrow, *oui*? It may surprise you what Saxon 'game' we flush out, sir." The man grinned.

"Nooo, not so soon, Francois. Wait a day or two. That way, if the lady suspected she was followed, she will think she got away with it when nothing happens. The same will hold true for our Saxon quarry."

"You risked your life by coming here tonight!" Eydmund whispered, caressing Lenore's cheek.

They had just made love and her beautiful face was sleepy and content in the shadows as she lay in his arms. His heart swelled with love. He would give his own life, and gladly, before aught ever harmed a single precious hair upon his true love's head.

"I implore you, beloved, lie low, until the Norman is done sniffing after you."

"I had to come. I could not help myself. It has been so long since I saw you—not since the night I gave you the ring, remember?"

The Norman had sent the amethyst and pearl ring to her at the priory, with the message that she should not act in haste, but should keep his token of love while she considered his offer of marriage.

Instead, she had given the Norman's bauble to Eydmund, urging him to sell it. Such a costly trinket would buy several weeks' food or weapons for his rebel band, and aid his cause.

"Besides, I waited almost a sennight!" she continued. "I *had* to see you, love," she murmured, snuggling up to him.

"What is it, Lenore? Something's troubling you, I know it! When we came together, it was as if your body was there, but your mind elsewhere."

"There is nothing. . . ."

"No? Then swear it! Look me in the eye—and swear it upon your love for me!"

"Please, love. Don't."

"Why? Because you cannot swear? *Tell me*. What is wrong?"

"Do not make me tell you, I beg you. You have worries enough. Oh, Eydmund, Eydmund." Tears glistened on her cheeks. "What will become of us?"

"That's an easy question to answer. You and I will become man and wife," he reminded her gently, his dark blue eyes tender as he looked down at her. "That is why there is no secret you cannot share with me, lady fair. So, tell me!" he insisted. He grasped her chin and tilted her head back, so that she had no choice but to look him squarely in the eye.

In answer, she took his hand and placed it on her belly.

"Here," she whispered. "Here is my secret. Your child grows here, beneath my heart."

"My child!" The joy in his eyes was all the answer Lenore needed.

Chapter Seven

"So. How do I look?" Madeleine asked Tabitha, anxiously eyeing her reflection in the dressing table mirror.

The gleaming midnight-blue satin was, perhaps, a little severe for an informal dinner party, intended to introduce her to neighbors and family friends of the de Hardcourts.

However, since Aunt Bea had always said the color was an excellent foil for her ash-blond hair and fair complexion, and that the style was becoming, she had decided to wear it tonight. After all, it was not as if she had dozens of suitable gowns to choose from! Country physicians' daughters were not, in the general rule of things, in great demand for dinner parties at the estates of the nobility.

"You look like a queen, you do, my lady," the

little maid assured her, smiling as she gave her mistress's simple coiffure a satisfied pat. "Rector Cargill will reckon he's dining with royalty t'night, he will, mum. And that Mrs. Cargill—well! This dinner'll give her something t'gossip about for the next six months, I shouldn't wonder, bless her!"

"And what about Sir Michael and Lady Sabina?" Madeleine asked curiously, replacing unused pins in the porcelain hairpin container. Sir Michael and Lady Sabina Latimer's estate, Five Gables, bordered the Hall on the far side of the old priory grounds. "Will they like me, do you think?"

She happened to look up and caught Tabitha's reflection in the mirror before her. She was wrinkling her nose.

"Tabitha? What is it? Do you not like the Latimers?"

"Never said I didn't like them, did I, my lady?" Tabitha shot back, looking uncomfortable and twiddling with the skirt of her apron.

"You don't have to. I can see it in your eyes," Madeleine said gently. "It's all right, Tabby. No one's going to sack you because you don't like someone. Or at least, I certainly shan't."

"I know, mum," Tabby agreed unhappily, hanging her head. "You're a good lady, you are. But that Sab . . . that Lady Sabina, she's as sour as spoiled milk, she is!"

"And Sir Michael? What about him?" Perhaps it was poor form to quizz the servants about their guests, but she was curious and there was no one else to ask.

When Justin had given her the guest list so that she could write and send the invitations, he'd told her only that he and Michael Latimer had been friends for as long as he could remember. As boys, they'd run wild over the Kent countryside together and landed themselves in all kinds of mischief. They also had boarded together at Eton, when the time came for them to be sent off to public school, as the sons of English nobility always were.

The rivalry between the two of them had been as fierce as that between many brothers, according to Justin. So fierce, he claimed, that to Michael's way of thinking, they had briefly been rivals for the same woman only a few years before.

"Fortunately for me," Justin had added with a faint, unamused smile, "Michael won the lady's hand in marriage—and her Papa's substantial fortune."

"I see," Madeleine had murmured, a little dismayed. There was an edge to Justin's tone that she couldn't quite put her finger on whenever he mentioned Michael. She would have been willing to wager that, appearances notwithstanding, the friendship between the two men was not without its problems. Was Justin still mourning the loss of Sabina, and angry that Michael and not himself had won the woman's hand—and, apparently, her heart? Or was there some other reason for that odd, flat quality to his voice?

"It . . . it in't my place t'gossip about me betters, mum," she heard Tabitha say evasively, only half her attention on what the girl was talking about.

"I'm sorry, Tabby. What was it you said?"

"I said 'tis not my place t'gossip, mum. Mrs. Fox doesn't hold with it. Nor does Mr. Digby, the butler."

"They don't? Then I shall have to find out for myself, won't I?" Madeleine murmured teasingly, startled by the panic that leaped into Tabby's gray eyes with her declaration.

"Tabby, don't! I'm just teasing you! It's all right. I won't say a word to anyone, I promise. Oh, and you needn't wait up for me tonight. I can undress myself," she assured the girl.

"Are ye sure, mum?"

"Very sure."

"All right, then, mum." Tabby looked as if she wished a huge hole would appear in the Turkey carpet and swallow her up. "My lady?"

"Yes, Tabby?"

"You will be careful, won't you?" the girl urged.

Her brows lifted. "Of my dinner guests? Are

they ogres, then? Surely they can't be so very frightening?"

Tabby slowly shook her head. "Not them, no. But there's . . . there's other things in this house, mum," she said in a rush, as if it was something she'd wanted to tell her for some time. "Things you don't know nothing about, mum. *Needy things.*"

"Needy things?" Madeleine's skin crawled as she echoed Tabitha's words. The fine hairs lifted at the back of her neck. What on earth could Tabby mean by such an odd comment?

Do not fear me, lady fair. . . .

"What things? Why are you telling me this?" she asked, ignoring the seductive plea of that other, inner voice.

"T'warn ye, mum! You're . . . you're a kind lady. A *good* lady. And the fact is, good people attract things they'd be better off *not* attractin', if ye get my meaning?"

It was the longest speech Madeleine had heard the girl make—and the most confusing one. What did Tabitha mean, that she attracted "needy things?"

"No, Tabby. I'm not sure that I do," Madeleine said honestly. "What exactly are you trying to warn me about? Tabby? Tabitha!"

But the girl would say no more as she scuttled from the room, although Madeleine knew Tabby must have heard her.

She had little time to dwell on the maid's odd comments, or her disobedience, however. No sooner had Tabitha left the bedchamber than the connecting door opened and Justin came in.

As always, excitement crackled between them like an electrical current as her husband joined her before the mirrored dressing table. Her heartbeat quickened as he came to stand behind her.

It had been that way from the very first, she remembered. Justin had only to enter a room, and her entire body responded, hummed, vibrated, like a fine instrument played by a master musician. And to think, she had disliked him intensely at first, finding him an austere, unfriendly man when they met, despite his stern good looks and those eyes of midnight-blue velvet flecked with gold that, in a certain light, were black and bottomless wells.

Tonight, he looked urbane, elegant, and lordly in a perfectly tailored black frockcoat and breeches. The bunch of snowy lace at his throat and the deep lace cuffs at his wrists were in striking contrast to his tanned complexion and jaws darkened with faint beard-shadow. His midnight hair, worn clubbed back into a handsome queue, was fastened with a narrow black grosgrain ribbon.

He would have been perfectly at ease in any of London's finest salons or elegant clubs. But instead of hobnobbing with his peers in the heart of London's social whirl, he chose to be here, with her, in this sleepy English backwater.

Standing behind her, he held up a slim black velvet box, meeting her indigo eyes in the mirror with a tender smile.

"Madeleine? It would please me if you would wear this jewelry tonight, *chérie*," he began, opening the box with a tiny key. "It belonged to my mother, la Comtesse Emilie de Harcourt. The necklace and the matching earbobs and bracelet were my father's wedding gifts to her. Tonight, they are mine to you. *Ma mere* would have been delighted to see you wearing the de Harcourt diamonds."

Justin lifted a necklace from the box. Three strands of glittering ice flashed star bursts of purple, silver and blue as they slipped through his fingers like liquid fire. But instead of heat, they felt like ice chips strung together on a chain, as Justin draped the necklace about her throat.

She gasped as he fastened the intricate gold clasp at the base of her neck, then kissed the downy skin just below it. She sighed.

There was, she realized, a large heart-shaped sapphire, set in smaller diamonds, suspended from the center of the lowest strand.

Justin bent and kissed her cheek. "Magnificent."

"Oh, yes. Truly magnificent!" she said in an

awed, breathy voice, unable to believe her husband had casually presented her with a fortune in diamonds. "Thank you, my love!"

She owned a few small pieces of gold jewelry—a simple crucifix she'd received from her papa on her twenty-first birthday, a set of pearl earbobs set in gold, a cameo on a slim gold chain that had been her mama's—but nothing comparable to this priceless set.

"I was referring to my wife, not the bloody necklace," Justin countered huskily, meeting her eyes with his own in the looking glass.

She blushed and quickly looked away, smiling as he idly stroked her hair. She had felt his long, intense look all the way down to her curling toes. As always, her senses quickened at his lightest touch. Dear God, she loved him so very much!

"Tonight, I want you to wear these diamonds when I make love to you, Madeleine," he declared huskily, stroking her throat with one hand as he bent to kiss her. She felt an answering stab of response, deep in her belly "And *only* these diamonds," he added wickedly, trailing his fingertips over her bare shoulder and down one arm.

"As you desire, *m'sieu*. I shall meet you here, after the last of our dinner guests has gone, yes?" she teased throatily as she clipped on the second earbob.

His words stirred a delicious frisson of sexual

hunger in her belly. Her nipples hardened, becoming exquisitely sensitive where they rubbed against her lawn chemise. Dear Lord, was she becoming insatiable? Perhaps. It still delighted— and surprised!—her that the act she had expected to find such a distasteful obligation as a married woman had proven deeply pleasurable, instead. But then, in Justin, she had a most experienced teacher, she was sure. . . .

"Only swear you will not breathe a word of our rendezvous to my lord husband!" she added, lowering her lashes seductively. "He is a jealous man who would not hesitate to challenge you to a duel, sir!"

Justin laughed, took her by the hands and raised her to stand before him. "Pistols on the heath at dawn, eh? Well, who could blame the poor devil? His wife is a very beautiful, highly desirable woman. But, never fear, this tryst shall be our little secret, *chérie.*" He kissed the tip of her nose. "Ours—and our four chaperones'!" he added teasingly, nodding at the stern wooden bedposts that guarded their marriage bed.

"Come. Let us go down and greet our dinner guests, shall we?"

Twelve of them sat down to supper at the long oak refectory table that evening.

The dining room of Steyning Hall was ablaze with the light of countless candles set in glittering Waterford crystal chandeliers. Their light winked off the beautiful old stained-glass bay window, off the finest crystal stemware and translucent porcelain, rimmed with gold. It flashed off highly polished silverware, soup tureens and serving platters, and off the dazzling array of jewels the women wore at fingers, wrist and throat. It bleached the Irish linen tablecloths and the monogrammed serviettes a dazzling white.

There was Rector and Mrs. Peter Cargill, Sir Michael and Lady Sabina Latimer, and Squire Dudley Walshingham and the Honorable Mrs. Walshingham from Steyning village and its environs. Lord and Lady Folkestone, Henry and Judith, and the Duke and Duchess of Dover, Percy and Agatha, arrived by private carriage. The elderly duke and duchess, friends of Justin's father, and the Folkestones, would be staying the night before returning home. Lastly, there were Justin and herself.

Mrs. Fox had reassured her countless times that she need not concern herself about the dinner party. The Hall's staff had done this dozens of times for his lordship. Every dish she had approved for the menu would be perfectly prepared by Mrs. Beaton, and exquisitely served by both maids and footmen.

Nevertheless, Madeleine was still very nervous as she took the high-backed chair the footman held for her at one end of the polished oak table, with Justin seated at the far end. The thought of presiding as the Hall's hostess for the very first time was intimidating, to say the least.

On her right sat Sir Michael, and on her left, Percy, the aging duke of Dover. Both men proved surprisingly charming dinner companions. In fact, Sir Michael—who was as handsome, in his own fair-haired way, as her husband—went out of his way to make her feel at ease, which she had not expected.

Lady Sabina, Sir Michael's wife, seemed to think her husband was spending far too much time conversing with their hostess, judging by the looks she was giving them from her place at the table.

"Justin tells me you and Sir Michael have children, Lady Sabina," Madeleine began, hoping to defuse any jealousy, although the woman surely had little reason to be jealous.

Sabina Latimer was everything Madeleine was not. Her features were stunning, with wide dark eyes set beneath delicately arched brows, high cheekbones that gave her beauty an exotic cast, a small nose and a lush-lipped red mouth. Her flawless complexion was creamy, in dramatic contrast to her mane of glossy black hair, which was elaborately dressed tonight and adorned with glittering ruby pins. Her gown was crimson satin, and of the latest fashion, possibly one of

Mr. Worth's own creations. Men, Madeleine thought, must adore such a beautiful woman.

Unfortunately, her lush red mouth was turned down tonight in an almost permanent expression of disapproval. Sour enough to curdle milk? Madeleine wondered, remembering what Tabby had said and wanting to giggle.

"How old are your little ones, Lady Sabina?" she pressed when Sabina did not immediately respond.

"Constance is five, and Charity a year," Sabina supplied offhandedly, with little apparent interest.

"Two darling girls!" Madeleine exclaimed, imagining two adorable cherubs dressed in spotless pinafores and dresses, with ribbon bows tied in their hair. "They must be such a joy to you and your husband."

"On the contrary, I make it a point to leave their upbringing to Nanny. Child-rearing is all well and good for the working classes and the poor who breed like animals, I daresay, but those of us with social obligation . . . well, we prefer to leave such matters to the servants. Besides, Michael wanted a son. He has no interest in the girls. In fact, he has as little to do with them as possible."

"I see. Then perhaps you'll have another? . . ." Madeleine began, desperately wishing she had chosen another subject—*any* other subject!—

for their conversation. The delicacies Mrs. Beaton had prepared for her and her guests' enjoyment suddenly tasted like sawdust on her tongue. "Who knows? It could be a baby boy, next time."

"There can be no other children. My physician was most adamant on that point," Sabina explained in a lower voice. "Should I carry another child, my own life would be in jeopardy."

"Oh. I'm so sorry. I do hope you'll accept my apologies for bringing up the subject. It . . . it must be very painful for you," Madeleine murmured. "Lady Walshingham. I've been admiring your coiffure all evening. The style is so very becoming, don't you agree, Your Grace?" she asked the elderly duchess, who was thin and long limbed, and reminded Madeleine of a gray-feathered heron. The illusion was aided by the osprey plumes in her hair.

"For my part, I'm disappointed to find a new bride fussing about coiffures and such nonsense when her husband has so recently returned from France," Agatha, the elderly duchess of Dover, scolded Madeleine sharply, looking down her beaky nose and lorgnette at Madeleine. "And likely to be sent back there at any moment," she added. "When I was a young gel, things were very different."

"His lordship is such a dear young man," cooed Althea Cargill with a flutter of her eyelashes. "If I may say so, Lady Madeleine, you are just like turtledoves." She sighed. "Exactly what Steyning Hall needed."

Madeleine smiled at the rector's wife, grateful for the woman's efforts to steer the conversation onto safer ground. For the wife of a clergyman, Althea Cargill applied rather more rouge and powder than was appropriate, and sported two velvet beauty patches on her cheeks, but it was impossible not to like the woman. Or at least, Madeleine found it impossible.

On the two occasions they had met to date Althea Cargill had endeared herself to Madeleine. She was always so enthusiastic about things, whether it was her plans for raising funds for the new church roof, the birth of her spaniel bitch's puppies, or the lives of her husband's parishioners. And unlike some, Althea Cargill never pretended to be something she was not, unless it was fluttery and useless. Despite outward appearances, Madeleine suspected Althea Cargill was neither.

"I agree with Her Grace. It is a miracle Justin has escaped with his head, time after time," Lady Sabina added with what Madeleine could only describe as relish.

The rest of the group chose that moment to abruptly fall silent. Sabina's words plummeted like lead shot into the void, yet each one struck the heart of its intended target: Madeleine herself.

Although she had known all along that Justin's government business in France was probably dangerous, to hear her worst fears voiced in such a callous way was frightening, to say the least.

The thought of Justin meeting a violent end was terrifying. Her stomach, already queasy for some reason, turned over. She felt so upset she thought she might actually be sick.

She wanted to spring to her feet. To run away and hide from these insufferably snobbish people—especially that spiteful Sabina. She was not up to this! In truth, she feared she would *never* be up to this. She should not have married Justin, no matter how dearly she loved him. She simply could not be the wife he needed and deserved, the perfect society hostess who knew exactly the right things to say to people like these.

From the far end of the table, Justin fixed her with a smoldering dark-blue stare. *"Trust me,"* his expression seemed to say. *"Answer only to me."*

"Surely you forget, Lady Sabina, Your Grace," he observed in a low, well-modulated voice that had everyone silent and straining to hear his every word, "that my own mother was French, as is my entire family on her side. One does not simply ignore the ties of blood. And as for my wife," Justin continued softly, gazing into her eyes over the dancing candleflames, "Madeleine knows that I love her with all my heart." A half smile curved his mouth, giving his dark good looks a wicked, almost saturnine quality. "Or should, by now. Nothing—I repeat, *nothing*—will keep me from coming back to her."

He grinned and raised his crystal wine glass. "Ladies and gentlemen, I give you my bride, Madeleine, Lady de Harcourt! My beautiful wife, the light of my life—and my only love!"

"Lady Madeleine! Hear, hear, sir!" The other gentlemen at table murmured polite agreement. There was a spattering of applause after they raised their glasses to her in salute. Only Sabina did not join in, she noticed.

Embarrassed yet touched, Madeleine blew her husband a kiss across the table, then smiled her thanks at the others. She was well aware that the duchess was scowling, and that Sabina looked even sourer than before. Sir Michael continued to eye her bosom over the rim of his wine glass whenever he thought himself unobserved—or was it her diamonds he eyed so avidly?

Flattering as they were, Justin's assurances did little to rid her belly of the sick, queasy feeling. It persisted.

She waited until the men retired to Justin's game room for billiards, brandy and cigars, then escorted her female guests into the drawing room across the hallway.

After seeing the ladies comfortably settled and pouring tiny demitasse cups of coffee, she excused herself briefly, on the excuse that she needed to fetch her fan. In reality, she desperately craved a few moments alone, in which to compose herself and settle her rebellious stomach.

"Please, ladies, make yourselves comfortable," she urged her female guests. "I shall be only a moment."

The huge bedchamber lay in shadow except for a small lamp left burning.

Going to the washstand, she poured cool water from the ewer into the basin, dipped a flannel face cloth into it and bathed her face.

The cool water felt wonderful, so refreshing on her burning cheeks. She wrung out the cloth, dabbed her throat and the back of her neck, and sighed. Better. Much better. Downstairs, she'd thought she might faint if she didn't get some fresh air.

As she was patting her face dry, she felt a prickly sensation at the base of her spine. A tingle that said she was being watched.

Help me!

The voice was very loud.

Straightening up, she slowly turned around, sweeping the room with a nervous glance.

Nothing. And yet, the prickly sensation lingered.

Carrying the lamp with her, she went to each of the chamber's corners in turn. Trembling as she did so, she raised the lamp high, so that the light dispelled the darkest shadows.

There was nothing there—as she had known, in her heart, there would be nothing. Or at least, nothing tangible. Nothing she could feel or see. Nothing real.

Silly goose! she scolded herself, but she was still trembling, nonetheless. The dining and drawing rooms had both been uncomfortably warm, but it was quite chilly up here. So chilly, gooseflesh had risen on her bare arms.

Do not fear me, lady fair!

She all but dropped the lamp. The voice was so loud, so crystal clear, so . . . so insistent! It came from inside her head, however. Not from some external being.

I don't fear you. And I won't listen to you. You're not real, she told herself sternly as she sank down onto the bed. She was shaking uncontrollably now. *Be silent! Leave me alone.*

A small posy of wilted wildflowers, tied together with a wisp of straw, lay upon the bolster.

Putting the voice out of her mind, she concentrated her attention on the posy, instead.

It was probably a country charm, intended to bring the occupants of the bed a sound night's sleep. A charming gesture, she thought, wondering who could have left it, then deciding it was probably Tabby, or if not her, Effie. It had not been there earlier, when she was dressing, she was almost certain. She frowned thoughtfully. The mauve flowers looked familiar, but for the moment, their name escaped her.

As she crossed the entrance hall at the foot of the staircase, she heard whispers and rustling in the shadows beneath the servants' stairs. They were followed immediately by an urgent, *"No!"*

She tensed instinctively, but unlike the eerie moonshadow she had glimpsed her first night at the Hall, or the voice she heard in her head, there was nothing in the least supernatural about these sounds! They were stealthy, yes, but robustly human.

"Who's there?" she demanded sharply, trying to see. "Show yourself!"

To her surprise, Effie, the chambermaid, emerged from the shadows. Red-faced, she thrust quickly past Madeleine, refusing to look her mistress in the eye as she fled up the back staircase, to her dormer in the attic. Her mobcap was awry, Madeleine saw, lips tightening, and the bib of her apron was rumpled.

A man followed Effie from the shadows, dabbing at his lip with a kerchief.

Madeleine's jaw dropped. She expected one of the footmen—perhaps that Trevor Fox!—to be Effie's secret sweetheart. But she was wrong.

Chapter Eight

"Sir Michael!" she exclaimed, genuinely shocked. "What business have you with my servants?"

The wretch actually had the nerve to grin.

"Come, come, dear lady. An explanation isn't necessary, surely?" He winked. "We are both adults, after all."

"Be that as it may, sir, please leave my maids alone," Madeleine suggested sharply, "and find someone else with whom to dally. May I suggest your . . . your wife?"

His smile vanished.

"I keep forgetting. You're not one of us, are you, Maddy, love?" he jeered. "If you were, you'd know when to keep your pretty mouth shut and leave well enough alone."

"How dare you talk to me that way!" she exclaimed.

"Your precious Effie's a little slut—a servant!" he said contemptuously, his pale eyes flickering over Madeleine as if he considered his best friend's wife of the same caliber. "Such drabs do what they must for an extra coin, and none the wiser. It's been that way for centuries—"

"That does not make it right!"

"Perhaps not. But a lady—a real lady, that is, one to the manor born, rather than one who married into the upper classes, would have ignored such an incident as beneath her."

"Any lady who ignores the welfare of those in her care, Sir Michael—especially her young female servants—is a lady in name only," she shot back softly. "Now, if you would please step aside, sir, I wish to pass." When, after several seconds, he made no move to let her by, she added, "Do not make me tell Justin—"

"Tell Justin? Tell Justin what?" Michael scoffed. "Jus and I have been as close as—closer!—than brothers since we were nine years old. You can't really imagine he'd believe a word you said against me, after the things we've done together? Just because you're his wife?"

"I do, without question," she said with quiet conviction, staring him down.

Latimer snorted—but he was the first to look away, she saw with a tiny surge of triumph. He was not as secure in his closeness to her husband as he would have liked her to believe.

"What's going on out here?" Justin's deep voice rang out into the hallway. Obviously, he sensed the tension between them, although he had missed their exchange.

The aroma of fine cigars and cognac wafted out into the hallway around her husband's tall frame, which was silhouetted by the smoky light in the open doorway of the game room. "Madeleine? Michael? Is everything all right?"

"It is, yes. And nothing's 'going on,' Jus, old boy, more's the pity!" Michael responded loudly. His lazy upper-crust drawl managed to sound amused, roguish, regretful—and in no way disconcerted. "I simply happened to be in the right place at the right time—just as your beautiful wife missed her footing on the last two stairs."

"Madeleine?" Justin asked. Concerned, he came toward them. "Were you hurt, *chérie?*"

"She's perfect. Not so much as a bruise! You owe me, de Harcourt! If I hadn't caught her, she might easily have snapped her lovely neck in the dark! Isn't that right, Lady Madeleine?" he asked smoothly.

"It's possible, yes," Madeleine agreed with reluctance, furious at herself for being a party to the man's easy lies. He would have touched the back of her neck, as if to give emphasis to his lies with the gesture, but she quickly jerked her head away. "Please, let me pass now, sir. My guests are waiting for me."

Michael Latimer bent to retrieve the fan she had dropped in her surprise. "But, of course. Your fan, dear lady," he murmured, making her a mocking bow.

She snatched the fan from him, tossed her fair head, then thrust past him, much as Effie had done.

Justin frowned. He caught her elbow as she hurried by him, turning her so that she was forced to look at him. "You look pale. Are you sure nothing's wrong?"

"Yes, of course," she insisted after a moment's hesitation, unable to meet his eyes. Feeling guilty, though for what she could not have explained, since Michael Latimer had been the one in the wrong, she rejoined her guests.

"You're a lucky devil, my friend," she heard him exclaim behind her. "But then, you de Harcourts always were."

"I've told you before, Latimer. Luck has nothing to do with it," she heard Justin's answer.

Was she imagining things, or was there a cold, angry edge to her husband's voice? Madeleine wondered as she closed the drawing room door behind her. And if so, was his anger directed at Sir Michael—or at her?

Chapter Nine

"God! I thought they'd never leave," Justin murmured, dropping down onto the bed beside her. He propped himself up on one elbow.

"Or retire for the night," Madeleine added, stepping out of the billowing cloud of navy satin that was her gown. She picked up the garment, shook it out and hung it tidily in the small wardrobe alcove that adjoined the bedchamber, enjoying the small personal task.

To think, there had been times at Rose Arbor, usually in the autumn, when she and Aunt Bea had been busy bottling and preserving jams and jellies from dawn to dusk, when they had both said how wonderful it must be to have servants at one's beck and call. But now that she had more servants than she'd ever imagined, Madeleine found she missed doing such simple tasks as hanging up her own gowns herself.

"Her Grace, Agatha, duchess of Dover, insisted that no fewer than three heated bricks be placed in her bed, before she would even contemplate sliding between the sheets," she disclosed.

"Three? in July? Good Lord! The woman must be as cold-blooded as a frog!"

Madeleine laughed. "Easily! And Mrs. Fox had the chamber maid put warming pans in her bed, too!"

In fact, upon reflection, Madeleine believed Effie must have been on her way back to the kitchens from the blue guest room when Sir Michael waylaid his reluctant victim under the stairs.

She went over to where Justin was sprawled and offered him her back. "I told Tabby she needn't wait up for me. Would you mind unlacing me?"

"My pleasure, *chérie,*" Justin sat up. "Poor Uncle Percy! I fear His Grace, the duke, can no longer keep Her Grace warm in bed, the poor old devil." He deftly unlaced her stays and tossed the corset aside.

"Mmm. Thank you." She sighed with relief. "That's much better."

"I'll say," Justin murmured, drawing her back against his chest and nuzzling her throat. He slid his arms around her, cupping both breasts. "Everything's so much more . . . accessible, without that wretched contraption."

Slipping both hands inside her chemise, he fondled her breasts, toying with the nipples until they grew hard as pebbles.

"Rest assured, my sweet, that the duchess's complaint is not one Lady de Harcourt will have for a very, *very* long time, hmm?" He reached lower, smoothing his hands down over her firm, flat belly and rounded hips.

Her breathing quickened. Her pulse skittered as his hot breath filled her ear. His tongue traced the delicate seashell whorls, bringing warmth and a rosy flush to her skin. She could feel his hardness nudging her bottom as he held her against him, and pressed backward to meet it.

"I certainly hope not, milord," she whispered. "For I sincerely doubt there are enough hot bricks in all of Steyning to warm this drafty bedchamber."

Laughing, she turned smoothly around to face him, standing now between his spread thighs as he sat upon the edge of the tester. Her eyes holding his, she stroked his broad shoulders, skimmed her fingers across his chest, traced his nipples with her fingertips until they stiffened into tight nubbins of flesh. She ducked her head, then nipped, nibbled and licked each one, until he groaned.

A narrow *T* of dark hair lay like a shadow across his chest and down his washboard middle. Firmly planting a palm on his chest, she pushed him down, onto his back.

"Uhhf!"

He went down without much of a fight, his eyes hot and slitted with lust as he lay there, watching her undress.

She did so very slowly, excited and encouraged by his sensual expression. As she lifted her arms above her head, her breasts swung forward like perfect snowy bells, steepled with hard buds that were the salmon pink of angelskin coral, surrounded by aureoles that had darkened to red.

She heard the breath catch in his throat. Felt his rigid staff buck beneath her fingertips as he cupped a breast, weighed it in his hand. "Madeleine, *chérie*. Have I told you how beautiful you are?" he whispered. "Or how much I want you?"

"A time or two, yes," she responded, smiling a lazy half smile. She wore only white silk stockings, lacy garters, and the de Harcourt diamonds now.

Tugging free of Justin's hands, she seductively removed her garters, then slowly rolled down the silk stockings, trailing the gauzy wisps across his body as she drew them off, one by one.

Her fair skin was luminous in the shadows. It had the creamy luster of pale pink pearls. The necklace and bracelet reflected the lamplight in brilliant blue rainbows, encircling her throat and wrist. The earbobs that dangled from each perfect ear trailed tails of light, like shooting stars.

As she knelt over him, he tugged the pins and combs from her hair, so that it spilled down her back in long ringlets.

"Come here, my lady fair." His voice was thick with desire, as he lay back, lifting her astride his flanks.

She cupped her breasts, then ran her hands down, over her body, seductively skimming her hips, her belly, then sliding down between her inner thighs. "What would you have me do, my lord?" She eyed him coyly, her head tipped to one side, her lips slightly parted and moist.

Justin wetted his lips, his mouth dry, his breathing ragged and shallow. "Ride, my lady."

"Ride?" Her laughter was throaty. "Forgive me, I do not know how, sir."

"Never fear, madame. I'll teach you," he promised.

Much later, they lay drowsily in each others' arms, their limbs entwined, the linens twisted about their naked bodies, exhausted by their lovemaking.

"Justin?" Madeleine whispered.

"Hmm?" he asked, lazily stroking her hair.

"Do you wish you'd married a duchess or a countess?"

"No."

"Why not?"

"Because I didn't marry a title. I married you. The woman you are. The woman I love." He kissed the top of her head."

"But wouldn't it be better if I had a title?"

"The only title I care about is the one you have. Mistress Madeleine de Harcourt, wife of Justin de Harcourt, Esquire." He nipped her earlobe with his teeth, then tunneled under the bedlinens to bite her bottom. "Lady Madeleine," he said, his voice muffled.

"But . . . ow! . . . a doctor's daughter has very little notion of how to behave in high society," she said in a small voice, squirming away from his teeth. "You must tell me when I'm doing something wrong. More than anything, I want to be the perfect wife for you. Justin, stop it!"

"You are the perfect wife, in every way," he drawled wickedly, kissing the second cheek, "but one."

"Oh?" She tensed. "And what way is that?"

"You talk too bloody much, *chérie!*"

"Justin! Be serious, please," she implored, pushing his marauding hands from their explorations. "I want to be the perfect wife everywhere, not only in . . . in bed!"

"You always underestimate yourself, my sweet," he said seriously, sliding up the bed so that they were face to face. "You are the perfect wife for me in every area of our lives because of the person you are. Intelligent, kind, caring, lively—all the reasons I love you. And you love me. Who the rest of the world thinks we should marry is unimportant—or at least, it is to me. When you married me, you made me the happiest man alive. And as for being a lady, no title could make you more of a lady than you already are."

He tunneled back to her side. His arms surrounded her. Her cheek was pillowed on his broad chest. She could hear his heart's steady beat beneath her ear, like the measured throb of a drum. How could she doubt him or his love, when her body was full of the sweet ache of his lovemaking?

Love overflowed her own heart—and with it, a new and terrifying emotion. *Fear.* The fear that she might lose him.

"What the duchess said about your work for the government? Was it . . . was it true?" she asked several minutes later. "Is it really very dangerous?"

He hesitated, perhaps trying to decide whether to lie to her or not. "Yes."

"Then why is it that everyone knows except me! I'm your wife, Justin. Why didn't you tell me?" she demanded, pushing herself up on one elbow.

"I didn't want to frighten you. I was hoping

we'd have some time together, before I was called away again, to explain about my missions. I certainly didn't expect to get orders during our wedding breakfast!"

"What . . . what is it that you do, when you're over there, I mean?" She had a fair idea, thanks to Sabina and the horrid duchess of Dover, but she wanted him to tell her himself.

He explained almost casually, as if helping prisoners marked for execution escape Paris's dreaded Bastille was not a particularly risky or even an unusual undertaking. "Since Father's death last year, I have carried out these rescues alone, except for the help of a friend or two in France."

"Were those you rescued members of your family?"

"The first ones, yes. My cousin, Armand, his wife Celeste and their small children, poor devils. They were condemned for no other reason than that they were members of the hated French aristocracy. You cannot imagine how it is in Paris these days, *chérie*. The madness . . . the sheer madness of it all!

"When it became known in certain circles that my father and I were able to bring about such rescues, we were contacted by our government. They asked us to engineer the escapes of certain individuals of their choosing. Ones the powers-that-be considered politically valuable."

"*Is that why you were in Whitchurch last spring? Because of these . . . émigrés?*" His explanation answered so many of the questions she had.

He nodded. "Yes." He hesitated. "Madeleine, there's something else you should know. I didn't fall off my horse, as I told you when we met. I was shot by a sniper as we came ashore at Dover. I managed to deliver my 'cargo' safely to Charles, but then—"

"—but then, your wound required the services of a physician. My father," she finished.

"Exactly. Doctor Lewis removed the ball from my back and treated the subsequent infection. And 'twas your good fortune that he did, my lady fair."

"Me? How so?"

"If we had not met, you would still be a spinster, gathering dust upon the marriage shelf!" he teased.

"Ha! You would like to think so, sir!" She punched him playfully in the chest. "I'll have you know that I was a spinster by *design*, not because no man has ever asked for my hand."

"Oh? And why is that?" he asked, idly winding one of her creamy ringlets about his finger.

"Because, sir, my Papa means to care for his beloved patients as long as he is capable of doing so, God bless him. And in order to do that, he'll need a housekeeper. Since Aunt Bea is not getting any younger, I thought if I did not marry, I could keep house for him."

"William must come here to us when he is ready to retire. He could treat the villagers. There's always someone that needs doctoring, and old Doctor Smythe is getting no younger. Write to him, Madeleine. Tell him he is always welcome in our home. I know his grandchildren will enjoy having their grandfather at the Hall, as shall I."

By *grandchildren*, Justin meant *their* children. A thrill ran through her at the thought of holding his baby in her arms.

"Thank you," she murmured, kissing Justin's chest. "That would be wonderful."

"Yes. But not nearly as wonderful as what I have in mind."

Chapter Ten

Steyning Forest
1067

Anger flared in Lenore as she wove her way between the last few trees.

Yet again, Hal and the other sentry had not challenged her as she approached the clearing where the Saxon rebels made their camp. Fugitives all, every one of them had prices on their heads. 'Twould have been safer had Eydmond chained hounds in the woods to sound the approach of strangers, rather than a brace of idle louts who sounded no alarm whatsoever!

Fuming, she pulled up short at the edge of the small clearing, stunned by what she saw there. Or rather, by what she *did not* see.

Eydmond's camp was gone! Not a horse, man-

tle, broadsword or pikestaff remained to show
that the rebels had ever been there at all.

She ran across the clearing, certain she must
have made a mistake. Surely this was the wrong
clearing? But she found the blackened ring
where their campfire had burned, and the leafy
bower between two low trees, where she and
Eydmond became lovers that spring.

A sob clogged in her throat. The thick grass
over which he had tenderly spread his mantle for
her to lie upon was still crushed from the weight
of their bodies.

Fighting tears, she looked around her. Yes.
This was the place. There was no longer a morsel
of doubt in her mind. It *was* the place.

She sank down upon a tree stump, knowing if
she did not, she would swoon. Her heart was
heavy with dread, and there was a sick coldness
in her belly.

What had happened here, she wondered? Had
their camp been discovered by Normans? Had
Eydmond and his followers been forced to flee
and make a new camp elsewhere?

Nay. If they had been attacked, there would be
signs, surely? The ashes of the fire would not
have vanished so tidily nor so completely. The
grass and earth would have been churned to mud
by the horses' hooves. And—she swallowed—
there would be *bodies*, too, as well as other signs
a foray had taken place.

She cradled her belly, as yet still flat as any virgin maid's, as if with hands alone, she could protect the fragile life within. *Eydmond, my love and lord, where are you? Where may I find thee?* she silently asked the giants of the forest that ringed the small clearing.

Her only answer was the whispery rustle of leaves as a sudden chill breeze stirred the oaken boughs.

She shivered. No birds warbled above her, for all that it was midafternoon, and the day was fair and warm. There was no sign of fox, badger or deer, either, nor any wild creature of the forest. Had something happened here to frighten them away? Or . . . was it simply the strong scent of man that caused the forest creatures to give the clearing wide berth?

Whatever the cause, the silence, the stillness was uncanny. Lenore crossed herself as she knelt upon a tussock of grass. Hands folded, eyes closed, head bowed, she said a fervent prayer for her Eydmond's safety.

The sun lay low upon the horizon when Lenore returned to St. Mary's. The sweet chanting of female voices, raised in plainsong, rose on the evening air.

She slipped in through the priory's gatehouse, which faced west. Not far from the gatehouse rose wooden scaffolding and the skeleton of the fine new castle the hated Norman was in the process of building, to the glory of William the Bastard and himself. As yet, only the lower levels were completed. The great rectangular keep rose from the slight incline upon which it perched like a great dark hawk, wings spread over its territory below—spread not in protection, but in threat and warning of its Norman might.

The stone masons and the young apprentices who usually scampered up and down the ladders or crawled about the scaffolding like spiders dancing on a web were huddled together this even', off to one side of the construction site. Their faces were long and unhappy, or so they seemed to her, and they spoke in hushed tones quite unlike their usual raucous bawdy banter.

Just before she passed under the gatehouse, into the priory, she happened to glance over her shoulder, and saw the reason for their melancholy.

One of their number lay dead upon the grass in their midst, sprawled lifeless on his back in a puddle of water. A livid bruise the size of a man's fist showed starkly against the drowned man's freckled forehead.

She recognized him, Lenore realized, filled with pity and sorrow. The red-haired, homely young mason had oftimes paused in his work to tug at his forelock and bid her a cheerful, "Good morrow, my lady," whenever she passed by. His cheeky, enagaging smile had more than made up for his unremarkable features.

A plump young woman—his wife, no doubt—knelt, weeping, at her dead husband's side. Two grubby children, clothed in little better than rags, clung to her skirts. One, a little lad with big blue eyes, had inherited his father's ragged foxy hair.

"Tell me, what were my Rufus a-doing there? He had no reason t'go t' the weir. None at all!" the goodwife sobbed, her face ravaged by tears, her speech thickened and all but incoherent with grief. "And how could he have drowned, tell me that? Swim, he could, aye, like a blessed fish, God rest his soul!" She broke down and sobbed as another of the masons' wives came to comfort her.

Uttering a silent prayer for the man's soul and his little family's survival, Lenore crossed the cloisters to the prioress's cell. With her own be-loved man missing, she knew what terrible sor-row the woman must be feeling.

At this hour, her aunt was probably at supper in the refectory with the other sisters. She would wait for her here, in the prioress's cell, she de-cided, pacing back and forth between the spartan walls in her agitation.

"My child! Where have you been?" Aelfreda demanded, hurrying into the cell some while later. Despite her concern, she took her niece's hands in her own and fondly kissed her brow in greeting.

"He has gone, Aunt! They are all gone!" Lenore whispered, tears slipping down her cheeks as she clung to the older woman for support. "Oh, sweet Mother of God, what shall I do? For the love of God, *what shall I do?*"

"Shh. Shh. Who has gone? Explain yourself, child," Aelfreda scolded, shaking her gently. "I can do nothing unless you tell me! What is it?" In truth, her niece's pallor frightened her as nothing else could. Her eyes were blank with shock and terror, too, her iips all but bloodless.

Haltingly, Lenore explained how she had gone to Eydmond's camp in the forest. She described finding the clearing deserted, with no sign of a fight having taken place, and not a blade of grass disturbed by either hoof or boot heel.

"It is as if they were never there at all, Aunt! But surely, if they had been forced to flee, there would be some signs left behind?"

Aelfreda nodded in understanding, her gray eyes deeply troubled. "There would, aye. But do not give way to panic, child. Come. Dry your eyes. Cease your weeping, my dearling," she murmured, drawing Lenore into her arms to comfort her. "I warrant Thane Eydmond suspected that the whereabouts of his stronghold had become known—could that not be it? Perchance he and his followers removed all traces of their camp in the forest before they found themselves another hiding place?

"When he is able to do so safely, I am certain your lord will send word for you to join him at his new camp. For now, you must be patient, my child, and wait."

"Prioress. Aunt. *Dearest* Aunt. You are my lady mother's own dear sister, and as precious to me as was that good lady herself. Because you are dear to me, there is something I must tell you."

"Anything, child. Anything. No daughter of my body could be dearer to me than you," Aelfreda murmured, stroking Lenore's fair head. "Whatever it is, you may tell me, have no fear that I shall judge thee."

"I am with child, Aunt."

Aelfreda bit her lip. "Dear God in Heaven! Are you sure?"

Lenore nodded. "My courses are but a sennight late, but yes, I am quite sure. A woman knows such things."

"And you told him this? The father, I mean? Your Eydmond?"

She nodded. "The last time we were together."

"Ah. And now Thane Eydmond is gone."

Anger flashed in Lenore's eyes. "I know what you are thinking, but it is not so, Aunt!" she cried sharply, pulling free of her aunt's arms. "Eydmond . . . Eydmond loves me, just as

I love him . . . with all his heart and soul. He would never desert me, or his child, I know he would not, as surely as I know that you and my mother are sisters. When I told him, oh, you should have seen the joy in his eyes! Joy . . . and love . . . for us both."

"I'm sure you are right. But . . . think of it, dearest child. He is young, your lord Eydmond, too young, perhaps to shoulder the burden of leading a rebellion against the conqueror and his Norman lords. Mayhap," the prioress suggested very gently, very carefully, "the added responsibility of a wife and child, in such uncertain times, became too much for him to—

"*No!*" Lenore hissed, her eyes blazing. She flung off the prioress's hands. "I cannot believe he has deserted us, Aunt! *I will not!*" She sprang across the cell to the doorway. She would have plunged through it in headlong flight, had her aunt's voice not rung out.

"Wait, child! There is more we must speak of. The Norman was here again today. He wanted you to go a-hawking with him. He was most displeased to find you gone."

"What . . . what did you tell him?" Lenore whispered, turning to face her. "How did you explain my abscence?"

"I told a lie. One for which I must certainly seek absolution at my next confession." A naughty smile curved Aelfreda's generous lips, lighting her handsome oval face. "I told him that you—devout Christian lady that you are!—had made a small pilgrimage to Canterbury cathedral, accompanied by two sisters of our order. Since I did not know where you had gone, I told the Norman you were not expected to return for two days, maybe longer. What else was I to tell him?" She shrugged, her face pale with worry beneath her wimple. "You must not show yourself for a day or two, child."

"Never fear, I will not. You did well, Aunt, and I thank you for it. But, what else happened? There is more. I can see it in your eyes, Aunt. Did the Norman tell you what business he had with me?"

"He did." The prioress wetted her lips nervously. "It is the same business as before. *Marriage*," Aelfreda murmured. "He also bade me tell you that . . . that he is eager to wed you, my dearling, and he is a most persistent suitor. Oh, child, he will not easily abandon his cause, despite your refusal! When he speaks of you, his eyes burn like flame." The prioress shuddered. "In truth, I fear him. Surely he is kin to the Devil himself!"

"A pilgrimage to Canterbury, you said? Then we have a day or two before he returns," Lenore murmured thoughtfully, her mind on more important matters than the Norman. "God willing, 'twill be more than long enough for my lord to send me word of his whereabouts. Meanwhile, I shall ask the travelers in the hospitium if they passed Thane Eydmond and his men upon the road, or if they heard anything in the taverns on their journeys."

"And if they did not? What then, sweet girl? What then?" Aelfreda's voice trembled with doubt. It was as if their positions, for the moment, were reversed, she now the maid, her niece the matron.

Lenore's lower lip quivered, yet she swallowed bravely over the tears that choked her throat, and squared her jaw, trying to be optimistic and hope for the best.

Yet somehow, she knew, in her deepest heart, as she had sensed in the forest from the moment she had seen the empty clearing, that the best was not to be. Her woman's intuition told her she would never again have word from her Eydmond. Would never again cradle his fair head upon her bosom. Never again taste his kiss upon her lips. Never again know the strength of his arms about her. Nor would their child ever know its father's love.

"Then, dear Aunt," she whispered brokenly, her trembling fingertips pressed to her belly, "then must we devise some other clever plan. And pray."

As, hands clasped, the two women knelt together, the chapel bell began to toll.

Chapter Eleven

As they sat at breakfast the Saturday following the dinner party, Justin announced that he was riding over to Five Gables to see Dark of the Moon, the new mare Michael had purchased.

"According to him, she's a Thoroughbred, a direct descendent of Eclipse." Justin's excitement simmered just below the surface, showing itself as a boyish gleam in his usually serious dark-blue eyes.

"Eclipse?" Madeleine repeated politely.

He nodded. "A descendant of the Darley Arabian."

"The Darley Arabian?" she echoed again, feeling like an idiot.

"One of the three foundation stallions," he explained. Seeing the puzzlement on her face, he clarified, "There was Lord Godolphin's stallion, then Byerly's Turk and the Darley Arabian. The four progeny of these first three stallions—Eclipse, Herod and his son, Highflyer, and Matchem—are the lines from which all Thoroughbreds today are descended. My intention is to breed Thoroughbred horses here at Steyning, you see. Michael hopes to be a part of that venture and by so doing, turn his fortunes around. To that end, he wants Saracen or Satan, Steyning's Thoroughbred stallions, to stand at stud for his mares, including this new one. The proceeds from the sale of any foals sired by Steyning's studs will be shared by both stables."

"That sounds like a fair proposition to me. What do you think of the idea?" Madeleine asked, flattered that her husband would discuss his business affairs with her. Most men didn't, from what she had heard, her sister Felicity's husband, David, included.

"I told him that I would consider his proposition, with reservations," Justin continued. "First, I must examine the new mare for myself, then go over her pedigree and the pedigrees of the other mares in Five Gables's stables with Nowles, before I commit our stables to anything." Justin had mentioned before that Nowles, Steyning's head groom, knew Thoroughbred horses, breeding and bloodlines better than any man he knew—with, perhaps, the exception of his late father and his father's friend, Jim Weatherby, who was researching pedigrees for the general stud book he hoped to make public very soon.

"You sound a little skeptical."

"I am. This horse-breeding venture is just the latest in a string of schemes by which Michael hopes to recoup his family fortune by hanging on to my coattails," Justin explained, tight-lipped. "You see, my father and I always hoped to start a breeding farm for Thoroughbreds. Ordinarily, I wouldn't give a damn if a friend wanted to come into the enterprise. But unlike myself, Latimer can't afford to lose money and chalk it up to experience if this falls through. I happen to know he's already squandered most of his inheritance at the races, you see, or at the gaming tables of the City's most notorious hells. I suspect most of Sabina's hefty dowry has followed it. The damned fool!" he finished. "He refuses to listen to reason and exercise a little caution."

"Then let's hope this mare is everything he claims, and the answer to his prayers," Madeleine suggested, dabbing her lips on a lace-trimmed serviette.

"I hope so, too. At times, he seems so bloody . . . what's the word? . . . desperate? I hate seeing a friend in his predicament, but after the last time, I told him there would be no further loans from me."

"You've done what you can," she murmured sympathetically. "Nobody likes to watch their friends suffer or go under. But there's only so much *you* can do for them. Friends or not, they must also help themselves, if they are ever to get out of trouble."

Justin reached out and squeezed her hand. "Nicely put, your ladyship. I know you don't care for Michael, but even so, not an unkind word from your lips!"

She laughed, embarrassed by his compliment. She was not nearly the saint he made her out to be. Thank goodness he could not read her thoughts! "What makes you think I don't like him?"

"Do you?" he challenged.

"Not really, no," she admitted, wrinkling her nose.

"I knew it. I could feel hostility in the air the other evening." He smiled. "In the hallway, remember? It was fairly crackling."

"Was it so obvious? I'm sorry. I'm afraid I found him—"

"Arrogant? Overbearing?"

"Yes." As well as a few other choice adjectives she could think of.

"That's Michael for you. You didn't happen to catch him with one of our maids, did you?"

She stared at him. "How on earth did you know about that?" She had mentioned it to no one, not even Effie, who had been so embarrassed since that evening, she had been avoiding her mistress. Madeleine had decided to ignore the incident, unless the girl approached her or brought it up herself.

Justin threw down his utensils in disgust, his expression furious. "I knew something had upset you. I should have called the rogue on it! Damn it, I warned him about bothering our people."

"Did you? Then that explains it."

"Explains what?"

"Why he tried to make me feel very much the outsider when I threatened to tell you. I expect he was afraid I really might! It was his way of trying to scare me off."

"I dare say it was." He looked fit to be tied. "What did he say to you?"

"Nothing much, really. He just implied that, in upper-class circles, it was quite all right to take advantage of innocent young girls. And that if I had been one of you, I would have known that without having to be told."

"Did he, by God!"

Lord help Michael if he rubbed Justin the wrong way that afternoon, she thought. "Must you take him to task about it? It's not important and I'd much rather you didn't say anything. Please?"

He frowned. "And let him think he can get away with that sort of behavior?"

"Better that, than have him thinking I went running to you about it."

145

"That's precisely what you should have done, my dear!" There was reproof in his tone.

"Perhaps. But . . . he's your friend. Your boyhood friend."

"Even more reason for him to treat my wife with respect."

"Please? I'd really just like to forget about it, this time. If Michael is given reason to resent me so soon after my arrival, we will always be uncomfortable around each other. The last thing I want to do is destroy the friendship between the two of you."

Justin snorted. "Obviously he doesn't give a damn."

"I'm sure he does, terribly. He just doesn't show it. Please, Justin? Just this once."

"Oh, all right. I'll spare the wretch this time." A faint smile played about his lips. "Since you pleaded his cause so prettily. I have an idea. Why don't you ride over to Five Gables with me, *chérie*?" he suggested, spearing a sausage with his fork. "It's high time you practiced riding somewhere other than the paddock."

His dark eyes kindled. She knew, her gaze meeting his, that he was thinking of something very different from the innocuous jaunt he was suggesting. She blushed and looked down at the rasher of bacon on her plate.

"Besides, it's only a half-hour's ride," he continued. "You could take tea with Sabina, while

Michael and I discuss horseflesh. I'm sure the poor woman must be bored, living so far from London. You two could be company for each other when I'm not here."

Madeleine wrinkled her nose. Perhaps it wasn't very Christian of her, or even very nice, but everything within her rebelled at the idea. She had no desire to befriend the woman for whose affections both Justin and Sir Michael had once been rivals. Nor, she fancied, would Sabina welcome any friendly overtures on her part. They had disliked each other intensely from the get-go. Nothing was going to change that.

"Do you mind very much if I don't come this time? I'm still stiff from my last riding lesson. Besides, I'd planned to make some brass rubbings for my father."

Her claim that she was still stiff was no lie. Her bottom felt numb, and her thigh muscles still ached from yesterday's riding lesson. She had lost count of how many times Justin and his head groom, the gnomish, bowlegged Mr. Nowles, had made her ride around and around the paddock—so many times, she had been quite dizzy when she dismounted. She'd had to perch with her right knee hooked uncomfortably over the wretched sidesaddle, her back poker-straight, her hands resting lightly upon the reins.

Why was it that only men were allowed to ride in the most logical, comfortable method, seated securely astride their mounts? When Justin rode, he became a part of his horse, the two of them moving as one. So much a part, he reminded her of a mythical centaur, half god, half horse. She, on the other hand, thudded up and down like a sack of potatoes on her mount's back, no more a part of the poor creature than a horsefly!

Still, despite her stiffness and the accompanying difficulties, she intended to persevere with her lessons. One day, she would be able to ride effortlessly with Justin over the countryside, and her discomfort would be forgotten. Riding and fine horse flesh were interests that the gentry—especially her husband—enjoyed very much. As long as he did not expect her to participate in one of those barbaric fox-hunts the gentry favored, she would do her utmost to become his companion on horseback.

"Is that your only reason?" he asked, his expression amused.

How easily he saw through her "No, not exactly. As I said, I've been telling myself I would make charcoal rubbings of the de Harcourt effigies ever since I heard about them, but I keep putting if off. Yesterday, I told myself today would be the day. My father collects rubbings, you know. He has them framed to hang in the library. He's been expecting these ever since I wrote to tell him about them."

A rare, wicked twinkle came into Justin's deep

blue eyes. "They are not, I hope, rubbings of his failures' final resting places?"

"His failures?" She did not immediately catch his meaning. When she did, she rolled her eyes heavenwards and exclaimed, "Oh, you. You are quite impossible, sir!"

"Impossible, perhaps. Nevertheless, you are madly in love with me, are you not, Lady de Harcourt?" He said it seriously, as if it was a matter of record.

"Why, yes, m'lud, I do believe I am. Very much so." Leaning over, she kissed his cheek, her own eyes twinkling.

Before their betrothal, she had never imagined that his sternly handsome, oftimes brooding appearance could house such an affectionate man. "Have a wonderful afternoon, messing about with your beloved horses."

"Hmm. Kiss me like that again, and there's an excellent chance I shan't leave this estate, beloved horses and your precious charcoal rubbings notwithstanding. . . ."

"Oh? And what about your promise to Sir Michael, hmm?" she asked, popping a piece of buttery toast into her mouth the very second before he could kiss her again.

"Michael? Who the devil's Michael?" he wondered aloud, then kissed a tiny smear of butter from her lip. "Mmm," he murmured appreciatively, licking his lips.

Plucking the half-eaten triangle of toast from her hand, he casually tossed it over his shoulder, letting it fall to the Turkey rug.

"Justin!" she exclaimed, shocked.

He cut off her next words by fitting his mouth to hers and kissing her even more soundly, until she squealed for breath.

Despite his teasing, he rode off alone soon after luncheon, leaving Madeleine to her own devices for the afternoon.

"Don't wander too far and get lost."

"Lost? I never get lost! I'll have you know I have the homing instinct of a . . . a carrier pigeon!" She grinned. He grinned back. She thought again how lovely it was to see him smile so often. Before their marriage, she suspected he had rarely done so.

"You will be careful, Madeleine?" He was not smiling now.

"I'm always careful," she said dutifully, shading her eyes as she looked up at him.

"And you feel all right?"

"I feel wonderful. Why do you ask?"

"I don't know. You look a little pale this morning."

"You don't," she retorted cheekily. "You look . . . magnificent!"

It was no less than the truth. Mounted and clad in a black riding coat, fawn breeches and black boots, he truly did look magnificent. His mount,

Satan, was a huge, glossy black Thoroughbred stallion that appeared to have been carved from polished jet. It was tossing its beautiful head and curvetting, eager to be off.

"Have you any special reason for so many warnings, sir?"

Was it her imagination, or did she see a flicker of something in his eyes? And if so, what?

"Nothing that should unduly alarm you. Trevor tells me he thinks a poacher's been hanging about the property. Or perhaps it was a tramp, looking for a dry place to sleep. Such people are usually harmless, unless they are in danger."

"I see. Then I shall be especially careful and keep my eyes open for anything unusual."

"Good enough," he said levelly. With a farewell salute, he lightly touched booted heels to his horse's sides. "Hup, Satan!"

It was the first time he had left her alone since his return from France, yet he'd kissed her goodbye as ardently as if he would be gone for a year, instead of only an hour or two.

Remembering his farewell, she touched her cheek with the back of her hand, a dreamy expression in her eyes.

She could still feel where Justin had kissed her, as if his lips had left an indelible mark upon her skin, just as they had upon her heart. She sighed. Surely it was tempting Fate, asking for trouble,

151

for two people to be so very happy and so deeply in love?

Donning a straw hat to protect her complexion from freckling, she armed herself with a worn wicker picnic basket from her trunk. The basket held her supplies for the charcoal rubbings: a roll of paper, a small wooden box of charcoal sticks, and a small whisk broom.

Telling Mrs. Fox where she could be found, if the houskeeper needed her, she left the house by the kitchen entrance, crossed the cobbled stable-yard and the carriage house, and followed the flagstone path around to the spice and herb gardens beyond.

The August sky was cloudless and bright blue, the sun dazzling. She was glad of her straw hat and the cool, airy fabric of her lavender day gown as she made her way down the path.

Those from other countries who deplored England's rainy climate had never seen long, golden summer days like this one. The halcyon days seemed to last forever, with evenings remaining light until nine, sometimes ten of the clock.

This afternoon, the warm air was filled with the lazy droning of honey bees, and with the heady scents given off by the herb beds: sage, rosemary, mint, chamomile, lavender.

She found the rusty side-gate that the game-keeper had shown her with little difficulty this time. As they had the first time, the wrought-iron hinges shrieked as she pushed the gate open.

She went through it, into the priory's tangled grounds. Broad-limbed trees cast pleasant shade over the cushiony grass, their leafy foliage like a lacy parasol. Daisies, poppies, buttercups and clover dotted the grass.

She picked a daisy and plucked off its petals, one by one, as she strolled along, chanting as she went:

"He loves me, he loves me not. He loves me, he loves me not," She plucked the last petal on, "He loves me," and smiled a small, contented smile as she twirled the daisy's flowerless stem between her fingers.

The priory grounds covered several acres of the Hall's sprawling estate. Once upon a time, according to Rector Cargill, the sisters of St. Mary's had raised sheep on the priory's meadows. In spring, they sheared their flocks, storing the fleeces in the huge undercrofts below the priory until they could be taken to the wool markets and sold. She frowned, trying to recall where Trevor had pointed out the headstones. It appeared her search for the earliest de Harcourt graves was going to be more extensive than she'd thought.

She walked as far as the woods in one direction without finding any sign of them, coming to an abrupt halt where the trees grew closer together. The dense foliage kept out most of the fierce sunshine. What light there was seemed somehow thick, green and mysterious.

A pretty path, flanked on either side by wild bluebells, wound between the trees. That path beckoned her into the woods, offering her shade and a brief respite from the hot sun that beat down upon her back.

She followed the path, the graves for the moment forgotten as she daydreamed.

Had Lenore followed this same path between the bluebells, on her way to meet Eydmond, she wondered? Had the Saxon thane met his bloody end not far from here, on the point of a Norman broadsword?

It was a sobering thought.

She halted, feeling suddenly chilly and uneasy. Lost. The back of her neck prickled. *She was well and truly lost.*

"The password, I tell thee . . . say it!"

"And if I will not?"

Then there is but one way. Enter this clearing over my dead body."

"As you will, Miller. As you will. . . ."

"Devil take you! Die, Norman dog! Ah, sweet Christ, deliver me! Jesu, I am dead . . . dead. . . ."

". . . under attack! To arms! To arms, all of you!"

"Over there! Look out!

"Nay! Behind you!"

"Ride, I say! Ride—Aaagh!"

She covered her ears with her hands. "No! Be quiet! Stop, all of you!"

The hoarse whispers were all around her. Did they tell the tale of Saxon rebels, murdered long ago upon this very spot? Or were they but the rustling of the leaves in a sudden gust of wind? Real—or her imagination, playing tricks again? Fact or fantasy, it was hard to say.

She swallowed, wondering—not for the first time—if she was going mad. The woods no longer seemed inviting or cool, but sinister and deceptive. A pretty snare for the unsuspecting innocents the cool green light lured into their shady depths.

In sudden panic, she turned around and fled back between the trees, the way she'd come. She tore down the path toward the glorious light as if it were the Holy Grail itself.

She burst from the shady woods like hot lead shot from a pistol, breathing heavily in her panic. The sun bathed her face in its warmth as she tilted her head back. She drank in its rays, trying desperately to catch her breath as she held the stitch in her side.

Gradually, the soothing sound of running water penetrated her efforts to control her breathing. Her fear, coupled with her hasty flight, had left her mouth dry, her throat parched. Eagerly, she hurried toward the sound.

Oh! How perfectly lovely!

Emerging from a spinney of graceful silver birches that formed a dainty lattice screen, she discovered the source of the sound. A weir, or dam, had been formed by placing large mossy boulders across the river, perhaps to redirect the flow of water toward a mill, farther downstream, or for some other similar purpose.

"What were my Rufus a-doing . . . by the weir?" she heard the Saxon goodwife of her dreams say. *"Swim, he could . . . like a blessed fish. . . ."*

She flicked her head to rid it of the widowed woman's words, determined those wretched dreams should not intrude here, in this pretty spot, as they had in the woods.

Several weeping willows bowed their long, graceful tresses over the swift-flowing water. Purple irises nodded lovely bearded heads upon its banks.

Kneeling down, Madeleine scooped water into her hands and drank. *Aaah. It was so cold.* She drank until she was refreshed, then wetted her kerchief in the shallows. Finding a comfortable, shady place, she swabbed at her hot face and throat with the kerchief.

Tugging the damp, clingy folds of her gown away from her sticky spine, she sat down to rest and watch iridescent dragonflies as they dipped and flashed over the water.

The river's noisy, endless song was fascinating. So were the misty sprays and eddies that formed as the water leaped over the rocky ledge before beginning its race to either mill-wheel or sea.

Reluctant to leave such a cool, refreshing spot, she took her time before gathering up her basket to continue her search for the graves. This time, she followed a rough bridle path that led through turf and heather.

Her new path wound to the headlands and the white chalk cliffs that overlooked the seashore. Below and away stretched the choppy white caps of the English Channel.

Taking off her straw hat, she stood upon the very edge of the cliff and drank in the pretty view of sea and sky, of screaming gulls and tiny fishing boats with dazzling white sails.

A warm wind blew inland, off the sea. It pressed her gauzy skirts tightly to her hips and thighs, and whipped strands of her hair in all directions.

She shaded her eyes. To the west, she could see the town of Dover, with its colorful huddle of fisherman's cottages, fine houses and magnificent Norman castle.

To the east, she was surprised to see the pointed rooftops and chimneys of Five Gables, the Latimers' mansion. It was much closer to the Hall than she'd thought. In fact, it could be reached quite easily in only a few moments by the seashore, whereas it took a good half-hour on horseback, following country lanes and bridle paths, according to what Justin had said.

As she turned back the way she came, the edge of the cliff crumbled beneath her heel.

Somehow, she managed to leap back, onto solid ground.

Craning her head over the ledge, she flinched as she saw the dislodged clump of earth bounce several times against the cliff walls before striking the beach below. Pebbles and chunks of earth showered from it each time.

That could have been me, she thought, shaken. *Dear Lord!* Had she stood there just a second longer, she might have fallen along with that clod of earth, she realized, offering up a silent yet fervent prayer of thanks that she had not.

Although still shaken by her brush with danger, she still intended to find the graves before returning to the Hall for afternoon tea.

Determined the afternoon should not be entirely wasted, she headed back toward the priory, lost in thought.

Rector Cargill had explained at dinner the other evening that the earliest de Harcourt graves had been in the vestry of the priory's church, but that the church that housed them had fallen into ruin several centuries ago. Where would that church have stood, in relation to the priory itself, she wondered?

Although it had met with no success, thus far, her search brought home exactly how important the priory must have been to the area in the eleventh century. Anglo-Saxon religious houses were not usually so large nor so fine as St. Mary's had once been.

Like so many other noteworthy historical buildings, the priory had been built over the ruins of an earlier priory at the end of the seventh century. An ancient king of Kent, King Wihtred had ordered it built to honor the Virgin Mary.

"If 'tis the graves you're looking for, they're over there, by the hedge, my lady." The gamekeeper's voice cut into her thoughts. "Remember?"

She gasped. He had come up behind her so quietly, his voice startled her.

"Right there? I don't remember them being so close to the Hall." She had wandered all over the estate for nothing.

"They were in St. Mary's vestry, at one time. But the old priory church is long gone now. A heap or two of stone is all that's left to show where it once stood, aye? All this were gardens once, and beyond, grazing for the sisters' flocks, and pasture for their cows and horses."

Madeleine shaded her eyes, squinting against the dazzling sunlight. As Trevor had indicated, there were two low mounds not far from the tall yew hedge that enclosed the Hall's spice and herb gardens. The graves were much closer to the Hall than she remembered, which explained why she had not found them sooner. She had passed right by them and begun her search too far from the Hall itself.

"Thank you. I see them now," she murmured, embarrassed that she'd needed the gamekeeper to point out their location for her. She didn't turn around to look at Trevor as she marched across the grass toward the spot. She didn't have to. She knew he would be grinning his cocky grin.

By the graves, she crouched down. Drawing the small whisk broom from her basket, she began brushing dirt and grit from the face of her subject.

This particular rubbing was not going to be easy, however, she realized, frowning. Although the grass around the effigies was emerald-green, and as short and weedless as any Turkey carpet, the lichened stone effigies were almost completely hidden beneath a cage of rambling blackberry brambles.

Drat! If she wanted to make decent rubbings for her father, the first order of business would be to pull aside the wretched brambles and completely expose the stone images.

Kneeling, she tugged the first long thorny red vine aside. It whipped back, scratching her hand. She sucked the stinging scratch.

"The priory church and the castle stood side by side, once upon a time, aye?"

She jumped, so engrossed in her task, she'd completely forgotten Trevor was still there. "They did?"

He nodded. "When the castle fell into ruin a few hundred years ago, the earl of that time built Steyning Hall on the original foundations."

Trevor crouched down alongside her. One arm dangling casually between his knees, he used the other to help her pull the brambles aside, adding, "The blasted fool used the old stones from the ruined castle t'build it."

"Why did that make his lordship a fool?" she asked, panting with her exertions. Should she scold him for calling the lord of the manor a fool? "I would have thought it was the clever thing to do. Think of all the expense it must have saved."

"Clever, perhaps. But there's some that say he should never have done it, savings or no," Trevor said, shooting her a dark look.

"Oh? And why is that?" she asked, breathing heavily as she fought to tug the stubborn, springy brambles aside. She kept doggedly at it, despite numerous deep scratches that welled tiny beads of blood. Her excitement over making a new rubbing was growing. Her efforts had exposed the almost undamaged likeness of an eleventh-century knight in full armor.

The figure lay on a low stone base, his arms crossed over his chest. His sword, inverted, rested upon his breast like a huge crucifix, although a small part of the hilt had broken off and was missing.

The handsome face of the knight wearing chainmail and breastplate was intact, except for the nose and the helm's noseguard, which were both missing. In fact, the effigy was remarkably undamaged by either vandals or time, she saw eagerly. Unfortunately, the man buried here was not, she saw, anyone whose name she recognized from her dreams.

The depth of her disappointment startled her. She had not realized, until this very moment, how deeply involved she had become with the characters that filled her dreams nightly. Nor had she realized—until now—how badly she wanted to hear that the lady Lenore had been wrong, and that she and her Saxon had found each other, after all, and lived happily ever after with their child.

She'd even been hoping against hope that one of these graves belonged to Eydmond of Lewes, although that was utter foolishness on her part. Thane Eydmond would never have been buried here at Steyning. He had been a Saxon rebel, after all, and Lord Giles, the lord of the manor, his sworn enemy.

So, where had Eydmond vanished that sultry

summer's day, Madeleine wondered for the umpteenth time since she'd had the dream? He and his band could not simply have vanished into thin air, like a magician's silver balls.

Had the Saxon chieftain left Steyning Forest, as the prioress suggested, and found a new hiding place? Had Eydmond been unable to shoulder the added burdens of wife and child, as well as leading a revolt? Or, had he fallen victim to a far more ominous fate?

Was it his voice she heard in her mind, beseeching her to help him? A voice that, somehow, managed to make itself heard across the barriers of time and even death?

Had the man even existed?

And what of the lady Lenore? What of the child she carried? Had it survived its birth and grown to manhood? Or had its desperate mother, finding herself alone and with child, thrown herself into the dark waters of the weir, or over the chalk cliffs, taking her own life rather than bear her illegitimate child?

Had Lenore even existed or, like Eydmond, did she live only in Madeleine's dreams?

The dreams. She had not had them for several nights now. Instead, she had fallen asleep in her husband's arms, sweetly exhausted by his lovemaking. Perhaps she would never know the end of the story.

"He should never have used the stones from

163

the old castle for the same reason country folk planted these brambles here, my lady."

Trevor's patient voice brought her sharply back to the moment at hand. "I'm sorry, Master Fox. I'm afraid I was wool-gathering. What was it you said?"

"I said that it was not by accident these brambles grew here. They were planted here. Brambles bind spirits t'a grave, where they rightly belong, you see. Same as betony, aye?"

Frowning, she asked. "What do you mean, brambles 'bind spirits' to places? As for betony . . . I don't believe I've ever heard of it before."

"Nay? And you a physician's lass, an' all, my lady!" Trevor scolded her, far too familiarly for any gamekeeper. Despite her disapproving look, he grinned and shook his head. His eyes and the golden earring in his ear both flashed in the sunlight. "According to herblore, 'tis betony that keeps ghosts from hauntin' the living. Am I right, love?"

"That you are, Trevor Fox," came a shy female voice from behind Madeleine. "Or so my old mother says."

"And when it comes to herblore, there's not much Mother Lee don't know, aye, lovie?" Trevor added softly.

Trevor was not alone, she realized belatedly. Tabby had joined him, their hands linked like sweethearts.

The pair were obviously walking out together on their afternoons off. Tabby looked very pleased with herself, too. So, come to that, did the gamekeeper, who looked even more like a Gypsy today than he had before, if that was possible, in shirtsleeves, a seamed black leather waistcoat, his moleskin breeches tucked into polished black boots.

At Trevor's feet sat a shaggy black-and-white collie. Tail wagging, the dog expectantly eyed the stick Trevor was holding.

"All right, then, 'Pie! After it, girl!" Trevor urged as he hurled the stick into the air.

Tongue lolling, the game little dog streaked after it, a black-and-white blur that soon vanished into the edge of the woods. Madeleine sternly resisted the silly urge to quickly call the little creature back, to sunshine and safety. What nonsense she was thinking today!

She forced a smile as she looked up at Tabitha. The girl's usually pale plain face was neither pale nor plain today. It was flushed and pretty. Her gray eyes shone, and her dress, of inexpensive deep-green cotton, sprigged with small white flowers that had yellow middles, was in flattering contrast to her bright carroty hair, which tossed on the wind like wild-fire.

Trevor, Madeleine saw, eyed the girl with pride—and no little affection.

"Then it was a posy of betony that you put in

my bed, Tabby?" she asked, absolutely certain now that Tabitha had put the mauve wildflowers there.

The girl did not bother to deny it. "Aye, mum. I wanted t'protect you, ye see. Ye've seen things, have you not? Or felt them?"

"Nonsense! I've done nothing of the sort," she lied. Confirming her imaginings would only give them greater substance. "Don't be foolish, Tabitha. Really. All this silly talk of ghosts and seeing things! 'Tis nothing but . . . but superstitious nonsense," she insisted.

"Ye can't pretend, not to me. See, I know ye've felt them, mum! I can tell by your eyes!" Tabby insisted, more outspoken than usual. "So troubled, they are, oftimes. And ye have this . . . this way of looking over your shoulder, as if ye expect t'see someone behind ye. Tell me, my lady. Have ye had the dreams yet?"

"The dreams! How could you know about the dreams?" Madeleine blurted out before she could stop herself. She had told nobody about her dreams, or even that she had dreamed at all.

"My old mother's the one ye should ask about them. She were in service here at the Hall when Lady Emilie was alive. Lady Emilie had the dreams, too, ye see? Before she died."

"She died? How did she die?" She was almost afraid to ask.

" 'Twere an accident," Trevor explained

quickly. "Nothing to do with dreams nor ghosts. The cliffs, mum. The poor lady rode her horse over the edge. They reckon it bolted while she was riding."

Trevor's answer, rather than reassuring her, filled Madeleine with alarm. She had almost fallen over the cliffs herself that afternoon. It was a sobering thought.

As if by mutual consent, no more was said of either death, dreams or ghosts. Despite her protests that they should not waste their free time in helping her, Trevor and Tabby held back the brambles, so that she could finish her rubbing of the effigy.

The knight who appeared in charcoal upon the pristine white paper was a handsome fellow. He wore a helmet, the noseguard chipped off, like his nose, and pointed shoes. His shield, bearing the de Harcourt heraldic coat-of-arms, lay at his side.

The charcoal made the Latin inscription on the beveled stones that surrounded the knight's effigy much easier to decipher than in stone relief, although some of the individual letters were chipped. Madeleine could translate a few of the words but did not know enough Latin to make proper sense of what it said, other than that the knight's name had been Lord William de Harcourt. Her papa would understand it better than

167

she did. She would write and ask him to translate it for her.

She discovered, when the brambles surrounding it had also been pulled aside, that the second grave belonged to a woman. Her effigy wore the veil, wimple and robes that were fashionable for noblewomen of the eleventh century. A filet, probably of some precious metal, bound her brow, and appeared to be studded with gems. A rosary and psalter, or psalm book, were clasped in her hands, which were folded across her breast, like the knight's.

She was not, as Madeleine expected, Lord Guillaume's—William's—wife, but a much older woman. The stone from which she had been sculpted did not dim the great beauty that had once been hers. Nor did it hide the determination and intelligence revealed by a wise brow and strongly molded jaw.

She had been a woman to reckon with, Madeleine decided, shaking her head to dispel a moment's dizziness. And a beautiful one, too, in her youth.

She eagerly pushed back yet another bramble. As she did so, the inscription at the foot of the grave all but leaped out at her:

*"LENORE
DE HARCOURT
LADY OF STEYNING.*

Moonshadow

b.1050-d.1100.
"Here lies in stone
Our ladye fayre.
Should ye disturb her sleep
beware."

A thrill ran down Madeleine's spine as if someone had walked over her grave. The charcoal stick slipped, unnoticed, through her fingers to the grass.

According to the inscription, Lenore had not only lived—she had *wed* the hated Norman! How could she have done so? How could she have been unfaithful to the memory of her love?

"My lady? My lady! Are you ill?"

Tabby's voice. It seemed to come from far away. The girl was shaking her shoulder. *Why?* she wondered. What did Tabby want with her? Why couldn't she leave her alone? Why did she keep shaking her?

An insistent ringing began in her ears. Colors swirled in her vision like bleeding watercolors on paper. *Sunstroke*, she decided in a still reasoning, still logical part of her mind. She swayed slightly. That would explain the odd sensations. The sun was so very hot!

"I'm quite all right," she reassured them. But even to her own ears, her voice sounded quavery and uncertain.

As she stood, brushing grass off her skirts, she

169

realized, with a sinking heart, that she was far, far from all right. Rather, she was weak as a kitten. Everything around her had an unreal quality to it, as if she was watching a play performed on a distant stage.

Oh, the sun! The heat! She passed a hand across her brow. All that tramping about in the fierce sunshine had been too much for her, that was all.

"Aaah!" A blinding white pain sliced through her skull. It pounded in her temple, fiercer than any headache she had ever experienced. Rather than feeling sweaty and hot, as she had but moments ago, her face was clammy now, drenched in an icy sweat. Her legs could no longer support her. In fact, she felt so dizzy, she thought she might swoon, or else be sick on the grass and disgrace herself before Tabby and Trevor.

"Tsk. Tsk. You're pale as whey, my lady," Tabby scolded, her gray eyes concerned. She cupped her mistress's elbow to steady her. "Why, ye look proper queer, ye do. Ye'd best sit down, my la—*Trevor!*"

Tabby's frightened cry and Pie's excited barking were the last sounds Madeleine heard. Her eyes rolled back in her head, then everything went black as she slipped into the abyss.

Chapter Twelve

She was suffocating, her mouth filled with terror, her lungs on fire!

Air!

Oh, God, oh, God! Where was the blessed air? Where was the light—the air!—the cool sweet air!

It was as if a thick black bag had been thrown over her head, cutting off light and air. A smothering black bag that reeked of lime. The vapors and the bag's thick folds plugged her nose and filled her mouth, cutting off her breath as effectively as if a great weight crushed her chest. Pressed it. Keeping out precious air. Closing her windpipe, her lungs. *Air*, oh, God, she couldn't breathe!

From somewhere close, she could hear animal sounds. Desperate heaves and wheezes. Gurgling, choking sounds. They were like the terrible final screams of a pig that has had its throat cut by the butcher. The whistling shriek of its last breath, rushing from its severed windpipe in a desperate, dying squeal. They were *her* sounds. The sounds she was making as she died. *She didn't want to die!*

"It's all right, *chérie*. Don't panic. You're safe now. Madeleine! Open your eyes!" Justin commanded sternly. Like Tabby's, his voice seemed to come from very far away.

". . . most unusual in such a young lady. . . . I suppose, a form of lung-ague," another male voice said.

She did not recognize the speaker.

"Help me," she managed to croak, with superhuman effort. "I . . . oh! . . . oh! . . . I . . . can't . . . I can't brea . . . breathe! . . ."

"Open your eyes, Madeleine. Open them and look at me. Hold my hands, *chérie*, and try to breathe slowly and deeply."

"I can't! I . . . can't . . . breathe!"

"Yes, you can. Open your eyes. Look at me. If you can speak, you can breathe. Slowly, *chérie*. Draw the steam deep into your lungs. Deeper."

Justin's voice was like a lifeline, filled with love and concern. It reached out to her, reeled her in to safety. He was the rudder that steered her back on course, the star by which she steered—steered desperately.

She concentrated, mastering her terror, little by little, forcing her mind to focus, her body to do as he commanded.

By some miracle, her breathlessness began to ease. She managed to draw a single, shallow breath, then another, then a longer deeper one.

The air she was breathing was moist and laced with camphor. It extinguished the fire in her chest. Opened her throat. Let lifegiving air into her lungs, inflating them like bellows.

She hung onto his hands, her fingernails digging half-moons in his skin. Gradually, the heaving of her chest eased as her breathing grew gentler, easier, deeper. The animal sounds she had made became low uneven sobs, then helpless weeping.

Gently, Justin drew her into his arms, stroking her hair. Tears flowed down her cheeks, to soak his shirt. She had felt as if she were suffocating! She had been so very afraid—so convinced she was going to die!

She wept until she had no tears left to shed. When her reddened, swollen eyelids fluttered open again, she saw that someone had drawn the hangings around the tester, enclosing the two of them as if they were inside a steam tent.

A brazier filled with ruddy coals had been placed close to the head of the bed. It held a big black kettle. From its long spout belched steam, scented with camphor, moistening and medicating the air she breathed. It was the combination of camphor and steam that had eased her breathing. That, and Justin's quiet confidence and unfaltering love.

As she stirred, his arms tightened around her. He looked disheveled and his eyes were frightened and dark with concern as he set her away from him and looked down at her.

"Better?" he asked hoarsely.

"Much." She gave him a wan smile.

"Thank God!" He drew her hand to his lips and kissed it. "You gave us quite a turn."

"Us?"

"Tabby. Trevor. The gardeners. Mrs. Fox. Me. Is there anything I can get for you, *chérie*? Water? Brandy?" He grinned and she knew he would have welcomed a brandy himself.

"Just . . . would you open the hangings, please?" she whispered. "Ever since . . . ever since I was a little girl, I've hated being enclosed in small spaces."

He squeezed her hand. "We all fear something, *chérie*."

Standing, he drew back the heavy brocade hangings, letting in the blessed light. He kept his face carefully averted as he moved about the room.

Why? she wondered. What was it he didn't want her to see there? How very frightened her sudden illness had made him? Was losing her what *he* feared most, she wondered, remembering his comment, just as she feared losing him?

She thought it was, for when he turned back to her, his stern features were carefully under control.

It was late afternoon, she judged by the patch of sky she could see through the mullioned panes. But of what day? The same day she had gone out to make the rubbings—or the next? How long had she been unconscious?

She was in her own bed, she knew that much. The same canopied tester that she and Justin shared in the master chamber of Steyning Hall.

There was a second older man there whom she did not recognize, as well Mrs. Fox. Of medium height and clean-shaven, his gray hair was clubbed back into a queue fastened with a floppy black bow. He was dressed like a country parson in rusty black frockcoat, frayed white stock, black waistcoat and old-fashioned yellow gaiters that made her want to laugh.

"This is the physician from the village, *chérie*. Dr. Smythe," Justin introduced him, seeing her frown.

"Doctor." She nodded politely, licking dry lips.

"Good afternoon, dear lady. 'Tis an honor to meet you. However, if you simply must see me, I would prefer we met at some social gathering in future, rather than at your ladyship's sickbed."

He smiled down at her, his brown eyes twinkling behind the lenses of his gold-rimmed *pince-nez*. A kindly man, she decided, smiling back.

"Unfortunately," Smythe continued, "a lengthy birthing out at the Hathaway's farm kept me absent from your dinner party last Saturday beven-ing. Mistress Smythe and myself were desolate to have missed such a delightful occasion."

Dr. Smythe lowered his gray head to Madeleine's ear as she tried to answer him. She could see her own pale face reflected in the lenses of his spectacles as he bent over her.

"What was that, your ladyship? 'Next time,' you say? Why, yes, of course. Quite so! Now, then. Your lordship? Mrs. Fox? If you will be so good as to leave us, I would like to examine her ladyship more fully, in an attempt to discover the cause of her fainting spell, yes?"

Mrs. Fox bobbed a curtsey and discreetly made her exit.

"Madeleine. Would you like me to leave?" Justin asked.

She shook her head, suddenly frightened. "No. Please, stay." If the physician had bad news to impart, she did not want to hear it alone.

"Very well. Let us proceed. I have a few questions to put to you first, my lady, if I may?" Smythe proceeded to ask them, ending with, "And what of your sleep, my lady? Do you sleep well?"

"Not lately, no," she admitted. "I dream almost

every night, you see. And such . . . such strange dreams, they are, too."

"Aah. By strange, you mean, nightmares?"

"No, Doctor, not nightmares. *Dreams.*"

"And what makes these dreams so unusual, my lady?" Smythe asked levelly. He pulled down her lower eyelids and peered into her eyes, frowning as if he wondered whether she might be a candidate for the wards of Bedlam.

"They are dreams about the past, doctor. Yet they unravel in perfect and logical order, with none of the distortion or random quality we expect of our dreams. And . . . they are about events that once happened here at Steyning Hall. The people who lived here centuries ago. Like . . . like the dreams your mother had, Justin, before the dreadful accident that claimed her life," she added, turning to look up at Justin, at the other side of the bed.

Although she knew that both his parents were dead, until today, she had no idea how or even when either of them had expired. Were their deaths the reason he'd seemed so withdrawn when she first met him, she wondered now? Was their loss the cause of the deep sadness he carried inside?

Justin smiled faintly. "You have been listening to the servants' gossip, *chérie.* I wouldn't put too much store in it, myself. Besides—" he shrugged—"who doesn't have strange dreams

177

when they sleep in a new bed in a new house for the first week or so, isn't that right, Doctor? It is only to be expected. You have been at the Hall only a short while, after all."

"Indeed, yes. Furthermore, if I may be frank, milady, milord, the Hall is no ordinary house, but one with a rather . . . sinister and brooding aspect, however misleading such an appearance might be," Smythe suggested cheerfully. "In my opinion, it would be odd if one didn't dream here, madam, all things considered!"

"But these are not ordinary dreams!" she insisted, her voice a little stronger. Agitated, she tried to sit up. "They seem to be . . . to be building toward some climax or other!"

"Shoo, shoo!" Making a clucking sound of disapproval, Dr. Smythe gently pressed her back down, then took her wrist between his fingers to count her pulse. "Please, lie back."

"Their story unravels like a . . . a play before my eyes," Madeleine continued firmly as Smythe counted, telling her story more for Justin's benefit than the doctor's. "Or . . . or like the chapters of a book, page after page. But this is a true story, I fear, for my dreams are peopled with characters who really existed, once upon a time, though I have never heard of them till now. There is the . . . the lady Lenore, whose grave is out there, by the yew hedge. And Lord Giles de Harcourt—"

"Lord Giles? Then you've heard of the wicked old reprobate?" Justin chuckled and winked down at her. " 'Tis as well that you know the full measure of the man you married, my dear. My darkness of character is bred in the bone—as was his!" he teased, trying to bring a smile to her face.

But Madeleine was not amused. She would not be cajoled out of telling him all, now that she'd begun.

"There was an Eydmond of Lewes, too. A Saxon thane, the leader of a rebel band intent upon mounting an insurrection against the Normans who had conquered and occupied the isle of Britain," she continued doggedly. "And . . . and the Prioress Aelfreda. She was the prioress of St. Mary's Priory at that time." She wanted him to believe her, but suspected he was hearing her out only to humor her.

"Eydmond? Never heard of him," Justin declared. "But the prioress . . ." His broad brow creased in thought. "I believe there actually was a prioress at St. Mary's centuries ago. Of course, there would have to be, wouldn't there? She was somehow related to my ancestor, the lady of Steyning, if my memory of the story serves. Her sister, I believe it was—"

"She was Lenore's aunt, her mother's sister—" Madeleine supplied in a whisper.

"But I could be wrong," Justin continued as if he had not heard her. "The de Harcourts' nefarious doings do not grace the pages of many history books. I fear we were a boring lot! There is only a paragraph or two devoted to us in my father's entire book collection. When you are feeling better, perhaps you would care to explore the library for yourself?"

"I shall, thank you. But, what of Lord Giles? Do you know anything of the man?"

"Only that he and his wife—your lady Lenore!—were married by Bishop Odo in St. Nicholas's church in the village. It would have been quite a feather in your lady Lenore's cap, to have married a Norman, although I expect her Saxon countrymen might have considered it a betrayal. Bishop Odo was one of William the Conqueror's favorites."

"Yes, I know. Go on!"

"There's nothing more to add. That's it. All of it. Or at least, all that I recall." His expression was concerned. "You should rest now, *chérie*."

"You don't believe me," she stated baldly, ignoring his suggestion. "Not about the dreams, not about any of it! You think I'm losing my mind."

"Not true, my sweet," Justin insisted gently. "And I do believe you have had these dreams, despite what you think. It's just that . . . well, I cannot believe they are anything other than simple fantasies."

"If that were true, how did I know the names

of your ancestors, before you ever told them to me? Answer me that, if you can, sir?" she demanded, eyes blazing. "How did I know of the priory's existence my very first night at the Hall, if you did not tell me of it?"

"Are you quite sure I didn't? That evening at Whitchurch, when I was telling you and your father about my estate?"

"I'm positive," she insisted. But his reminder of that night had planted a tiny question in her mind. She'd completely forgotten that evening, for it had been memorable for quite another reason. It was that day Justin had asked her to marry him, as they sat in the rose arbor of her father's garden.

"My lady, forgive the interruption, but may I ask when your last . . . er . . . courses were?" the physician cut in apologetically in a low, discreet voice.

"My what?" Madeleine frowned. "Oh. *Those*." She wrinkled her nose. "Let me see. Not since before our marriage, doctor," she realized, frowning. Had it really been so long?

Thrusting both hands under the bedcovers, Dr. Smythe palpated her belly, poking her so firmly in some areas, she yelped in protest. "Have you noticed any tenderness to your breasts, my lady?"

"Why yes, I have," she admitted, surprised by his question. Her breasts had seemed a little swollen and been quite tender for a week or more, but she had blamed the tenderness on their lovemaking. When she bathed, she noticed that the aureoles surrounding her nipples seemed a darker pink, almost brown, and she could see veins as faint bluish lines under the skin of her breasts.

"Have you felt any nausea upon rising, my lady?" Dr. Smythe asked.

"No, not that I recall. I've felt dizzy and a little queasy in the evenings, sometimes. At our dinner party the other evening, I had to leave my guests because of it."

"You should have said something," Justin scolded her.

"It didn't seem that important at the time. I just put it down to a silly attack of nerves about, well, about meeting your friends for the first time."

The physician nodded knowingly. "The condition doesn't affect all women similarly, milady. Morning or evening, the nausea usually has the same cause, however."

"Oh? And what cause is that?" Justin demanded sharply. "What is wrong with my wife, doctor?"

"Nothing whatsoever, your lordship. Quite the contrary, in fact. I am delighted to report that Lady Madeleine shows every evidence of being with child. Congratulations, milord. And congratulations to you, too, my lady."

Madeleine sank back on the pillows, open-mouthed and too stunned to comment. *A child!* She was going to have a child! She had been so wrapped up in her new marriage, so . . . so absorbed in those wretched dreams, she had ignored all the signs and symptoms. Of course!

Justin leaned down and kissed her. "Thank you, *chérie*. You've made me the happiest man in England!" His dark blue eyes shone as he squeezed her hand. His smile was fond and irrepressible. "Let me accompany Doctor Smythe to the door, all right? I'll be back in just a moment."

She did not question why her husband would choose to see the physician to the door personally, rather than having the butler usher the man out. Instead, she lay there, lost in a lovely rosy reverie, her palms pressed lightly to her belly.

Her sister, Felicity, had been safely delivered of an infant daughter just the week before. She had written to tell Madeleine of baby Elizabeth's safe arrival, adding how wonderful it had been to see their father's face when he first beheld his little granddaughter. Felicity promised she and her husband, David, would visit Steyning Hall when Elizabeth was old enough to travel and her mama fully recovered from her lying-in. However, since it was some distance from Colchester to Steyning, it would not be for a while yet.

Madeleine sighed. What a miracle it was, to know a tiny life was growing beneath her heart. A life that she and Justin had created from their love. Only a moment ago, she had not even suspected the baby's existence. But now that she knew, she loved her little son or daughter, sight unseen, without a word or a touch or a glance ever needing to pass between them. Instantly. Wholly. Unconditionally.

The knowledge of her condition sang inside her, filling her with a warm glow of contentment and happiness. "Oh, thank you, God!" she whispered as happy tears flowed down her cheeks. "Thank you."

"I wouldn't put too great a store in her ladyship's fantasies, if I were you, my lord," Smythe reassured Justin over the glass of Canary his lordship poured the doctor to celebrate his impending fatherhood. "Women in Lady Madeleine's condition—especially, if I might say so, women who do not marry at an early age—are oftimes prone to . . . er . . . how shall I put it? Excessive imaginings? Odd fancies? Peculiar cravings?—when they are carrying a child. I can only speculate that the changes going on in their bodies somehow affect women's minds, temporarily. I once had a female patient in the same delicate condition who persisted in eating lumps of coal, right out of the blasted scuttle! Why, the poor creature couldn't get enough of the wretched stuff, until after she was delivered. Can you imagine? Her husband was beside himself, poor chap!"

"And what of the choking? Have you any explanation for it? Is there anything we can do to keep it from happening again?" The memory of Madeleine's pale, terrified face, mottled blue from lack of air, filled his mind. In that moment, he had known the true meaning of terror, the like of which he had never felt before. It made the work he did for the government seem like a Sunday picnic.

Smythe shrugged and looked perturbed. "I'm afraid not, no. I must admit, that choking fit or whatever it was is a mystery to me. Her lungs sound perfectly clear, and she has no sign of either a lung-ague or grippe of the chest. Thank God, whatever it was, it is over, without lasting effect. You might consider taking her ladyship away on a little holiday, milord. Rest and a change of scenery would perhaps do her a world of good. Somewhere by the seashore, where the salt air can open her lungs."

"I know just the place," Justin said thoughtfully. Smythe was still citing other examples of the bizarre behavior of women who were with child as he clambered up onto the driver's perch of his dogcart. He gathered his reins in hand.

"A good day to you, milord. And once again,

my heartiest congratulations! Do not hesitate to send for me, should your lady have need of my services."

Justin was deep in thought as he went back inside. Digby, the butler, cleared his throat, discreetly announcing his prescence without startling his master. "I couldn't help hearing that her ladyship is with child, milord. May I be one of the first to congratulate you, sir?"

"You may, Digby. Thank you." Justin grinned broadly.

Digby return his master's rare smile with an even rarer, broader one of his own. "You are quite welcome, sir. Is there anything I can bring you, sir? Anything you would like me to do?"

"Not at the moment, thank you, Digby," Justin said, running his hand through his hair.

Now that the initial surprise was beginning to wear off, he was suddenly and acutely aware of how exhausted he felt, and how relieved that Madeleine's fainting episode had an understandable—and happy!—explanation. If only her choking and inability to breath could be as easily written off.

"You might ask Mrs. Fox to send a tray up to her ladyship. Something tempting and light, I suppose, under the circumstances. Oh, and tell Trevor I wish to see him tomorrow, in my study, immediately following breakfast."

"Very well, sir," Digby promised, inclining his head.

Justin was headed back upstairs when he all but ran into Michael Latimer, standing in the hallway at the foot of the stairs. "Michael? What the devil are you doing here? Digby didn't announce you."

Michael laughed easily. "That's because Old Digs doesn't know I'm here. When you and Nowles raced off, I followed you back, then sneaked in through the kitchens. Queen Bea's always glad to see me, even if you aren't." The cook, Mrs. Beaton, had always been fond of him. "How is she? Your Maddy, I mean?"

"My *Madeleine* is much better, thank you. It seems she had good reason to faint." He grinned. He couldn't help himself. "According to Smythe, I'm going to become a father in the not-too-distant future."

"Are you, by Jove! Congratulations!" Michael exclaimed, pumping Justin's hand and grinning. "With your luck, I wager it'll be a boy!" he added enviously.

Justin shrugged. It was no news to him that Michael had as little as possible to do with his two small daughters, nor that he was disappointed and bitter that Sabina had not given him the heir he craved. "Son or daughter, I don't give a damn, Latimer. It will be my child. Mine and Madeleine's."

Michael grinned. "Ah, well. I should have expected that sort of attitude from you. You've always been far nobler than I ever could be. Remember Old Merle's mathematics exam?" He chuckled.

"How could I forget?" Michael had filched the answers to the exam from Professor Merle's study, but the accusation of cheating had fallen on Justin. Along with it came the threat of being expelled from Eton in disgrace, the de Harcourt honor besmirched. Some things were forgivable, but cheating was not one of them.

Justin had known immediately that Michael was somehow involved, but his personal code of honor prevented him from betraying his friend— any friend—even one in the wrong.

Fortunately for him, Professor Merle had known both him and his ability in mathematics well enough to know he had no reason to cheat, and that it was not in Justin's character to do so. The professor had quietly dropped the matter, thrown out the first results and made the entire form retake the exam. Michael, of course, had flunked miserably, still blithely unrepentant that Justin had almost been expelled for his wrongdoing.

"Well? Aren't you going to offer me a drink to celebrate?"

"Hmm? No. Not this time." Justin grinned.

"Go home, Latimer! I promised my wife I'd rejoin her after I saw Smythe out."

"All right. Run along. If you're in such a bloody stingy mood, I'll see myself out."

"You do that." Justin shook his head, but he was grinning as he said it. "You come and go here as if you owned the bloody place!"

"No such luck!" He paused, his smile fading. "Jus, about the mare. You won't reconsider?"

Justin's face hardened. "I can't. Michael. I wish I could. I'm sorry. I don't believe that pedigree is the genuine article. Dark of the Moon's a fine animal, but she's no Thoroughbred."

Michael nodded. "That's alright. I understand. Be sure to pass on my best wishes to her ladyship, won't you?"

"Of course."

Chapter Thirteen

To Madeleine's surprise, Tabby woke her early the following morning from a deep—but dreamless!—sleep.

"You're to wake up straightway, mum, and I'm t'see that ye dress comfortably, for traveling. The master says he has a surprise for you," Tabby confided with a broad smile.

The maid talked to her very gently, as if she was an invalid—or a blathering idiot!—who should not be flustered or upset in any way. "Oh?" she murmured, annoyed. "Does he, indeed?"

"Aye. And very mysterious about it all, he was, too, his lordship! So, come along, now, mum. Up with you! Oh, I was so excited when I heard about the baby, mum! I said t'Trev—Master Fox—that it's been ages since there's been a little one here at the Hall. Not since his lordship was a nipper . . ."

Her surprise, Madeleine discovered after a carriage journey of about an hour, was an old Tudor-style farmhouse. It stood back from the king's highway, between the coast road and the seashore.

It was so unlike the gloomy Hall and its environs, they could as easily have been on the moon.

"What a charming place!" she exclaimed.

The house was long and low, nestled comfortably in the cup of a hollow. Its traditional pink-plaster walls were charmingly accented with dark beams in the Tudor style of two centuries before. A half-dozen pretty trees stood protectively about the place. Both they and the gardens were enclosed by a low wall built in the old country way, with stones placed carefully on top of each other, without mortar to bind them together.

It looked like such a cozy place to live. Safe, too, she added silently, releasing the long breath she had not known she was holding, until then.

Safe. What an odd thought. Had she felt so unsafe at the Hall, then? Tabby's odd comments, made moments before she fainted, came back to her. Had she felt unsafe, as well as seeming pale and frightened to others?

"To whom does this house belong?" she asked, forcing herself to concentrate on the moment at

Thrill to the most sensual, adventure-filled Romances on the market today...

FROM 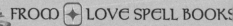 LOVE SPELL BOOKS

As a home subscriber to the Love Spell Romance Book Club, you'll enjoy the best in today's BRAND-NEW Time Travel, Futuristic, Legendary Lovers, Perfect Heroes and other genre romance fiction. For five years, Love Spell has brought you the award-winning, high-quality authors you know and love to read. Each Love Spell romance will sweep you away to a world of high adventure...and intimate romance. Discover for yourself all the passion and excitement millions of readers thrill to each and every month.

Save $5.00 Each Time You Buy!

Every other month, the Love Spell Romance Book Club brings you four brand-new titles from Love Spell Books. EACH PACKAGE WILL SAVE YOU AT LEAST $5.00 FROM THE BOOK-STORE PRICE! And you'll never miss a new title with our convenient home delivery service.

Here's how we do it: Each package will carry a FREE 10-DAY EXAMINATION privilege. At the end of that time, if you decide to keep your books, simply pay the low invoice price of $17.96, no shipping or handling charges added. HOME DELIVERY IS ALWAYS FREE. With today's top romance novels selling for $5.99 and higher, our price SAVES YOU AT LEAST $5.00 with each shipment.

AND YOUR FIRST TWO-BOOK SHIP-MENT IS TOTALLY FREE!

IT'S A BARGAIN YOU CAN'T BEAT! A SUPER $11.48 Value!

Love Spell ✦ A Division of Dorchester Publishing Co., Inc.

GET YOUR 2 FREE BOOKS NOW—AN $11.48 VALUE!

*Mail the Free Book
Certificate Today!*

TWO FREE BOOKS

Free Books Certificate

YES! I want to subscribe to the Love Spell Romance Book Club. Please send me my 2 FREE BOOKS. Then every other month I'll receive the four newest Love Spell selections to Preview FREE for 10 days. If I decide to keep them, I will pay the Special Member's Only discounted price of just $4.49 each, a total of $17.96. This is a SAVINGS of at least $5.00 off the bookstore price. There are no shipping, handling, or other charges. There is no minimum number of books I must buy and I may cancel the program at any time. In any case, the 2 FREE BOOKS are mine to keep—A BIG $11.48 Value!

Offer valid only in the U.S.A.

Name_____

Address_____

City_____

State _____ Zip _____

Telephone_____

Signature_____

If under 18, Parent or Guardian must sign. Terms, prices and conditions subject to change. Subscription subject to acceptance. Leisure Books reserves the right to reject any order or cancel any subscription.

A $11.48 VALUE

Get Two Books Totally
F R E E —
An $11.48 Value!

▼ Tear Here and Mail Your FREE Book Card Today! ▼

PLEASE RUSH
MY TWO FREE
BOOKS TO ME
RIGHT AWAY!

Love Spell Romance Book Club
P.O. Box 6613
Edison, NJ 08818-6613

AFFIX
STAMP
HERE

hand, and put everything else out of her head.

"To me, at the moment," Justin admitted, carefully watching her face. "To you, after our little holiday, if you would like it? I thought I'd have the deed made over to you when we get home. That way, you'll always have this place, should you need to get away from Steyning from time to time. You know, to breathe the sea air." He grinned.

"You're . . . you're giving me a house? An entire house?" she asked, round-eyed. Her voice was squeaky with surprise.

He laughed. "Why not? 'Tis but a small gift, compared to what you are giving me." He caught her to him and planted a kiss on her forehead. "Ah, Madeleine, my dear sweet Madeleine. Thank you."

" 'Tis a gift I give you freely, my dearest. And with love," she murmured, touched by his tenderness. "Besides, this child—our baby—would not exist, were it not for the love we share, would it?"

Dark blue eyes tender, he rested his hand fleetingly upon her belly for a second or two, before he caught her about the waist and swept her up into his arms. Ignoring both her efforts to escape and her girlish, giggling protests, he strode down the path and across the stableyard, and carried her inside.

The farmhouse consisted of only four rooms;

the biggest, the great room, was where all the cooking and hearth-gazing were done, with vaulted ceilings, smoke-blackened rafters, and a wide hearth of natural stone. Before the hearth was a shabby rag rug, in which one or two small holes had been burned by stray embers.

Alongside the fireplace was a highbacked settle, softened with faded chintz pillows. It was a place that cried out to be filled with red-cheeked children, cats, kittens and lop-eared hounds, huddled up to the hearthstone and to each other.

In the second chamber stood a wide tester bed. Unlike the one at Steyning, this had tall, elegantly turned posts at each corner, but no hangings. It was spread with a quilted coverlet of blue-and-white-sprigged cloth, the squares sewn together in the country fashion and heavily embroidered.

There was a braided rag rug beside the bed, and an ancient armoire against one wall. A dresser held a simple white china ewer and pitcher. The fireplace was of scarred but robust oak, with a mantlepiece of local fieldstone.

Behind the farmhouse was a flower and herb garden. Tiny walkways of stone meandered between the flower beds. The air was perfumed with the scents of lavender, sweet peas, phlox, sweet william and snapdragons. On the other side were herb beds, and a vegetable plot, a pump, a well, and a small carriage house.

Outside the wall, there were other outbuildings, and beyond those, hedgerows and meadows dotted with wildflowers that dreamed in the sun. If she listened, she could hear the crash and boom of the nearby sea as it beat against rocks and shore, as well as the joyous warbling of birds in the hedges and trees.

It was a delightfully rustic spot, and she said as much, adding, "But why are we here?"

"I thought, milady, that you were in need of the honeymoon I promised you before we were wed. The one that, thanks to the blasted government and its perverse sense of timing, you were denied when I took ship for France."

"A honeymoon? Really? Just the two of us?"

"Just you and me, my sweet." With that, he tugged the ends of the bow that fastened her bonnet beneath her chin. Its ribbons unraveled, and he plucked the blue silk creation from her head. His eyes held hers willing captives as he did so.

"I do not know if you are of a similar inclination, my dear, my sweet, my darling little bride," he teased, drawing the white shawl of Honiton lace from about her shoulders, "but I would relish some time alone with you here. Imagine, my love! Just the two of us. Long, lazy days in which to swim in the sea and feel the water's caress upon our bare skin. Or to walk and fill our lungs with brisk salt air while we explore the flotsam and jetsam of the shore. Or—" here his dark blue eyes kindled—"each other."

"Justin, I—"

"Shh. Hear me out, woman. Can't you tell? Your husband is trying—desperately—to seduce you. I want to make love to you in a hollow of wet sand, Madeleine. To lay you down beneath me in the meadows out there, among the tall grasses, surrounded by wild poppies and daisies. Or right over there, upon the rugs before the fire, as a summer storm rages. What say you, my lovely Madeleine?"

His voice was hypnotic, his words erotic—poetic, almost. His touch stirred little shivers and lightning darts of arousal in her body as he freed the tiny buttons that closed the back of her high-waisted gown.

"What could I say, milord, but 'yes,' " she asked softly.

Her heart was in her eyes as she looked up at him.

Chapter Fourteen

The next fourteen days and nights were idyllic ones for the two of them. They passed in a lovely golden blur, each glorious day melting into a glorious star-spangled night, which in turn became yet another glorious day.

As Justin had promised, they strolled along the beach every day, holding hands like sweethearts. Sometimes he chased her with garlands of seaweed that reeked of fish and iodine, which he threatened to stuff down her neck. In and out of the rocks, they ran, leaping between curls of white foam that lapped at the golden sands like a sailor's cat.

In the mornings, the light was so bright, it hurt their eyes, bouncing off the glittering water in sunbursts as they walked along the wet sand—a difficult pursuit while wearing sturdy shoes, she discovered on the first day. Before long, Justin made her take a seat upon a rocky ledge. He knelt at her feet and removed her sturdy boots and hose.

"What are you doing? Don't!" she protested, squirming away as he rolled down her stockings.

"Didn't you ever paddle in the sea as a child?" he asked. "No? Then today is your lucky day! However, in order to paddle, milady, you must first remove your shoes and stockings. It's easier to walk along the sand barefooted than it is wearing shoes."

She laughed in delight and shook her head, tearing off the second stocking herself. "I've never paddled before. We lived too far from the seaside when we were growing up. My sister and I learned to swim in the river. No, I take that back. It was actually in the village duckpond." She shuddered and made a horrible face. "Complete with ducks and duckweed and lots of horrid green slime. Uggh. Swimming in the river came later. After that, we learned how to punt, too."

"You punted?" He snorted with laughter. For some reason, he could not imagine his lovely delicate bride poling a flat-bottomed craft along the Thames.

She thumped him in the chest. "Why are you laughing? I'll have you know that after church on Sunday morning, my sister and I used to spend many lazy summer afternoons, boating on the river with my mama and papa." She smiled. "Those were such happy times. 'Memory-making times,' Felicity used to call them. Like this one. Like every day we spend together."

"We can paddle another time. It's so hot today! Come on. Let's swim, instead!" he challenged. Without waiting for her answer, he lifted his full-sleeved shirt over his head and began unbuckling his belt and unbuttoning his breeches.

He was such an exciting man! His deep blue eyes sparkled with challenge in his wind-browned face. His dark hair and the full sleeves of his shirt furled in the brisk salt wind that blew inland off the sea. In this setting, he could easily have been mistaken for a pirate or a wicked buccaneer, she thought. All he needed was a golden earring in one ear, like Trevor Fox.

"All right," she replied with a giggle. "Let's!" She stripped off her gown. Letting it fall about her feet, she stepped from its folds and took the hand he offered.

Together, they ran down the sand, with Madeleine wearing only her gauzy chemise, and Justin as naked as nature intended.

Despite the heat of the day, the water felt freezing, at first. She gasped as it surrounded her, plastering the filmy chemise to her body. The wet cloth accented the full curves of her breasts where it was dragged taut over the hard nubbins that crowned them. "I want you," he said hoarsely, straightening and kissing her hair. Wet, it was the color of honey, and molded slickly to her head.

"God knows, I want you, too. But can we . . . here, I mean? In the water, like this?"

In answer, he lifted her astride his flanks. Anchoring her legs around his waist, he slid his hands beneath her derriere. "You tell me, *chérie*," he said thickly, his eyes dark with desire as she took him deep inside her body. "Can we? Here? Like this . . . and like this . . . and like this?"

As he spoke, he moved strongly inside her, his mouth drawing upon her breasts, nipping the tiny buds through the folds of wet cloth, tugging the fabric aside with teeth and lips to suckle the bared nipples.

She moaned softly in delight, then let the man she loved—and the silky water—take her where they would.

That first day set the pattern for all that followed. They walked for miles along the beach, over the Downs or through the dappled woods, where the sunlight was thick and green and the air was filled with the smell of mosses and ferns and fresh, growing things. They swam. They played on the sands like children. They built crackling bonfires on the beach at night and made love wildly, passionately, by the light of leaping flames and the silvery glow of the moon.

Other nights, when the rain pattered over the thatched roofs, they built a huge log fire in the hearth of the farmhouse, and made love in the wide poster-bed there, wallowing in feather mattresses and pillows stuffed with eiderdown and in the sensual pleasures of their bodies, and being together that way.

Their appetites—for each other, and for food—were voracious. When they were hungry, they raided the farmhouse larder, or else tramped to the nearest village, about a quarter of a mile away, and ordered victuals in the taproom of the local tavern.

Everything they ate at the Crown and Anchor tasted twice as good as it would have done elsewhere. Their appetites were honed to a keen edge by the salt air, brisk walks and their lovemaking, which was frequent, energetic—wonderful!

The tavern keeper's wife served them hot and cold roasted chicken, with slices of savory pork-sausage stuffing, seasoned with parsley, thyme, sage and onion. There were pink slices of lamb, cooked with rosemary and pearl onions. Roast pork with delicious crisp crackling, gravy, and tiny roasted potatoes, pork pies and Cornish pasties, juicy blackberry pies with fresh sweet cream or baked apples with vanilla custard.

Nor was the farmhouse's larder ever entirely empty. The tavern keeper's daughter Maisie came each afternoon, bringing fresh produce for them. Fresh creamy milk, golden wedges of cheese, crusty bread loaves to be slathered with farmhouse butter, hard-boiled eggs, salads of lettuce, spring onions and other fresh greens, picked from their farmhouse garden.

Madeleine tucked into every bite with gusto. Her appetite was enormous with the child growing inside her.

"Had I suspected you were such a trencherman, my sweet, I would have thought twice before I married you," Justin teased one evening, laughing as she polished off the last mouthful of raspberry tart and fresh cream with obvious relish and a contented sigh.

"You would have? Really?" She looked hurt.

"Of course not, silly girl. But I would have had a bigger bed built so that I'd have en—*whoa!*" He yelped as she launched herself on him. "Quarter! Give quarter!"

"Never, you impudent rogue! Take that! And that!"

The last evening, they walked home from the Crown and Anchor arm in arm, their path lit by moonlight, starlight and the light of the storm lantern Justin carried.

As they walked, they talked, Justin telling her about growing up at Steyning and his boyhood scrapes with Michael, Madeleine reminiscing about her mother.

"She passed on seven . . . no, eight years ago," Madeleine explained. "Poor little Felicity was so distraught. She was just eleven years old, an age when a girl needs her mother, I believe."

"And you were the advanced age of . . . what?"

"Thirteen." She sighed. "Mama and I were closer than most mothers and daughters. We were best friends, too. I still miss her dreadfully, every single day. And yet . . . I would not have wanted her to live one moment longer than she did, not with the illness she had, and the pain it caused her. As it happened, it was a blessing. She simply went to sleep one night and never woke up again."

"While my mother supposedly rode her horse over a cliff."

"You sound skeptical."

"I am. Very." He hesitated, as if debating whether to say more. "You would have to know the superb horsewoman my mother was to understand why. She had ridden since she could hardly walk. There wasn't a horse in our stables at Steyning she couldn't ride—including the stallions. The day she was killed, she was riding her own mare. An animal with a sweeter, more even disposition never lived."

"If it wasn't an accident, what do you think happened?"

He shrugged. "I don't know. There was talk,

because she was such an expert horsewoman, that she killed herself."

"Oh, surely not! Was it something she might have contemplated? What reason would she have had for doing so?"

"The magistrate felt it was a possibility because she had been recently widowed."

"How recently?"

"Just a few months before. My father was shot during one of our missions for the government, you see."

"Oh, Justin, I'm so sorry. Another accident, coming so soon after the first. To lose both parents in just a few months' time. . . . How terrible it must have been for you."

"Father's death was no more an accident than my mother's. The bastards were lying in wait for him at Calais."

"The French? And you saw it happen! That's even worse!"

"No, I didn't see it. I wasn't with him, not that last time. I'd come down with food poisoning the night before he went over to France, you see. He left without me, and I was too bloody ill to do anything about it. Had I been there, with him, it would never have happened. I would have made sure of that. We watched each others' backs, you see?"

When she saw his bleak expression in the moonlight, Madeleine's heart ached. He had been close to his parents, just as she had. She squeezed his hand a little tighter. "You don't know that. Had you been there, you might well have been killed, too. Please. You must not blame yourself. There was nothing you could have done."

"How can you say that with such certainty? How can anyone? The fact remains that I wasn't there, so I will never know for sure, will I? I let my father down, and he died. And perhaps because of his loss my mother died, too. That is the knowledge I must live with for the rest of my life."

He was quiet and withdrawn for the remainder of the walk home. She knew that he was thinking about his parents and blaming himself for their deaths. Poor Justin. She had not realized he had lost both parents in such a short time. The circumstances surrounding their deaths and his feelings of guilt explained why he had seemed to sad and withdrawn when they first met.

When she was undressed for bed, he kissed her dutifully, promising to join her soon. But he did not, just as she had known he would not.

After an hour or so, she rose and padded barefoot through the shadowed farmhouse.

She found him outside in the little kitchen garden, where every leaf and blade was rimmed in silvery moonlight. Night-dew sparkled on petals like crystal tears. The perfume of the flowers was heady on the languid night air.

Justin was seated on a rough wooden bench, gazing up at the starlit sky. He did not seem surprised to see her there. When she curled her arms around his neck and brushed her mouth against his own, she tasted tears on her lips.

"Come to bed, my love," she whispered.

He looked up. Their eyes met. Held.

He nodded slowly. "All right. Lead on, *chérie.*"

Taking his hand, she drew him inside.

She took the initiative that night, wanting to heal his grief and ease his sorrow, hoping he would lose himself, for a little while, in the pleasure of her body.

Later, as his broad shoulders rose and fell rhythmically above her, as he filled her again and again, she thought how very deeply she loved him. How devastated she would be to lose him, as Lady Emilie had lost his father! Perhaps, despite what Justin believed, his mother really had taken her own life, rather than live without her beloved husband.

Their lovemaking had a keener, sharper, bittersweet edge that night because of their unspoken fear of losing each other. She clung to him a little tighter, gave herself a little more freely and eagerly, kissed him just a little more fiercely, until, with a great shout of triumph, he claimed his climax with one last, deep thrust.

In almost the same instant, pleasure pulsed through her own body.

They clung together, limbs entwined, hearts thundering, until, still whispering I-love-you's, they fell deeply asleep in each others' arms.

The next morning, they piled their belongings into the carriage and climbed aboard for the return drive to Steyning. The glorious honeymoon was over.

Chapter Fifteen

Steyning Keep
Year of Our Lord, 1067

The Norman had asked her a question. Yet had her very life depended upon her answer, Lenore could not have given him one.

Instead, she stared down at the bare fingers of her left hand, her mind gone blank with fear.

Like her sweetheart, the braided ring of Eydmond's hair was gone now. She had hidden it carefully between the pages of her psalter for safety, while she came to Steyning Keep.

She had resorted to this desperate measure only out of dire necessity; to protect the life of her unborn child. *Eydmond's child.* Yea, and it had cost her a fortune in courage to do so! After all, no lamb willingly entered the wolf's lair!

When the steward announced her and her escort—one of the nuns who was serving as her chaperone, in lieu of a lady-in-waiting—the Norman had greeted her in a benign yet cordial fashion. He showed no surprise that she bearded him in his own den. It was almost as if he was waiting for her.

"Welcome, damosel, welcome!" he greeted, his English heavily accented. There was an unspoken question in his dark eyes. "At last, you see fit to grace my new hall with your loveliness."

"Milord, you are too kind," she murmured politely, placing her palm over the back of his hand as he guided her across the hall.

Her skirts whispered over the rushes as he led her to the lord's high table. There, he invited her to partake of the evening meal with him. Bidding his steward pour wine for them both, he bade her sit at his left side, the perfect host.

Throughout the meal, he kept up a stream of light and oftimes witty conversation, inquiring after her health and such, while he served her the choicest morsels from his platter, skewered upon the point of his knife. There was a sliver of game pie, a succulent bite of capon, a morsel of golden-crusted bread made in the Norman manner, with fine white flour, so different from the coarse black bread to which she was accustomed.

During the meal, his steward plied her with heady Norman wines. Although unused to them, she drank freely, needing the courage of the grapes. After her first sip, she was not afraid of growing tipsy. French wine, she discovered, was not nearly as potent as Saxon mead. It did not go to her head nor addle her wits, but it did bolster her courage, just a little.

After the simple fare the sisters of St. Mary were served in the priory's refectory, the victuals at the lord's high table should have tasted like manna from Heaven. Instead, every crumb was like bitter herbs on her tongue, for she could not rid herself of her fear that de Harcourt would see through her ruse. Or that the Norman's legendary temper might, at any moment, explode, and rain murder and death all around her like arrows.

"Damosel?" Giles de Harcourt was staring at her expectantly. "My token. Pray, what became of it?" he asked softly.

His reminder jerked her back to the present. Whatever did he mean, she wondered desperately? What token did he ask after?

The *ring!* That was it, she realized, weak with relief as she found herself staring down at her unadorned hand. He had asked what matter had brought her to his keep, and what she had done with the amethyst and pearl ring—the love-token he had given her, not once, but twice. The first time, she had hurled it back in his face in contempt; the second time, she had kept it and given it to her love, to buy food for his rebel band or to help fund the insurrection he planned. The last time she saw him, Eydmond confided that they were not without allies among the conqueror's followers. A Norman knight, Count Eustace de Boulogne, was reputedly disenchanted with his countrymen, and eager to aid their rebellion. And where there was one Norman rebel, Eydmond had been convinced there would be others.

"Forgive me, my lord, but I no longer have your gift in my possession." She whispered the words, hanging her head as if in shame at the admission, while her mind raced for an answer to give him. The thunder of her frightened heart seemed loud in her ears. Could he hear it?

"You have left me no choice but to confess, sir. I gave your pretty token away! There. Do with me what you will. I have no excuse to offer."

With those challenging words, she defiantly raised her head and met him, eye to eye, letting none of her loathing for him show. It would work, or it would not. She would soon find out.

"You did what?" Instead of the angry outburst she expected, his black eyebrows rose. His dark eyes glinted, as if in amusement, though that could never be.

"I . . . I gave your ring away, milord," she repeated, small chin jutting obstinately. "Nor am I sorry for it!"

"Are you not? Then may I ask, damosel, the

identity of the lucky recipient of your—*my!*—generous gift?"

"Anon, my lord de Harcourt. First, I would have you know that I did not come easily to my decision to break off my betrothal and accept your suit in its stead," she began, the lies spilling from her lips in a rush.

"The decision was made only after days spent in fasting, and nights passed in prayers that the Blessed Virgin would guide me. I also made a short pilgrimage to the town of Canterbury, in the company of two of the priory's holy sisters. That ancient town is the very heart of our mother church here in England, you see."

"*Oui, oui,* damosel. I know this. And your piety is to be commended. But you have yet to answer my question," Giles reminded her sharply, impatient now. "Go on, pray. Tell me. *To whom did you give my gift?*"

"During my brief pilgrimage, I visited the old church . . . the church of St. Michael, where our beloved Saint Augustine first worshipped when he came to England. You see, sir, it was at St. Michael's font that I received my baptism as an infant—"

"*Non,* my lady, I do not see at all!" Giles said impatiently. He sounded bored. Irritable. "What has all this nonsense to do with the ring?"

Lenore smiled her apology, her cornflower-blue eyes meeting his for a long, smoldering moment, before, with a sweep of dark lashes, she quickly looked away.

"Forgive me, my lord. I am no eloquent man, like yourself. We women are inclined to . . . how shall I put it? To *meander* a little, before we come to our point," she explained, her thoughts racing for an explanation that would satisfy him. "But, I shall dissemble no more. The truth is, my lord, that I gave your ring to the . . . to the Church."

For a second, there was utter silence, like the lull before a great storm. But instead of erupting in fury, as she feared he would, the Norman instead threw back his short-cropped head and laughed.

"The Church? Did you, by God?" he roared. "Did you, indeed!"

Taking up his goblet, he tossed back the dregs of his wine, then wiped his lips and beardless chin upon the back of his hand. "Pray tell, *ma jolie* damosel, why would you do such a thing, when the ring was not yours to give?"

Lenore humbly bowed her head. "By your leave, *monsieur*, I acted upon impulse, not by deception or design—or even ingratitude. You see, it seemed only right and proper that I make that small donation to the Church, since it was in God's House that my prayers were answered."

"*Oui?* And what prayers were they, my lady?"

the Norman asked, rising to the bait like a fine fat trout to the fisherman's hook.

"I prayed to the Blessed Virgin. Implored her to show me how the . . . how the sons of my body might someday be great, in these troubled times," she said simply. "You see, my lord, the flower of England's nobility is either dead, or has been taken in chains to France by your countrymen. My former betrothed, once a . . . a Saxon thane in his own right, with both keep and lands, is now lord only of hedgerows. All that he once owned has been razed or wrested from him. So were my father's name, keep and lands lost in the battle at Hastings."

"His name? How so?"

"The seeds of his immortality were cut down. His sons—my brothers—who carried his name are both dead and gone. I am all that is left of his line."

"And you are filled with ambition to preserve that noble line yourself, my lady?" He sounded surprised.

"I am, sir, yes. Not for myself, but for the children I shall have some day. But I digress. Whilst yet in Canterbury," she continued her story, "I beseeched Our Lady to give me a sign. To tell me how my purpose might be accomplished."

"And? Did the Virgin send you some heavenly omen?" Giles asked, almost holding his breath. There was the hint of a sneer in his tone, yet despite himself, he was intrigued by her story. This was not, in all honesty, the tale he had expected to hear, yet its rambling quality gave it the ring of truth. 'Lord of hedgerows,' she had called her Saxon betrothed. He chuckled. Now, there was a fine jest, if ever he had heard one. *Not even that, lovely damosel. . . .*

"Indeed She did, my lord," she answered him. "Her sign is what brought me here." She toyed prettily with the girdle of gold and scarlet tablet embroidery that rode low upon her hips. " 'Tis the reason I have broken my betrothal to the Thane of Lewes and . . . and am now free to wed you, sir, should you still desire me for your wife and lady."

The lie dripped from her lips as smoothly as melted butter, yet she felt neither guilt nor shame for it. If, as she fully believed, her beloved Eydmond was in Heaven, looking down on her, he would understand full well that she did this for their child, because of the love she bore them both. Had he lived, she would never have forsaken him. Nor, in her broken heart, did she truly forsake him now.

If, God willing, her plan worked, and she was able to wed the Norman and convince him that Eydmond's child was his, the Norman would have no babes of his own—at least, not from her womb. She would employ vinegar douches and

216

herbs whenever he lay with her, to make quite certain he did not . . .

"The sign, woman! *Mon dieu!* You are as slow as a little snail! *What was the blasted sign?*"

"It was overcast that day, as I recall," she began, as unruffled as a quiet pool, despite his heated urging. Or, perhaps, because of it. "But as I knelt there, before the altar, the sun came out from behind the clouds. A single ray of sunshine, brighter than all the rest, pierced the stained glass window like an arrow. That shaft of glorious light fell upon my hand, sir. It shone directly upon your ring. 'Twas then I knew what I must do."

"That was it? A single ray of light that chanced to fall where it would? That was your Heavenly sign?"

"It was, my lord." Her chin came up. "Surely you do not question the Virgin's ability to perform miracles?" she asked him in a pious, accusing tone, her blue eyes wide and innocent.

Ah, *oui*, so very innocent, he noted, his groin tightening. Was he a fool to question the sign that would deliver her to his bed, as surely as a whoremonger delivered a virgin, bought and paid for?

"On the contrary," he lied smoothly. "I was merely . . . astounded . . . that such a simple portent could yield me my heart's desire!" He took both her hands in his and drew them to his lips.

"By accepting my proposal, *ma chere damosel*, you have made me the happiest man on this damp, wretched little island."

She let him kiss her fingers, hiding her revulsion beneath a sugary smile. If her plan succeeded, he would do far more than kiss her anon. 'Twas best she learned to mask her disgust from the very first . . .

"You shall not regret it, Lenore," he said thickly, lust in his voice and in his hot eyes as he drew her into his arms. "Marry me, and you shall have the child you crave within the twelvemonth—and I, a son and heir for Steyning!"

As she looked up at him, her smile was radiant, dazzling. It was the smile of a victor. A conqueror. Mayhap the Normans ruled the isle of Britain, but here, at Steyning—by the Grace of God, in this very keep!—the purest of Saxon blood would one day rule. *Her father's and Eydmond's blood!*

"Nothing could make me happier, my lord," she murmured, inclining her fair head. A half-smile played about her lips. She looked innocent, yet seductive. Full of allure.

He had underestimated her, Giles decided, claiming her lips in a possessive kiss to seal the agreement between them, before leaning back in his carved chair with a sigh of satisfaction.

Over the jewel-encrusted rim of his goblet, he admired the charming picture Lenore made, ivory skin delicately flushed, lips red and swollen from his kisses. Her beauty was timeless, bred in the bone. 'Twas not the fleeting comeliness to be found at court in Paris. A superficial prettiness that went hand in hand with youth and faded 'ere a month or two had passed. Lenore, on the other hand, would age gracefully and well, remaining beautiful long into old age.

Even now, hardly more than a girl, she looked every inch the great lady, framed by the French tapestries that graced the walls of his new hall. Walls that were as yet unsoiled by smoke, and still smelled of the fresh mortar and lime used to build them, he noted with pleasure.

Other knights would envy him his beautiful wife. Aye, and William would applaud him for taking a Saxon woman as his bride, and by so doing, winning their enemy's acceptance. Perhaps, as a result, his king and friend might shower more honors upon him, as he often did his most favored knights.

Moreover, pious as the flaxen-haired Saxon beauty seemed, her ambitions for her future offspring approached his own.

Ambition.

'Twas an unusual trait in an unwed woman, especially one of such tender years. This unexpected facet of her character fanned his lust, just as a random wind fanned the spark in a hayrick to a fine blaze. Ambitious women were she-cats when it came to bedsport. Together, he fancied, they would go far.

He smiled, eyeing the way fine tendrils of hair stirred about her lovely face, like delicate filaments of gold wire. His hot gaze shifted lower, to the ripe breasts that rounded out her scarlet surcoat. His mouth was dry with the impulse to the bear her down, to the table, on her back, and slake his obsession. To make her his, in deed as well as word, and purge his flesh of its craving for her.

"When?" he asked hoarsely, lewdly pressing her thigh beneath the trestle tablet as the steward splashed red wine into her goblet.

When she did not pull away, he resisted the urge to crow like a cock in his triumph. He had been very careful, very patient in this matter, and he had been rewarded with the prize: Lenore. A man could prevail over any rival, as long as the object of the woman's affections was never allowed to become a martyr. Women, with their soft little hearts, were too often moved to support the underdog. . . .

Biding his time, he had reminded her of his suit a time or two, then withdrawn, allowing the lady ample time and opportunity to come to her senses, and decide for herself that she had been deserted by her betrothed.

He smiled. Lenore was beautiful, but she was also well past the marriageable age of fourteen years, lacking family and means in a country ruled by conquerors from a distant land. Once Eydmond of Lewes had . . . abandoned her, her options had been few. The lady's instincts for self-preservation had overidden any lingering loyalty to the Saxon rebel. Nor had joining the priory as a Bride of Christ been an option she would choose. *Non!* Not Lenore. She was too alive, too sensual to be cloistered as a nun.

And so, she had turned to him—as he had planned from the first. It mattered not whether she ever grew to love him, or he her. He had wanted her from the first moment he saw her, and he would have her—*oui*, and often. Once they were wed, she would be under his rod, according to the law; subject to her husband's every desire.

"I ask again, my lady," he murmured, reaching beneath her kirtle, fondling her supple thigh. "When shall we be wed?"

Plucking his hand from her body, she drew away from him with a great show of maidenly dismay, yet her eyes bade him come hither—and more.

"I shall be yours as soon as may be, my lord Giles—but not until *after* we are wed." Her husky tone, the way her dark gold lashes swept down, promised him all manner of delights to come, once they were man and wife.

"Then shall I summon the bishop forthwith,

my little plum. And be warned, *ma chère.* You shall find me a most ardent bridegroom," he promised thickly.

"As you will, my lord," she murmured, inclining her head.

Giles wetted his lips in anticipation, like a hungry wolf licking its chops before the sheepfold.

As the chatelaine of Steyning Castle, lady wife to one of King William's favorite knights, her belly swelling with his sons year after year, she would soon forget the rebel bastard she was once betrothed to wed. A sly, secretive smile curved his fleshy lips. *As had he. . . .*

"Blessed Mary in Heaven, where have you been?" the Prioress Aelfreda demanded in a hoarse whisper when Lenore returned to her cell later that evening, her lips bruised and swollen from the Norman's kisses. " 'Tis late . . . I feared the Norman had forced you to his bed."

"I have been busy setting a snare, Aunt," Lenore murmured, her eyes a hundred leagues away.

"A snare? What sort of snare?"

"A snare for a Norman wolf."

"Have you, indeed? And with what is this snare baited?" As a good Christian woman, a woman who had taken orders, she was not certain she wanted to know the answer to her question, but she asked it nonetheless.

"My maidenhead," Lenore said softly. "My woman's body. What else should I use to catch a Norman?"

"Sweet Blessed Mother!" Aelfreda exclaimed, crossing herself. "And when shall this trap be sprung?"

"De Harcourt and I are to be married as soon as may be. On the morrow, the Norman will send a messenger to William's bishop, Odo of Bayeux, requesting he come here to perform the nuptials. My betrothed is most eager to claim his virgin bride." Her lip curled in an expression of disgust.

"Virgin? But . . . but you are—"

"—already with child, and no longer a maiden by any man's measure?" A bitter smile curved her lips. "Yea, Aunt, I know it full well." Her eyes met her aunt's. "But . . . the Norman does not." She gnawed her lower lip. "I have heard rumors . . . my mother's women, they used to talk. They said . . . I overheard them whispering that there are ways if a woman wants to . . . convince a man that he . . . that he is her first lover. Ways to make him think that he has broached a virgin's maidenhead."

Aelfreda's features puckered like a miser's purse. She shrugged, her expression one of disapproval. "Perhaps there are. I know nothing of such things myself . . . and nor, I warrant, do any of the sisters. I know. We must send for Eartha in the village. She will help us."

Eartha? Lenore frowned, trying to put the woman's face to the familiar name. "The one whose brother drowned in the weir? What was his name? Rufus?"

"Aye, that's her, God Bless her. Eartha is a harlot, God forgive her. She does what she does, and seeks charity from no man. Yet, sinner or nay, what she does puts food in the mouths of her brother's widow and children, as well as her own and her old mother's. Some might think 'twould be better they all starved and died rather than take their nourishment from such a source. I do not share that view, however."

An image of a red-haired fresh-faced wench filled Lenore's head. Eartha had a bold eye and a saucy way of swinging her hips as she walked. When she'd strolled past the spider's web of scaffolding to bring her brother his noon-day victuals, the men had whistled and called to her.

"Can she be trusted to hold her tongue?"

"With her life, dearling! With her life. She has no love for the Normans. They are the reason she must do what she does now. The good Lord knows, no decent man would take her to wife, not after what de Harcourt's men did to her when they first rode into the village. Passing her from man to man, and her sobbing and screaming!—" The prioress shook her head and crossed herself. "The poor child. Her own betrothed turned his back on her, after that, for all that they

224

were to have wed within the twelvemonth!"

Lenore nodded soberly. The Normans had much to answer for, across England. "Summon her here as soon as may be, Aunt. If all goes well, she will never again have to earn her living on her back. I shall make her nursemaid to the Lord of Steyning's heir!" she crowed.

"His . . . his *heir?* But your child is not his g—!" Her hand flew up to cover her mouth. "Oh, Sweet Mother of God! How foolish of me. Now I see it!" Aelfreda exclaimed.

The prioress laughed, despite her horror at her niece's bold plan, and what could befall her— both of them—if Giles de Harcourt were ever to learn of it.

Lenore laughed, too, yet it was a hollow, bitter sound, to Aelfreda's ears. Her eyes were full of pity as she stroked her niece's fair hair. In truth, Lenore's heart had broken in two with her beloved Eydmond's desertion, despite the air of bravado she maintained so bravely for her child's sake. Unlike her niece, Aelfreda was not entirely convinced that Eydmund had been killed by de Harcourt.

"And if you fail? What then, dearling? What if the Norman discovers your secret?" she pressed gently.

"Then I have lost nothing I have not already lost, except my life. And that, dear Aunt, means little to me now, without the man I love to share

225

it. At daybreak, send for Eartha, if it please thee."

"Very well," Aelfreda promised.

Leaving her Aunt's cell, Lenore crossed the quadrangle to the Lady Chapel.

Even at this late hour, the tall lighted candles that stood in silver holders before the altar spilled gentle pools of radiance across the marble floor. Their flames were longer than her hand, yet burned with slender tongues of steady fire.

Sinking to her knees before the altar, Lenore began to pray. "My dearest lord and love, forgive me. . . ."

When she was finished, her heart was sore in her breast. Her throat ached, too, yet her eyes were dry, her tears all shed. The agony of grief remained; a pain that she would carry with her, always.

"Where are you, Eydmond?" she whispered into the scented stillness, in which there was not a whisper of a draft. "What did the Norman do to you, my love?"

On either side of her, the flames guttered and went out.

Chapter Sixteen

Still only half awake, Madeleine lay drowsily in her bed, staring up at the brocade canopy above her. Her mind was troubled. Her thoughts were confused. Her heart still raced in the aftermath of her latest dream.

Could the story be believed, she wondered? For if so, it meant that the hateful Norman, Giles de Harcourt, was not Justin's ancestor at all. Her husband was descended from Thane Eydmond of Lewes, a Saxon lord—thank God!—if the babe survived its birth, and all went according to its mother's plan. . . .

Stop it! she told herself sharply, remembering Justin's loving admonitions to abandon this obsession with her dreams. *Forget this foolishness! Think of our child!*

Justin had warned her she would make herself

ill again if she persisted in getting wrapped up in what he called "this fanciful nonsense."

"They are dreams, nothing more, nothing less, my love. Think about something else. Imagine, instead, how it will feel to hold our baby in your arms."

She had tried. God knows, she had really tried! And—until last night—she believed she had succeeded. She'd told herself the dreams were a thing of the past, gone, never to return. She'd had good reason to believe it was true.

They had been back at Steyning for three full weeks now. Three weeks of blissfully dreamless nights. And, although she thought often and with longing of their little farmhouse by the sea, and of the idyllic honeymoon they had shared, she truly believed she had succeeded in putting the dreams behind her.

She had awakened each morning feeling rested, refreshed and ready to take on the world. Eager to fill Steyning—and her marriage to its master—with the light, laughter and happiness that Justin needed and craved. It would take time for his wishes to be fulfilled. The sorrow that Steyning Hall had absorbed had taken centuries to seep into the stone. It would not simply leach out of the walls and be replaced by happiness in the space of a few weeks or even a month or two.

Until the day came when gloomy, forbidding Steyning took on a cozier, happier atmosphere, she and Mrs. Fox had put their heads together. They came up with a plan of action intended to banish the gloomy oppressive atmosphere of the ancient manor.

Every room, every stick of furniture, every Turkey rug and floorboard, had been scrubbed, beeswaxed, polished, dusted and beaten in turn, until even the smallest alcove or forgotten corner sparkled.

Flowers of every type and color had been cut and brought in from the gardens; purple delphiniums, white sprays of lilac, pink and white roses. Brass and silver bowls had been polished until they shone, then filled with the blooms. With one or more bowls in every room, the musty old house was filled with the glorious scents of summer.

Mirrors and looking glasses in carved gilt frames had been brought down from the attics and stategically hung in gloomy corners to take full advantage of every ray of light.

Casement windows had been thrown open to the sun, and the draperies drawn back, allowing sunshine and summer breezes to fill the house with the fresh green smells of the woods and gardens, and the briny scents of sea and wind. The number of candlesticks and candelabra lit each evening were increased, too, so that golden candlelight was reflected off every polished surface.

Unlike her predecessors, Madeleine had

launched herself wholeheartedly into the process, insisting to an alarmed Mrs. Fox that, despite her condition, she was not such a milksop that she could not wield a feather-duster to good account, or buff up a brass bowl until it gleamed. She would leave swoons and such theatrics over what was, after all, a very basic, very common human condition, to ladies of the nobility, she declared gaily.

Her light-hearted laughter and good humor were infectious. Mrs. Fox had reluctantly acquiesced, on condition that her ladyship take frequent rests and refreshment. Madeleine agreed that she would, with some reservations.

"They must be very small quantities of refreshment," she warned the housekeeper laughingly, "for while we were away, his lordship remarked that my condition has made me something of a trencherwoman! Should I grow plump, I fear he will turn me off and take a . . . a beanpole as his wife, instead!"

"On the contrary," Justin observed, catching her last remark as he came into the drawing room, where she and Mrs. Fox were going over the household accounts. "I have discovered I heartily dislike beanpoles, and instead have a decided penchant for ladies of the well-endowed variety. Moreover, I have come up with a way to keep mine nicely rounded."

He wickedly jiggled his eyebrows and tossed a

lecherous wink at Madeleine. His expression left no doubt as to what way he was implying.

Madeleine turned bright pink and burst out laughing. She would never have expected such a bawdy comment from her serious husband.

"Oh, sir!" Mrs. Fox exclaimed, deeply shocked by his ribald wit. "Oh my, oh my!" Her cheeks were very red. "What a wicked thing to say! And in front of my poor lady, too! And you a gentleman, sir!"

"Indeed, I am, Mrs. Fox. Would you care to hear more?" he inquired, trying to keep a serious expression.

"I certainly would not, sir!" that good woman said huffily. She hefted her generous body out of a wing chair with considerable effort, and bustled to the door. "Perhaps we could continue our business later, madam, *after* his lordship leaves."

She had given Justin such a pointed, disapproving look, that Madeleine had wanted to laugh, but hadn't, for fear of hurting the poor dear's feelings.

"If you need me, I shall be in my room, madam," Mrs. Fox said, before closing the door behind her.

"Hmm. Probably having a nip of gin," Justin murmured after the housekeeper was gone. "And it'll be *my* gin she's nipping, at that! I've long suspected somebody was filching it. Now we know who."

"Poor Mrs. Fox. She's such a dear. You are a terrible rogue to upset her so," she scolded. "And while she may be a trifle prudish, I'll have you know she definitely isn't your gin-nipper!"

And so laughter began to find a place at Steyning Hall. Dr. Smythe and Justin had both been right, she decided. Her silly dreams had been a result of her early pregnancy. Nothing more than the foolish flights of fancy that her condition sometimes engendered in certain women, like a sudden passion for strawberries, say, or shrimp.

But now this latest dream had changed everything again. She was back where she'd started— or was she?

"That's it. It's not going to work anymore," she muttered, tossing aside the bed linens and swinging her legs over the side of the bed. "Do you hear me, Eydmond of Lewes, or whoever you are? Or should I say, whoever *you were*. Get out of my head! Get out of my dreams! Get out of this house! Go! Be off with you!"

Taking up a silver-backed hairbrush, she bent forward, so that her tangled hair almost swept the floorboards. She brushed her hair with furious, almost violent strokes.

When it was free of tangles, she raised her head again, tossing her long hair back, over her shoulders, like a mane.

Her actions brought her face to face with her reflection in the looking glass . . .

. . . and a stranger's face beside her own.

A pale face, male, and limned in light, framed by ragged fair hair. He wore the garments of another time.

An icy chill sluiced down her spine.

Eydmond?

The silver hairbrush fell from her nerveless fingers. It struck the edge of the dressing table, and thudded to the floorboards. Her pin box followed, shattering as it landed.

She was too scared to think, could hardly breathe. She could only stare. Logic said Eydmond could not be there, because he did not exist, except in her mind. *In her imagination.* Justin had said so, and she had agreed.

So why were the fine hairs standing up on her neck and down her arms? Why had the blood drained from her face as their eyes met in the looking glass—and held.

Find me, lady fair! And in the doing, save thy self—!

"Where are you?" she managed to whisper. "What did de Harcourt do to you? How can I find you unless you tell me where you are? Help me!"

His eyes were the saddest she had ever seen. She could not bear to gaze too deeply into them, for fear his sorrow was contagious. And yet, she *had* to know whether he was flesh and blood, or spirit.

233

Slowly, she turned her head.

There was no one there.

And when she turned back, that other pale face in the looking glass was gone—if it was ever really there. She saw only her reflection, pale and wide-eyed. The frightened face of a woman who cannot believe what she has seen.

Reaction set in. She was trembling as the adjoining door opened. Justin came in. He was half-dressed, his jaws and cheeks half-hidden beneath shaving soap. He carried a razor in one hand and a linen cloth in the other.

"What the devil was that racket?"

"I dropped something," she whispered.

"I could have sworn I heard you talking to someone. Is everything alright?"

She nodded without turning to face him, afraid he might read the truth in her eyes. She desperately needed a moment to compose herself.

His quick glance took it all in. The silver hairbrush on the floorboards. The shattered Wedgewood pin box. The hairpins, strewn in all directions. Her pallor. The way her hands shook when he set aside the razor and took them in his.

"Madeleine. Your hands are freezing. What's wrong?"

Gradually, as if she had just awakened from a dream, she lifted her head. She looked at him, then quickly averted her eyes. He would guess the truth if she let him look too closely. And of course, she could not tell him what had happened. He would be convinced she was going insane if she were to say, *I saw a face in my looking glass. 'Twas the ghost of one of your ancestors, I believe. A distant* Saxon *forebear*.

No, he must never suspect the truth. He might have her locked in the attic, like a crazy aunt.

"Just a . . . a little dizziness, that's all. I was bending over, brushing my hair, and straightened up too quickly. The blood . . . the blood must have rushed to my head, I suppose. I staggered and knocked some things off my dresser. That's all it was. I must remember not to do that again."

He grunted in response, then knelt, picked up the brush, and returned it to the dressing table. Carefully, he collected the broken pieces of sharp porcelain and tossed them onto the hearth, out of harm's way.

"Those pieces look sharp," she warned. "Careful you don't cut yourself."

He looked at her curiously. Was she talking too much? She couldn't seem to keep from babbling. "Never mind me. What about you? Your foot is bleeding."

"It is?" She was surprised when she saw all the blood. "A sharp piece must have flown when it shattered. How odd. I didn't feel a thing."

"Perhaps you were preoccupied with something else?"

"Perhaps." She still could not meet his eyes.

"Step over those sharp pieces and sit on the chair," he instructed.

While she did as he ordered, he poured water into the basin and dipped a face cloth in it. Taking her foot in one hand, he gently wiped the blood from her instep with the other. It was a small wound but had bled profusely. "There. It's hardly bleeding now."

"Oh, stop it! That tickles!"

"The blood?"

"No, silly. Your hand on my instep. I'm very ticklish there, remember?" she reminded him flirtatiously. He had held her foot like this at the beach, when he took off her shoe so that they could go paddling in the shallows. Only then, he had kissed her arches, nibbled her toes . . . and more.

"Don't try to steer my thoughts elsewhere," he told her, scowling. He had seen through her little ruse.

"Justin. Why on earth would I do that?" she asked in a wounded reproachful tone.

"I don't know, Madeleine. You tell me. Why would you?"

He regarded her very seriously, his dark blue eyes intent, searching, his features looking very stern on one side, hidden by lather on the other.

She wanted to giggle, but dared not. Lather or no, it was as if he could see right through her. As if he knew her every thought.

"Is there something you'd rather I didn't know?"

She frowned. "Don't be foolish. You are my husband. I have no secrets from you."

"Then you are telling me the truth? You haven't had any more of those dreams? No odd flights of fancy since we came home to Steyning? Perhaps last night . . .?"

She crossed her fingers within the folds of her nightgown, so that the lie would not count as a sin. "No! Nothing."

"You were so restless, tossing and turning. You would tell me if you had, wouldn't you?"

"Of course!" she insisted brightly, flashing him a dazzling smile.

"Honestly? Then why do your lips say one thing, but your eyes another?" he queried, shooting her a hard, questioning look.

"Are you implying that I'm lying to you?" she demanded in an indignant tone. For some perverse reason, she *wanted* to quarrel with him. To push him away, keep him at a safe distance. If she let him come too close, he would know he was right. That she was lying about the dreams. That they hadn't stopped.

"Why? Are you, Madeleine?"

"No!" she insisted, her fingers curling into

237

hard little fists. "What reason would I have to lie to you?"

"None that I know of. Why don't you tell me?"

"Oh, you're impossible!" she cried, springing to her feet. "If you won't believe me, I can't make you, can I?"

"Careful!" he growled, grabbing her wrist before she could step onto the tiny slivers of broken china.

"Let go of me. Don't touch me," she ground out, throwing off his hand.

"Someone has to keep you from hurting yourself!"

"I'm quite capable of taking care of myself. Now, let go of my wrist. *Immediately*."

He released her. His expression was cold now, his eyes glacial and remote. "Very well. Perhaps by this evening, you'll have come to your senses and be ready to tell me the truth."

"Why? So that you can tell me that I'm losing my mind? Or that the . . . the . . . that our baby is the reason for what is happening to me, when I know the one has nothing to do with the other?"

"Ah ha. Then you *have* had more dreams!"

"I didn't say that."

"You don't have to." He grasped both of her upper arms and shook her once, very gently. "Madeleine. *Chérie*. Please. Stop dwelling on these . . . these fantasies. These people, if they ever truly existed, are dead and gone. You cannot bring them back, nor right the wrongs that were done to them. No-one can. My sweet, you will make yourself ill if you persist in trying. If you won't stop for my sake, then do it for our child! For our little daughter or son."

Tears stung behind her eyes. He made her feel so uncaring, so foolish. "Don't you think I want these wretched dreams to stop? Don't you think I would put a stop to them myself, if only I knew how? But, short of staying awake each and every night, I can think of no way to end them. And as for the other, I!—" She caught herself just in time. Another second, and she would have blurted out what she'd seen in the looking glass. "Oh, never mind."

"No, go on. Tell me! The other what?"

"Nothing. It's not important." But even as she said it, in her mind's eye she could see Eydmond's reproachful eyes in the mirror. Such anguished eyes! Could hear his voice inside her head, beseeching her to help him. What had he meant, that in finding him, she would save herself? Was she in danger? She shivered. If so, from what? From whom?

"Everything that concerns you is important to me, *chérie*. Don't shut me out. More than anything, I want you to be happy," Justin said in low, earnest tones.

"And what about *your* happiness. Why would

239

I willingly burden you with my petty problems, when you already carry more than most men could ever bear?" Her voice broke.

His jaw became granite. "I decide what burdens to shoulder in my life, Madeleine. Not you, nor anyone else. I'm a man, damn it. You don't have to spare me."

"Why not? You would spare me, if you could! Besides, I'm your wife, am I not? Your partner in life. Your helpmate. We are supposed to share the bad things life hands us, as well as the good, remember? 'For better or for worse'?

"Then again, perhaps you feel a . . . a lowly country physician's daughter is incapable of understanding the lofty problems that are an earl's lot in life?"

Even as she said it, she knew it wasn't true. But she said it anyway, wanting to push him away. To keep him at a distance, where he could not read her every thought. *Or know her every dream.*

"Damn it, woman! You are being ridiculous. And don't put words in my mouth! What the devil has me being an earl to do with your blasted dreams? To do with any of it, for that matter?" he exploded. "I could not love you more were you a . . . a duchess, or a bloody empress, and you know it! Or should, by now! Any inferiority you feel because of the differences between us are in your head . . . and of your own invention, Madeleine. They are none of my doing! Now. May I suggest we discuss this again later, when you are in a more . . . reasonable frame of mind?"

With that, Justin returned to the adjoining room, presumably to finish shaving, since he was swabbing the lather from his face and neck as he went.

Although his parting comment left her fuming, in her heart, she was glad to see him go, for the time being.

They went down to breakfast separately, and took their seats with stony expressions. They sat at either end of the long oak refectory table, instead of beside each other, as they usually did. The expanse of Irish linen between them was as wide and unbreachable as any chasm.

For the first time since their marriage, the meal they shared was a silent one, the chill between them thawed only by overly polite requests for condiments to be passed. The delicious array of grilled kidneys, scrambled eggs, sausage, ham, porridge and other morning fare remained all but untouched. The small quantity of food they transferred to their plates was toyed with, but largely uneaten.

Luncheon was more of the same. The meal ended very quickly, with Justin muttering that he needed to speak to Nowles on some urgent matter or other. Quickly excusing himself, he disappeared in the direction of the stables.

Left to her own devices, Madeleine changed for walking out. Fending off Tabby's offer to accompany her, she headed toward the village of Steyning alone, with no definite destination or purpose in mind, other than that of removing herself from the house and the immediate presence of that unreasonable, dreadful, hateful man.

Somehow, she found herself at Rector Cargill's door, surrounded by Althea Cargill's spaniel puppies.

Now several months old, they were squirming, energetic roly-poly bundles of liver and white fur.

Between petting velvety heads and fondling floppy ears, she found herself asking the rector's wife where she would find Mother Lee, Tabby's mother, who lived in the village.

"Peg? She lives in the small cottage at the very end of the village High Street. You cannot miss it, my lady, for the quantity of purple foxgloves that grow about the door. She uses them for remedies, you see? But I believe you may catch Peg in the church at this hour, your ladyship," Althea explained loudly over the excited yips of the pups. She was glowing with the honor of having Lady de Harcourt call personally upon her at the manse.

"Mother Lee and some of the other ladies from the village take turns cleaning the Lord's house for the parish, you see, madam? Today, 'tis Mother Lee's turn."

"Thank you, Mistress Cargill." She turned to leave.

"Your ladyship? Lady Madeleine? Would you . . . I mean, I don't suppose you would care to take a dish of tea with me?"

"Tea? Why, yes, that would be lovely, thank you," Madeleine exclaimed, glowing with pleasure. Not only did she welcome the invitation, she was grateful for any reason to stay away from the Hall—and Justin—for as long as she could.

She knew, in her heart, that she had been at fault, not him. She also knew that she had created their quarrel as a red herring, intended for one purpose and one purpose alone: to put distance between them, so that she would not have to tell Justin the dreams had returned, or be called to account for having them. That was the reason, pure and simple. She was obsessed by Lenore and Eydmond and their lives, and loath to distance herself until she discovered what had befallen the Saxon thane.

"I'll come back after I've spoken with Mother Lee, if that would be all right?" she suggested.

"Oh, yes, my lady! By all means, do. I would be honored. I'll have Polly put the kettle on."

Mother Lee was polishing the huge silver candlesticks that stood in front of the altar when

Madeleine went into the empty church. Her footfalls seemed very loud in the still air, which smelled of candlewax, beeswax and flowers.

Dust motes danced in the colored light that fell through the stained-glass windows. The rays patterned her gown and the marble floor with ruby, sapphire, emerald and topaz. Though she had told herself she would think of them no more—and had given Justin the same promise—she could not help remembering her dream of Lenore, and the miraculous "sign" from the Virgin that she had invented for the Norman's benefit. Here, it was easy to imagine a single ray of sunshine falling through the stained-glass window to touch an amethyst ring with its light.

The old woman turned and bobbed her a curtsey.

"Mother Lee?" The woman at the altar was as tiny as a brownie, a pixie person with sharp bright eyes and quick deft hands. She reminded Madeleine of a small bird. A robin, perhaps, or a sparrow.

"Aye, milady. And you must be Lady de Harcourt, Master Justin's pretty wife."

"Yes. Yes, I am. I'm so happy to meet you, at last, Mother Lee. You see, a few weeks ago, your daughter, Tabitha suggested I speak to you."

The woman nodded. "Aye. And I can guess what it is you want to ask me about, my lady." She squeezed Madeleine's hands between her own. "The answer to your question is, aye. I felt him, too, when I was in service up at the Hall. Many times."

"You did? But who is he?" she managed to ask, a little unnerved that the woman had known her question, even before she asked it.

"Come, come, now, my lady. Don't you be after playing games with Old Peg. You already know the answer to that question, without me having to tell ye. 'Tis Eydmund. The ghost's name is Eydmund. Though Eydmund who or Eydmund what, I could not say. You would know that part of it far better than I."

She swallowed. "You . . . you have seen him, then?"

Mother Lee shook her head. "Felt him, aye. Seen him—no. But I always knew when Eydmond was about. The air changed, aye? Colder, it was. And no amount of logs could warm that chamber when he were about, not even in midsummer."

"He didn't frighten you?"

"God bless you, no, my lady. Poor lad. He was not one of them that seek to scare the living. Naaay. But . . . I've felt his sadness. And his longing, if you will. Ye must take care, my lady, for he *is* needy. And his will has proven strong enough to survive the grave this many years. What he wants, he will have, nor will he rest until he finds it. If he has shown himself to you, surely

245

you must know what that something is?"

"He wants to be found," Madeleine murmured, although she had not known, consciously, what it was Eydmond sought, until that moment. "He wants his remains found, so that he can be with Lenore."

The knowledge seemed to come from a deeply buried part of her, some half-forgotten memory.

"He wants her . . . the lady Lenore . . . to know that he did not abandon her or their child. To be beside her in death, through all eternity, as he could not be in life."

"You see?" Peg said, patting her arm. "You know more than you give yourself credit for. Small wonder he chose you and my dear Lady Emilie to put things right. Lovely gentle ladies, both of you. I warrant poor Eydmond was drawn to the light that shines from you."

The light within her? *That is what Justin once said*, Madeleine thought with a pang of guilt. "Is he . . . is he dangerous, do you think?"

Mother Lee shook her head. "Bless you, no. Only the most powerful emotions survive the grave. One is hate, the other, love. 'Twas sadness that I felt from Eydmond. Sadness . . . loss . . . and great love."

"But, what about Lady Emilie's death? She had the same dreams, did she not?"

"She did, God bless her, my poor dear lady."

"Yet she rode her horse over a cliff!"

Mother Lee smiled faintly. "So folk say. I'm not one t'believe it, though, nor do I put great store in gossip. The dreams have naught to do with what happened to her. The cause of Lady Emilie's death lies with the living, not the dead. Take care not t'become so preoccupied with those who are spirit that you forget to protect yourself from the living. Of the two, they are far more dangerous."

"What are you saying? That Lady Emilie's death wasn't an accident? That she didn't take her own life?" Madeleine asked, exasperated, confused and, if truth were told, a little frightened.

"I'm saying only that ye should be careful, my dear lady. A little less trusting than it is your nature to be. Think of the child. Aah, such a fine little lad, he'll be." The old woman took Madeleine's hand in her own and kissed it. "God bless you both, and his father, too."

"He?" Her hands strayed to her belly. Both palms cradled the hardness that was the child growing inside her. "My baby's a boy?"

Mother Lee smiled. "Aye. Then again, it could be a little lass." Her gray eyes—so like her daughter, Tabitha's—twinkled. "If you must know before your time, ask my daughter. She'll tell ye true! Such a gift she was born with, though some might call it a curse! Now. I must get on with my cleaning. A very good day to ye, your ladyship."

Madeleine let herself out of the church. She was walking back down the pathway of flagstones, towards the vicarage, to take tea with Althea, when she noticed a vault, close to the church, with an ornate door that stood ajar. Above the name "De Harcourt," which was etched into the stone above the door, soared two small stone angels—guardian angels.

Through the open doorway, she could see a lighted torch, propped in a sconce. The flame guttered in the draft, lighting a gloomy flight of steps that led down into the bowels of the earth, and to the de Harcourt family vault.

She swallowed uneasily, remembering the story Cargill had told her, about the ground below the vaults having shifted almost three hundred years earlier, with disastrous consequences. Fact—or fiction, as he'd so charmingly claimed? By some chance, could Eydmond's remains be down there, she wondered? It was most unlikely, but not impossible. He had, after all, been of noble Saxon birth.

She looked about her, but whoever had left the door ajar was nowhere to be seen. Should she wait until the person who'd lit the sconce returned, so that he could accompany her? Or take a quick look for herself, just to set her mind at rest? A quick look would do, she decided, lifting the torch from its sconce and raising it aloft. It would only take a moment, and it was possible whoever had lit it was still down there.

God, how she hated places like this, she thought as, taking a deep breath, she gingerly started down the stairs to the crypt below.

Her giant shadow partnered her as she went down into the gloom.

Chapter Seventeen

The torch's guttering light revealed a large crypt chamber, built like a square within a square. The outer walls held three levels of large niches. Each niche contained a stone sarcophagus or a brass-trimmed wooden casket. More niches were set in the four faces of the stone square in the center of the crypt, to her right.

Madeleine inched along, pausing to read the inscriptions in the flare of the torch she raised aloft. Her fear of enclosed places was forgotten as she read each name, each date of birth and death, and tried to sort out the de Harcourt family generations in her head.

Among the earlier stone sarcophagi there was an inscription that read, "Here lies our most pious lady, Rowena, blessed wife of William, earl of Steyning, and their infant daughter. Amongst the angels."

Lady Rowena must have been the wife of the Wiliam who was buried beside his mother, lady Lenore, on the priory grounds. There was an effigy of Rowena on the lid of the stone casket, and another of Rowena and William's son and heir, Richard, the third earl of Steyning, who had married Matilda of Folkestone, mother of Godfrey, the fourth earl.

She also found Lady Emilie's casket of polished black walnut, and that of Lord John, the eleventh earl of Steyning. Justin's father.

She paused before these last two, bowing her head to say a brief prayer. Tears choked her throat for their son, who had loved them dearly, but blamed himself, she knew, for their deaths.

She moved on to the vacant niches. This was where—in the very, very distant future, God willing—her and Justin's remains would spend eternity.

She shivered. The thought gave her goose bumps. It was difficult, if not impossible, to confront her own mortality here, now, with this new life growing inside her, and a happy future with the man she loved still ahead of her.

She moved on, her shadow enormous on the wall before her. As she went she cast a hasty glance at the nameplate or inscription upon each sarcophagus or casket she passed. But what she saw only confirmed what she'd expected. Eyd-mond's remains were not here.

She wrinkled her nose. The faint smell of centuries-old flowers, of dust and candlewax and a smell that was indefinable lingered on the still air. It was not so much the smell of death, of mold, or mildew, or even the ever-so-faint sweet whiff of decay, as it was a complete *absence* of human life. The combination of time, great age, sorrow and loss wafted a dank bouquet beneath her nose.

She shivered as the torch suddenly guttered wildly. A current of cool air kissed her cheek, making the shadows leap and dance like der-vishes. Immediately, a single loud *"bang!"* sounded, sharp as a pistol's report. The explosive sound echoed hollowly through this place of death and sent her heart galloping out of control!

It was only after the fact that she realized: the sound was that of a heavy door slamming. *The crypt door!*

"No!" she shouted, her cry ringing on the hush.

Turning, she fled back the way she'd come, blundering into corners in her panic, not stopping until she reached the short flight of stairs. Holding the torch aloft, she saw that, as she dreaded, the door at the top was closed.

Drawing a shaky breath, she flung herself up the stairs, her breath coming in frantic sobs, her chest heaving, the torchlight writhing. *'Twas only the wind*, she told herself. The door had just blown shut. There was no earthly reason it should be locked. She would still be able to get out . . . wouldn't she? Oh, God, *wouldn't she?*

Her frantic fingers anchored around the latch. She shook it furiously. "Come on, open!" she urged. "Come *on!*" The latch rose and fell with loud metallic clicks, but the door still refused to budge. Against all odds, it really was locked.

Replacing the torch in the sconce, she threw her shoulder, then her upper body against the door, then hammered and pounded it with her fists.

"Help! Someone! Help! I'm stuck in here! Open the door!"

She screamed, shouted and hammered until she was exhausted and defeated. A sheen of sweat slicked her face. The cloth of her gown stuck to her spine. More frightening, it was hard to breathe. Her chest hurt. The air going in and out of her lungs sounded as tinny as a penny whistle. She would suffocate down here if she didn't get out soon.

"Help!" she wheezed as she sank to the ground.

"Please! Somebody!" *Oh, dear Lord, what is happening?* The place seemed to be getting smaller by the moment. The walls and the dark were closing in around her.

It seemed as if she huddled there forever before she heard sounds on the other side of the door. By then, the torch had gone out, plunging her into suffocating blackness. Almost paralyzed with terror, she hauled herself to her feet as the door opened. A bright bar of sunlight illumined the darkness, blinding her momentarily.

"Oh, thank God!" she sobbed. "I thought I'd never get out of there!"

"Lady Maddy? Good Lord! Whoa! It's all right. You're quite safe now," Michael Latimer declared as Madeleine tottered out of the shadows, literally falling into his arms.

"Oh, God, I hope so!" She shuddered, her chest heaving. She was trembling and her pale face was shiny with moisture in the bright light of day. Her palms were clammy, too. "I was down there . . . and then the door slammed shut. Someone . . . somebody locked me in!" Her indignant voice trailed away.

"Hmm. Not very likely." He sounded doubtful. "Then again, I supposed George—he's the sexton—might have closed it, not realizing anyone was down there. George keeps the crypt in order, you see. Then again, it's more likely to have been the wind."

"Yes. Probably. Whatever happened, thank you for . . . for coming along and letting me out," she murmured, a little embarrassed now. "I don't know what I would have done if you hadn't heard me."

He grinned, thrusting a lock of fair hair off his brow in a boyish, charming gesture. "I must admit, it gave me quite a turn to hear someone demanding to be let out of the crypt! To be honest, it wasn't entirely a coincidence that I happened by, though. You see, I was looking for you. Your maid said you had taken a walk into the village and that I would find you here, somewhere."

"Tabby said that?"

"Actually, it was the . . . um . . . the other maid. Effie. I say. Are you sure you're all right? You do look pale." His face, dappled by the sunlight that fell through the leaves, was really very handsome, she noticed. And he seemed so genuinely concerned about her, too.

"I'm much better, really I am, thank you. Why were you looking for me?"

"Hmm? Oh! That." He rolled his eyes. "Well, there's something I've been telling myself I'd do for weeks now, but I've kept putting it off.

"The first time I mustered my courage and slunk over to the Hall with my tail tucked between my legs, you and Justin were away on honeymoon. So, I decided it was today, or never— but there you were, gone again. The elusive Lady Maddy." He grinned. "Madam, you are as difficult to catch as a will-o'-the wisp!"

"My name, sir, is Madeleine, not Maddy." Her

voice was stern, yet she could not help laughing at his boyish grin. He had not been nearly so engaging as this when she'd surprised him with Effie under the stairs. "Pray, tell, sir. What favor would you ask of me that requires such courage on your part?"

"No favor at all, madam. I ask only that you accept my deepest, humblest apology."

"Your apology! For what, sir?"

"As if you did not know! For my appalling manners that evening at the Hall."

"Oh. But that was weeks ago!"

"I know. That's how long it has taken me to bolster my courage to offer it. You really are very intimidating, you know, Lady de Harcourt."

"Me? Intimidating? Nonsense!"

"Oh, but you are. You see, I'm accustomed to the unprincipled jades of the ton. Unlike yourself, they are very accepting of behavior like my own that night. They would never have called me to account for it, as you did."

"Oh, but—"

"No, please. Let me finish. Maddy . . . Madeleine. It was only right and proper that you did so. I am supposedly a gentleman, after all. I have no excuse to offer, other than to tell you that my marriage is . . . well, it is less than the idyllic match that you and Justin have found together. The two of you are to be envied! Madeleine, since you are a married woman, may I speak with you frankly?"

"Please, do."

"After Charity's birth, I was warned by Sabina's physician that having another child could kill my wife. Consequently, I have been—how shall I put it delicately?—forced to seek satisfaction for my masculine . . . needs elsewhere." His light blue eyes flickered over her, an unfathomable expression in their depths.

"I had been given ample cause to believe that your maid, Effie, would welcome my advances." He shrugged. "Clearly, she had a change of heart at the last moment. Or perhaps I was in error?"

"So it would appear, yes."

"That being the case, I deeply apologize for any unpleasantness I caused you that night, dear lady. Furthermore, let me assure you that it will never happen again. I should like very much for you and me to be friends, Madeleine, as Justin and I are friends. Can you . . . could you . . . find it in your heart to forgive me, and let us start over? Please?"

He was so charming, so contrite. How could she possibly refuse? Her shoulders slumped. Laughing, she held out her hand. "Sir Michael? How do you do. I'm very pleased to meet you. I am Lady Madeleine de Harcourt, Lord Justin's wife."

"Delighted to meet you, dear lady. Delighted,"

Michael declared, playing along and kissing her hand as if they had only just met. "Lady Madeleine, may I have the honor of escorting you back to the Hall?"

"Actually, I was going to the vicarage to take tea with Althea Cargill. But, I thank you for your kind offer."

"Aaah. Here's that good lady now. Mistress Cargill. A very good day to you," he said as Althea came scurrying toward them down the path.

"Sir Michael." Althea nodded. She turned to Madeleine. "Is everything all right, madam? You were so long. I couldn't think what had happened to you."

"I'm quite all right, thank you, Althea. I did something rather foolish, I'm afraid. I went down into the de Harcourt crypt. While I was down there, the door blew shut and I was locked inside. . . ."

"Locked?" Althea began, frowning. "But—"

"Her ladyship meant stuck. Not locked. The door is very tight, you see? I had the devil of a time opening it."

"Aah. My poor lady. What a fright that must have been for you!"

"I'm afraid I didn't help matters much," Madeleine explained ruefully. "You see, I have this stupid fear of enclosed spaces. When I couldn't get out, I panicked."

"Oh, my. Come along then, my lady. A hot

dish of tea, well sweetened, will do your shattered nerves a power of good, I shouldn't wonder."

"Thank you. I'm sure it will," Madeleine agreed gratefully. "Sir Michael? Thank you again for coming to my rescue. A good day to you, sir."

"My name is Michael. And a very good day to you, too, Lady Madeleine." He inclined his head and smiled. "Friends?"

She laughed. "How could we be otherwise, sir, on such a brief acquaintance?"

Catching her hand, Sir Michael drew it to his lips and kissed the knuckles. He held onto it as he gazed long and hard into her eyes. "Thank you. I cannot tell you how happy this makes me."

It was then that Madeleine saw her husband, over Michael's left shoulder. The urge to guiltily withdraw her hand from Michael's was overwhelming, but she resisted it. After all, she had done nothing wrong. There was nothing to feel guilty about.

Justin sat his black stallion, Satan, beneath the lych gate. He was wearing a full-sleeved white cambric shirt beneath a brown-and-gold brocade waistcoat, and dark-brown breeches. From the furious scowl he was wearing, she knew he had witnessed the little exchange and that it displeased him to find his bride holding hands with his best friend.

Michael, on the other hand, tossed her husband a jaunty wave before he slipped inside the church.

Justin clicked to his horse. He followed the wrought-iron palings that enclosed the church-yard, until his mount had drawn level with her and the rector's wife.

"Justin? What is it?" Something was wrong. She could see it in his stern face, which looked as if it was chiseled from flint. It was also in the stiff-necked way he held his head and shoulders.

"Government business. I've been called away, Madeleine."

"Oh, no! Not again! When must you go?"

"Tomorrow. At first light. What business did Latimer have with you?" His eyes were narrowed.

"Michael?" She smiled for Althea's benefit, determined not to discuss their business in public. "Just to offer his congratulations. You know, about my condition?" It was not, strictly speaking, the truth, but there was no reason for Mistress Cargill to be privy to Sir Michael's marital problems, or anything else, for that matter. She would explain to Justin when they were alone.

Her husband frowned, clearly wondering what it was she was not telling him—and perhaps jealously assuming the worst, thanks to the silly quarrel she had instigated. She sighed. Surely he couldn't imagine she and Michael could have a *tendresse* for each other? Just the idea of it made her want to giggle. How foolish men could be. She would dispel any such notions he might have at the earliest opportunity. . . .

"Would you care to join us, your lordship?" Althea Cargill asked shyly.

"Madam?" Justin frowned.

"Lady de Harcourt has been kind enough to say she'll take tea with me at the manse this afternoon. You are most welcome to join us, milord?" Now that she had obtained the promise of a visit from Lady Madeleine, Althea had no intention of letting her prize slip away without a fight.

A grin broke through Justin's scowl. "Thank you for your kind invitation, Mistress Cargill. However, I doubt that my thirst could be appeased by tea this afternoon. On the contrary. I fear that will require a much stronger libation! Perhaps on some other occasion, if I may make so bold?"

Althea blushed and bobbed him a curtsey, beaming from ear to ear. "Oh, yes! I would like that very much, milord."

Her gushing, girlish reaction nettled Madeleine, for some obscure reason.

"Come, Mistress Cargill," she snapped crossly, shooting Justin an irritable glare. "I find myself quite parched, after all that shouting and banging. I shall see you back at the Hall, my lord."

Refusing to meet Justin's querying expression,

she continued on down the pathway to the manse, with Althea hanging on her every word.

She could feel Justin scowling after her, every step of the way.

The mood between them remained cool throughout dinner, Justin's attempts to engage her in conversation and her own best intentions notwithstanding.

She was seated before her looking glass, brushing out her hair and mentally kicking herself for not mending their quarrel before he left for France when the adjoining door opened. Justin came in.

His upper torso was bare and he was wearing only his breeches as he came to stand behind her. His hair, she noticed, was damp and he smelled of soap. Drops of water clung to his muscular body like amber beads in the lamplight. He placed a hand on each of her shoulders and ducked his head, dropping a kiss in her hair.

"Madeleine. *Chérie*," he murmured, his eyes meeting hers in the mirror. "I can't leave like this. Not with such coldness between us. My work is too dangerous. A moment's distraction could cost me my life."

"Then don't go. Stay here with me, and devil take everything else!" she said impulsively, knowing how childish it sounded, but suddenly fearful for him.

"Aaah, Madeleine, if only I could," he murmured, sliding his arms around her to cup her breasts. He buried his face in her perfumed hair, then kissed her silky shoulder. "I'd have to be insane to want to leave this. To leave you."

She leaned back against him, arching her head back, offering her throat for his kisses. He groaned. His hands caressed her breasts throught the soft fabric of her gown. Drawing the nipples between his fingers, he kneaded the soft mounds as he nuzzled her ear, or nibbled a tender earlobe.

His caresses filled her with intense sexual pleasure. She ached for him to make love to her. To make her forget that he must leave at dawn, or that his dangerous mission would lead him into enemy territory where his life could easily be forfeited. She must tell herself that what he did saved innocent lives from the guillotine. She must try to bear it, to be brave, until he came home to her.

She uttered a low murmur of pleasure, deep in her throat as he pushed her nightgown down, off her shoulders. Sweeping aside her fair hair, he rained kisses down her spine, over her shoulders, across her collarbone as she sat there, fully aroused, her body aching, yearning for his. She watched, as jealously as any voyeur, while their reflections made love in the looking glass before her.

His tanned hands were so dark and male, so sensual as they caressed her white breasts, smoothing the satiny skin, teasing each rosy nipple. His damp tongue traced the delicate knobs of her spine, lower, lower, until he was kneeling at her feet. He halted his sensual journey only when the soft fabric that was rucked about her waist impeded his lips.

"Let's get you out of this, shall we?" he asked huskily, taking her hands. As she stood, the nightgown fell about her feet in a pool of white silk. Grasping her derriere, he pulled her hungrily to him, kissing her fiercely as held her, pressed against his straining flanks.

"Yield, *chérie*," he growled, planting kisses along the lovely line of her jaw. "Let me love you tonight, before I must go."

She nodded mutely. Tears stung behind her eyes as she curled her arms about his neck. "Ohh, yes. I love you, Justin. I always have, I always will, come what may. Never doubt it. Never forget it. And remember that when you are away, you take me and my love with you in your heart, wherever you may go. As I will keep you and your love in mine."

There was nothing more to say. Nothing more that could be said. He swept her up, into his arms. Carrying her to their bed, he placed her upon the feather pallet as if she were spun crystal, delicate, fragile, and followed her down.

His hand between her thighs, he resumed the delicate foreplay she loved, touching her in those places that gave her greatest pleasure. He felt her breathing change. It grew shallow and breathless with mounting desire as he kissed her deeply. His tongue warring with her own, he plied her with his fingers.

The brush of his lips, his scent, his touch, the heat of him, everywhere, everywhere, made her shiver with delight.

Her senses still reeled as he mounted her, entered her, began thrusting strong and deep, inside her. He pinned her hands above her head, so that she was helpless to escape him, even had she wished it. Which, of course, she did not. His heavier male body, cradled on her belly, lodged squarely between her thighs, was a sweet burden, rather than a punishment; part and parcel of the wondrous pleasure they shared.

With a kittenish purr of contentment, she arched up, matching her rhythmn to his driving thrusts. The excited little sounds she made, deep in her throat, were enough to drive him over the edge.

"I love you, *chérie*," he ground out as his climax shuddered through him. Gripping her hips to hold her fast, he drove against her, time and time again.

"I know," she whispered, running her hands through his hair. It was all there in his eyes. The love, the need, the desire—even the raw lust. All of it. "I know. Come home to me, Justin. Come home safely."

With a shudder, a groan, he covered her mouth with his own and let passion take them both.

She awoke from a deep sleep to find their positions reversed. She was now sprawled across Justin's body, her fingers knotted in his silky black hair, her head cradled upon his broad chest. She could hear the measured beat of his heart, strong and steady beneath her ear—along with another pounding, this one as loud as thunder-claps, and farther away.

"Justin?" she whispered urgently. "Wake up! Justin! Someone's at the door." Still half-groggy, she lifted her head. Something was not right. . . . But what was it?

Ruddy light leaped and danced across the shadowed wall. It was like the flickering light the bedroom fire cast—except it came from the wrong direction!

Her head snapped around. An orange glow filled the section of window she could see through an opening in the draperies.

"Oh, God! Justin—*fire!*" she screamed. Springing off him, she snatched up her wrapper and ran to the door, dragging it on as she went.

Sliding the bolt, she saw Digby, the butler, standing there, about to knock again. He was still wearing his nightshirt and cap, and was clearly agitated.

"Madam, the stables are burning!" he cried. "Wake the master!"

"The horses!" came Justin's hoarse voice as he leaped past her, wearing only breeches and boots.

As the two men hurried below, taking the stairs two at a time, Madeleine tore off her wrapper, threw on her nightgown and followed them. Pulling the wrapper on again as she hastened downstairs, she raced through the kitchens and out to the burning building.

The scene that met her eyes was like something from a horrible nightmare.

Hellish flames leaped up into the cold night air. Showers of sparks whirled and eddied like orange fireflies above the carriage house, swirling on the blaze's roaring breath. And the sounds! She could hear the crackle of flames, terrified animal screams, and the thunder of the horses' hooves as they kicked out at boxes or stalls, trying to escape the smoke and the terrifying smell of burning wood and straw.

The shouts and yells of the men mingled with the clanging and jangling of buckets and bridles.

Fortunately, the first men to arrive on the scene had managed to pull Justin's fine black coach free of the inferno, while others had raced to fill buckets. The coach now sat in the middle of the stableyard. Its yellow-painted wheels and the gold de Harcourt crest gleamed upon its doors.

Despite the men's best efforts, great flames continued to spear up from the carriage house. They cast their leaping light over the cobbles, shimmied over the Hall's ivy-strewn gray walls in a macabre dance.

A chain of men and women, including Tabby, Mrs. Fox, Mrs. Beaton, Effie, and the other maids and scullery girls, all clad in voluminous night-gowns and wrappers, worked frantically, filling buckets at the pump, then passing them down the line to extinguish the blaze.

The stable lads, all shirtless, the gardeners, the footmen and Justin led terrified, screaming horses from the stables to safety. Most of the Thoroughbreds had been blindfolded to keep them calm. Their handlers turned the animals out, into the exercise paddock, then plunged back into the smoky building to lead those still trapped to safety.

Only a few feet from the blazing carriage house, the stable building was smoky but mer-cifully not ablaze, or at least, it had not caught yet.

Trevor Fox, Andrew Cox, and the groom, Mr. Nowles, worked like demons to fill still other buckets and douse the roof and walls of the sta-bles in a desperate bid to keep them from igniting, too. Their faces were grimy with soot. Obviously they had been among those who had plunged into the burning carriage house to haul out the coach.

Just after the last horse was led free, a rider clattered into the stableyard and leaped down from his mount. His white shirt was unfastened, his fair hair long and loose about his shoulders.

"You can see the blaze from Five Gables!" Michael Latimer exclaimed. "Where can I be of use, Jus?"

"Give us a hand to soak down the stables, and keep them from catching. The carriage house is past help, I'm afraid, but I want to save the stables, if I can, with winter coming on," Justin shouted over the noise.

"All right. Some of my people are on their way," Michael added.

"Their help will be appreciated," Justin said. "As is yours."

Michael nodded as he flung a bucket of water against the half-stone, half-timber stable walls. "You needn't play the gracious victim for me, Jus. You know damned well you would never let me forget it if I didn't lend a hand!"

Justin shot him a grin. "That's right. I need all the help I can get."

"Do ye know how the fire started, milord?" Trevor Fox asked, pausing in his tireless routine to catch his breath. His face, already swarthy, was streaked with dirt and smoke. His eyes were red-rimmed and streaming.

"Nowles thinks a stable lad was courting in the carriage house. He found an overturned lantern—and young Peter Betton's nowhere to be found. He probably panicked and ran."

"And what of the wench?"

Trevor shrugged and mopped his sweaty face on a soaked kerchief. "No sign of her, milord. Unless, of course, she's one o' our lasses." He nodded at the bevy of Steyning maids who made up the bucket brigade at the pump.

Justin's eyes narrowed. "Who sounded the alarum?"

"Tabitha Lee. She saw the blaze from her attic window and woke Digby, then ran to Nowles's quarters and roused him, then myself."

"Well, then. That's it. There's your wench!" Michael Latimer declared with a decisive air.

"That's not possible, Sir Michael," Trevor cut in, looking as if he would like to throttle Latimer with his bare hands. "Since Mistress Lee and myself are t'be wed next year."

With that, the gamekeeper turned on his heel and joined the other firefighters.

"Ill-tempered fellow, that!" Michael declared. "Dangerous, too, I shouldn't wonder. You should watch your back around him."

"On the contrary," Justin replied. "I'd trust

Trevor Fox with my life—or anything else I hold dear, come to that."

Michael shrugged. "On your head be it, then. Don't say I didn't warn you when the lout loses his ugly temper and injures someone."

With that, he sauntered over to where Mrs. Beaton was doling out dippers of water for the thirsty men, whose throats were raw from the smoke.

"Aaah, there she is. My Queen Bea! Goddess of the water bucket! A goblet of your elixir, if you please."

"Oh, sir, you are a one," Mrs. Beaton declared. She was flustered by his flirtatious banter, despite her age.

Shaking his head, Justin resumed his efforts, frowning as he noticed his wife energetically lugging buckets, slopping with water, despite her condition. The way she had pitched in to help warmed his heart, but he was not about to let her continue, as much for her sake as their child's.

"Cox!" he shouted to the under-groom.

"Sir?"

"Take my place, would you?"

"Right away, sir."

"The horses will stay in the paddock for the night. Thank God, the stables weren't damaged. The carriage house is easily rebuilt. Things could have been worse."

"What if the fire rekindles?" Madeleine asked worriedly as he cupped her elbow and drew her away from the rest of the bucket brigade, toward the Hall.

"Two of the lads will keep watch for the rest of the night, just to make sure it doesn't blaze up again."

"My poor Justin. Look at you! You've hardly slept. Must you still go in the morning? You must be exhausted." She was loath to mention it to him, but she had a queasy feeling in the pit of her stomach. A premonition, almost, that said something dreadful was going to happen if he left. "Can't the wretched government send someone else's husband?" She frowned, worrying her lower lip.

"I'm afraid not, no. But you don't have to worry about me being tired. I can easily catch a few winks on the boat over." He cupped her face and kissed her lips. "My sweet girl. You're always so concerned about everyone and everything else." He smiled. "It's time you started worrying about yourself—and my precious daughter."

She laughed. "So it's a girl. Is that what you think?"

"Yes. Definitely Or . . . it could be a boy." He grinned. "One or the other. I don't mind which."

"Now you sound like Mother Lee!"

"God forbid!" He laughed. "Come along. Back to bed with you, Lady de Harcourt" he urged.

Swinging her up into his arms, he carried her across the stableyard, to the kitchen entrance.

"Put me down, sir! I'm perfectly capable of walking, I tell you!" Madeleine insisted, pretending to be angry. Her loud protests drew Michael Latimer's attention. "Justin! Don't! Put me down, I say!"

"Silence, wench!" Justin growled in proper baronial fashion, managing to sound deliciously wicked as he rubbed his bristly cheek against her tender neck. "Should I hasten to my donjon tower, there may yet be time to have my wicked way with thee once more!"

"There might?" She squealed with laughter, her foreboding forgotten, replaced by a much more delightful prospect as he mounted the gracefully curving staircase. "In that case, milord, lead on! I am your willing victim."

Chapter Eighteen

Steyning Keep, Candlemas
Year of our Lord, 1068

Outside, in the bailey and beyond, in the surrounding countryside, snow lay upon the ground in powdery drifts, white as marten furs. The trees cast stark witchy moonshadows, their bony skeletons stripped bare of any softening leaves. Moonlight glinted on frozen ponds and on lakes, like candlelight that shone on mirrors of polished silver, and crystal ice-draggers hung from the castle's eaves.

Within Steyning's great hall, huge log fires blazed upon both hearths, casting their leaping light over the stone walls and illuminating colorful French tapestries. Hounds and men alike huddled close to the fires' warmth. They talked of days gone by, and of battles long-since fought and won—or lost; of summers yet to come and of women and maids still to be wooed, as they sipped hot mead and mulled wine.

In the highest tower of Steyning Castle, where Lenore, lady of Steyning, had her chamber, glowing braziers burned, adding their warmth to that of the fire that blazed on the hearthstone. Wolf and bear skins were strewn across the icy stone floor to warm the feet. Yet the heavy brocade hangings that kept the drafts from invading the bed had been pulled back, and most of the coverlets stripped away for the laboring woman whose low moans and gasps of pain occasionally rent the air.

"She is such a little thing," Aelfreda murmured to Eartha, her expression one of concern. "In truth, I fear for her."

"Don't. My mistress is small, aye, but strong nevertheless, God bless her," Eartha murmured with fond pride, casting the lady Lenore an affectionate glance. "The babe will be as lusty as my wee Gwen. Ye'll see, Mother Aelfreda."

Eartha had delivered a daughter, Gwendolyn, some two months before. The baby slept now in a basket close to the hearth, where it was warm and not far from her mother's watchful eye. Eartha loved her little daughter with all her heart, even though she did not know what man had fathered her. The man's identity mattered little to Eartha.

On the morning the prioress had sent for her, over seven months past, she had promised to wet-nurse the lady's Lenore's child, along with the one she was carrying herself. Thanks to the lady of Steyning, she would never have to earn her daily bread upon her back again, nor take any man to her bed unless she chose to. As nurse to the lord of Steyning's child, she would be able to provide—and provide well—for herself and her daughter.

"And what of Lord Giles de Harcourt? What if the wretched Norman returns too soon from Normandy?" Aelfreda asked.

"Then we tell him the tale we decided upon. That the babe was early. We'll tell him our lady's labor was brought on by a fall, that she slipped on an icy stair and fell all the way to the bottom. Pah. What do men know of infants, other than how to plant the seeds for them! One week or one month, his lordship will be none the wiser, unless the child is very large at its birth."

For herself, Eartha doubted the baby would be overly large. The lady Lenore had not grown as heavy or enormous with her pregnancy as some women were wont to do, which was fortunate for her plan. Even better, her mistress had passed the expected time of her delivery, and gone into the month following before beginning labor earlier that day.

That, coupled with convincing proof of his wife's virginity upon the sheets on the night of their wedding—courtesy of a chicken bladder filled with pig's blood—should convince Giles de Harcourt the child was his own get, she thought with a pleased grin. He would never suspect.

"I have an idea," Eartha suggested. "If he asks, I will tell Lord Giles my lady were up on the battlements, watchin' for his ship when she fell. His child's early birth was all because our lady was eager for the sight of his ugly Norman face!" Eartha nudged the prioress, made a hideous grimace, and chuckled.

"Aye. And my lord husband will believe you, too, because it is what he wants to believe, he has grown so enamored of me," came Lenore's husky voice from the bed.

"Enamored is not the half of it, my dear child!" Aelfreda exclaimed, hurrying to give her niece a sip or two of watered wine. "I have never seen any man so obsessed by a woman. Nor, I think, one so in love with his own wife."

"I am glad. It is a fitting punishment," Lenore said bitterly, her tone hard as flint now. She grimaced as another birth pang drew her belly up to a point, before taking a deep breath and continuing. "To love a woman who loathes and detests him with every fiber of her being, with never any hope of that love being returned! And the more he loves me, the more I shall despise him.

"I shall wait until he is on his deathbed, one foot in this world, the other in hell. Then I shall avenge my lord Eydmond. Only as the light of life fades from his eyes will the Norman know the truth. That the child he has raised and loved as his own—the child that will inherit his every possession!—was not of his blood, nor of his seed. But even so, it will be more truth than that . . . that devil incarnate has granted me," she added, a sorrowful shadow flickering over her weary face.

She had yet to discover what de Harcourt had done to her beloved. However, her conviction that he had done something to Eydmond and his men remained unwavering.

As the long night inched towards the dawning, Lenore became drawn and weak with exhaustion. She slept between her labor pangs, however, and those few precious moments of rest served to revive her and give her the strength to continue.

Her fair hair was limp, damp with the sweat of her labor. But although exhausted, she was far from defeated. Soon, God willing! Soon, she would cradle Eydmond's babe in her arms. It was her reason for living now.

The morning star was paling from the sky, the moon a fading crescent of light, when the urge to push came over her, hard and strong, unrelenting.

Eartha had tied strips of leather to the posts at the foot of the bed in readiness. Lenore wound her fists in the thongs. She pulled hard upon them as she bore down, grunting and turning as red-faced as any peasant woman in her efforts to expel the child from her body.

" 'Tis a wee lad," Eartha crowed as the baby finally slithered free of its mother.

Blond-haired and bloody, the child was perfect, but unmoving, Aelfreda saw. Its skin was bluish and shriveled. It looked, to Aelfreda's uncertain eyes, to have been stillborn.

"What is it? What is wrong?" Lenore asked, reading her aunt's pitying expression. "Why does my son not cry? Give him to me! Let me see him!" she cried.

After the last surge of blood had pulsed from the mother's body to the child's, Eartha tied and cut the birthing cord. With trembling hands, she quickly cleansed the limp infant's tiny nostrils and mouth with a moistened rag, and chafed the tiny limbs.

"Breathe, little one. Breathe!" she whispered urgently. 'Twas but a moment since the infant had emerged, yet it seemed a lifetime to her anxious heart.

When the infant remained limp, she did as she had once seen her mother, a former midwife, do. She grasped the infant by both ankles, turned him upside down and smacked his tiny arse, once, twice, thrice.

The child gave a gurgling gasp, coughed, hiccuped, then drew a shuddering breath. Immediately, he changed from bluish-gray to bright pink as air rushed into his lungs.

The newborn's strident wails filled the chamber, along with his mother's delighted laughter and his great aunt's tears of happiness.

"Do you see, Eydmond? Your son is born!" Lenore murmured as Eartha handed the infant, now swaddled in a warm blanket, to his mother. "The future lord of Steyning!"

The baby's face was bright red now, his eyes tightly shut yet tearless as he wailed, his mouth wide open. Tiny golden curls clung to his perfect scalp, like a cap that had been fitted to his nobly shaped head. Ten tiny toes. Ten tiny fingers—and a miniature hand that curled fiercely about his mother's finger and hung on. From the moment she set eyes upon him, it seemed to Lenore that the babe had done the same thing to her heart.

A fierce surge of love filled her to overflowing. She had lost her lord and love, yet in no small measure, God had given her back a part of him to love, with the birth of this child. *Eydmond's son!* His chance for immortality. And through that son, the Thane of Lewes would live forever.

The cries of the newborn infant awakened Madeleine from her dreams—or so she thought. When her eyes fluttered open, she saw the maid, Effie, standing over her. The girl was holding a candlestick in one hand, and shaking her arm to rouse her with the other. Her cheeks were flushed, her sole-black eyes dark and glittering in the candle's light.

"My lady? Madam, you must wake up! the maid whispered urgently.

"Yes, Effie? What is it?" Madeleine asked. Much of her grogginess was instantly dissipated when she saw the maid standing over her. The infant's wails had been a part of yet another dream, she realized, but Effie was real.

Her stomach turned over, filling her with a flutter of dread. Something must be very wrong, for Effie to be waking her in the middle of the night. It was like reliving the night she had awoken to an orange sky to hear Digby pounding at their bedchamber door. Please God, not another fire in the stables, not with Justin still away, and not a word from him since he left over a week ago.

"Is it another fire?" she asked anxiously.

"Not this time, no. It's the master, milady. He's come home, and needs you right away. Hurry now, madam. Out of bed with ye. Quickly!"

"What is it? What's happened?" She hastily sat up, tossing aside the bed linens. "Has someone been hurt?" Perhaps one of the émigrés Justin had spirited away from Paris had been injured during the escape?

"I wouldn't know, madam," Effie whispered. "His lordship only said for me to wake you, and to be quick about it, and tell no one else. He's waiting for you in the old priory ruins."

"The ruins? At this ungodly hour?" She padded, barefoot, to the window, and drew aside the draperies.

Sure enough, she could see a dancing flicker of light in the direction of the ruins, as if someone was carrying a storm lantern as he moved about.

"But . . . why can't his lordship come up to the house himself? Why all of this secrecy?"

"I didn't ask, my lady. Begging your pardon, but it's not my proper place t'question his lordship's orders either," Effie reminded her mistress with a sniff.

"No, no, of course it isn't," Madeleine agreed, preoccupied with fears for her husband as she dragged on her wrapper and hurried to the door.

"Effie, wake Trevor Fox or Mr. Digby for me, would you? Better yet, get both of them up and bring them to the ruins. And Effie? Hurry, do!" she added as she left the chamber.

"I will, madam," Effie promised.

Quickly, Madeleine moved through the shadowed house, hastening along the upper gallery, down the curving staircase, and across the black-and-white marble chessboard foyer. She passed the niches with their busts of playwrights, explorers and poets as she went.

Taking the rear door out, through the deserted kitchen with its gleaming copper pots hanging in tidy rows, and the dull red glow of the banked fire, she ran out, across the stableyard.

The cobbles were slippery with frost beneath her feet, yet she paid them scant attention. She was shivering as she hurried through the herb and spice gardens, her trembling caused by a combination of brisk night air and apprehension.

What would she find, she wondered anxiously? Justin, badly wounded? Dying? Was that why he hadn't been able to summon her himself?

She offered up a quick, silent prayer for his safety, and another that he would be unharmed, her fears for him unfounded.

Quarrels seemed so petty and insignificant now, when she considered how deeply she loved him. Of course he had been concerned about her and her obsession with dreams about people who were dead and gone! It was only natural that he should be, and that he would want them to stop, especially if he believed they were making her ill. He loved her, after all, just as he loved their un-born child.

To her surprise, the gate that opened into the priory gardens swung wide before she touched the top rung, shedding rusty flakes as it skimmed silently over the grass.

As she stepped through the narrow opening, into the priory's once hallowed grounds, the thought crossed her mind that one of the gardeners had oiled the groaning hinges. A chill wind and a handful of autumn leaves followed her inside the tangled gardens.

Above her, in the indigo sky, a gibbous moon scudded, high and free. 'Twas a full Halloween moon. A moon for goblins and phantoms. The light it shed rimmed everything with silver. Frost sparkled on blades of coarse grass, forming a crust of rime beneath her bare feet, which were turning blue with cold, she realized. She shivered. What had she been thinking of, to come out here, barefooted? She should have donned shoes and shawl before venturing outside.

By moonlight, the priory's grounds seemed sinister, very different from how they looked by day. Being here at this hour was like stepping back, into the past, she thought with a shudder. She could hear nothing, not the hoot of an owl, nor the yip or snuffle of a fox, a badger, or any other creature. Even the night seemed to be holding its breath, afraid to breathe. Perhaps the Hall *was* waiting for someone, as Justin had once said, in a rare fanciful turn of mind, though for whom it waited she did not know—and would rather not find out.

Caught up in the eerie spell of moonlight and mystery, Madeleine was breathing shallowly as she made her way down the path of worn flagstones. Each step carried her ever closer to the flicker of light she had seen from her casement window. And, God willing, closer to Justin.

Her long hair drifted on the night wind like the curling mist that rose from the ground as she glided over the frosty grass. Her eyes ached, heavy with exhaustion. The dark smudges beneath them were the result of sleepless nights and uneasy dreams, vividly remembered come the morning. Was she really awake now, she wondered, her nightgown billowing behind her like diaphanous fairy wings? Or still asleep, and dreaming . . .

"Come, Madeleine . . . leine!"

The voice calling her name was high, clear and oddly sexless, like the neutral chimes of a glass bell. It scattered her thoughts like beads from a broken rosary.

She halted, violet eyes wide, a metallic taste

on her tongue. Her imagination, she wondered? Or Eydmond's voice, echoing down through the ages, warning her that her life—and with it, her unborn babe's—were in jeopardy, as his had once been?

Impossible, logic insisted.

Yet her heart slammed painfully against her ribs in response. Placing a protective hand on her hard belly, she slowly turned around.

"Who's there?" Her voice cracked as she called out in the frigid hush. "Justin? Is that you? Where are you?"

"you . . . you!"

Laughter raised the fine hairs on Madeleine's neck, one by one.

"Justin? Say something! Is that you?" She ran toward the ruined cloisters, her wrapper floating out behind her.

But although she searched the crumbling nave with its rose-mullioned window, the cloisters, the stone rubble—all that was left of St. Mary's Priory and its church now—she could not find the owner of that bell-like voice.

Because there is no one to find! she scolded herself. *The voice—like the face in the mirror—is only in your mind! If you believe otherwise, you are surely mad! What other explanation is there, unless one believes in . . .*

. . . ghosts?

Perhaps she really was losing her mind? She

must be. Sane women did not hear voices. Sane women did not imagine a baby's cries, or reflections, or anything else.

Was she a victim of some ancient curse, she wondered? Destined—like the lady Lenore all those centuries ago—to become the bride of shadows, just as she ha—

"*Chérie.*"

Her heart leaped with joy in her chest. The child stirred, a flutter of wings in her belly.

"Justin! Oh, thank God!" She whirled about, relieved and concerned at one and the same time as she saw him.

He was leaning against a pile of crumbling stone blocks. The tricorn he wore and the lantern he held aloft cast his features in heavy shadow. The folds of his cape flapped about him in the night wind. *Like ugly dark wings*, she thought with a shudder of foreboding. A bat's leathery wings . . .

"Maddy? What's wrong? What is it?"

She frowned. Justin's voice sounded hoarse and strained. It sounded . . . *wrong*.

She took another uncertain step closer, frowning as she tried to make out his features. "Justin? Is that really you?"

"Of course, *chérie.*"

"Could you . . . could you come a little closer? I need your strong arm to—to lean on. To help me get back to the house.

Go to him, like a lamb to the slaughter, when all her senses screamed at her to run? To run, and not look back?

Never!

Still several feet from him, she turned and tried to bolt. But, like a striking snake, he leaped forward. His arm flashed out. His fingers caught and anchored around her wrist. He squeezed so cruelly she yelped in pain.

"Let go, damn you! You're not Justin!" she hissed, her violet eyes blazing.

"More's the bloody pity," Michael Latimer ground out through clenched jaws. "If I'd had that bastard's advantages, things would have been very different, let me tell you. I would be— whoa, stop that! Don't fight me, my dear! Tsk. Tsk. Not very neighborly of you, is it, Lady de Harcourt? Nor very ladylike."

"I'm not a lady—remember? You said so yourself! So let go of my hand," she demanded. "Release me, and I won't speak a word of this to Justin. It'll be . . . it'll be our little secret," she lied.

"Sorry, Maddy, love. That's not in the cards. I can't risk your getting away from me, you see. Not when I'm so bloody close to bringing that bastard to his knees."

"Justin?" She didn't understand, and Michael's calm, reasonable tone was frightening.

"Who else?" Removing his tricorn, Michael smiled. He cut her a mocking half-bow. In the moonlight, his face was otherworldly, the charming face of a fallen angel. A lock of golden hair flopped boyishly over his brow. His queue was clubbed back in an extravagant black bow, perfectly tied. The bunch of lace at his throat was a dazzling white in the moonlight. He was the very portrait of masculine beauty—yet utterly evil.

"Your desertion will be the perfect *coup de grace* I've been looking for, my dear. The final blow that will destroy my dear old friend Jus's spirit, once and for all. And then, I shall kill him."

"But why? Why are you doing this?" she asked brokenly, her voice hoarse with shock and horror. "What has Justin ever done to hurt you? It makes no sense!"

"Can't you guess why?" he asked bitterly. "Surely it's obvious? It is because he is always the best, Maddy darling. The best at everything, ever since we were children. No matter what we did, no matter what I tried, or how hard I tried, he was always better than I. At mathematics. At Latin. At Greek. At riding. Boxing. Fencing. Womanizing. At breeding horses—*everything!*"

"But . . . Justin doesn't care about things like that. He considers you his friend. Ask him for help, and he will help you, I know he will. It is not in him to abandon his friends or to make others feel small."

"You're right. It isn't. But then, it is easy to be honorable, to be noble, when you're the one on top! *I* cared, though. Oh, yes. I cared very much, Maddy, love. You can't imagine what it was like, caring and still getting nowhere. All those years of being second best. Of watching and hoping that this time, things would be different. That it would be my turn. Years of never being quite good enough. Never first, never Number One, never the winner!

"And as if that wasn't enough, Justin had the perfect family to come home to. Parents who loved him. A father who was proud of him. A mother who believed the sun and moon revolved around her precious son.

"My father loathed me. He squandered away my fortune, drinking and dicing himself to death. He blamed me, you see," he explained bitterly, "because my mother had died bringing me into this world."

"You killed them," she whispered in horror. "Oh dear God! It was you! You killed Justin's mother and father!"

He didn't even bother to deny it. Something flickered in his pale, pitiless eyes—satisfaction? Pride? Pleasure? Whatever it was, his silence was more chilling than any admission of guilt.

He had killed Justin's parents. He had probably shot Justin, too, before she met him that day at his Cousin Charles's residence in Whitchurch. It had been from Michael's shot that he was recuperating. Not a French sniper's. His friend and schoolboy companion was a cold-blooded killer. He would have no qualms about killing Justin's wife, either—especially now that she carried something very precious, very dear to her husband's heart: *his first child.* His son and heir, if Peg Lee's prediction was to be believed.

She had to get away! Had to warn Justin!

"What about Sabina?" she stammered, playing for time. "She's very beautiful, of good pedigree—a proper lady. Not like me, a physician's daughter. I'm sure countless men envy you your beautiful wife and little daughters," she said, hoping to lull him into thinking she was resigned to her fate, and would not try to escape. Effie would be here with Trevor and Digby at any moment. *Oh, hurry, hurry!* she implored silently.

He snorted, sounding amused. "Justin could have had Sabina, and her fortune, too, if he'd wanted her. God knows, she wanted him! It wasn't until much later, after I'd married her for her fortune—and to keep Justin from having her—that I learned she had tricked me. Justin had never cared for her. *Never!* Nor had she ever cared for me. She had been using me, pretending she cared for me in an effort to make Justin jealous. But by then, it was too late for both of us. We were to be married, and the joke was on me, once again. I married a cold bitch who was in love with my best friend, who can't even give me a son!"

Suddenly, Madeleine twisted sideways, hoping the sudden move would catch him unawares and she could wrench herself free. Michael merely tightened his grip on her wrist, twisting her arm up and behind her back.

She let out a choked sob as sickening pain slammed through her. Tears spilled as bone grated against bone. She had succeeded only in angering him.

"Be still, I say," he rasped. "Stop struggling . . ."

"What's going on here?"

Effie's voice. Oh, thank God! Thank God!

"Haven't you done it yet? What on earth are ye waiting for?" Effie demanded querulously. "Sunrise?"

Madeleine's relief turned to shock and a sinking feeling. Michael and Effie. There would be no rescue, not from the maid, nor Trevor or Digby. She was on her own.

"For you, Effie, my pet!" Michael said. "I was waiting for you! Do you have everything?"

"All we talked about—and more." Effie laughed coarsely, a high braying sound, like a donkey. "With this lot missing, along with a carpet bag or two, his lordship will believe his precious wife ran off and left him," she crowed, hefting the bulging bags. "Tut tut. Had words before his lordship went away, didn't you, my lady? A lover's spat that sent you running home to Papa. Pity you never arrived, innit?"

The girl was, Madeleine saw, wearing one of her own gowns—the deep-blue satin gown she had worn for their first dinner party in July. A hooded velvet cloak, also belonging to Madeleine, had been thrown over it.

"And the diamonds?" Michael asked eagerly. "Did you find them? They weren't in the safe in his study, or his armoire."

"What do you think I am? Stupid? Of course I got the bloody diamonds! So. How do I look? Like a hoity-toity lady of the ton?" She drew back the folds of her dark cloak. Her eyes were hard and glittering in the moonlight, like wet stones.

Madeleine saw the strand of fiery ice-chips that encircled her throat. The great sapphire that was the color of Justin's eyes was nestled where her cleavage began. *The de Harcourt diamonds.*

"You look ravishing." Michael grinned wolfishly. "A proper lady! Tut, tut, Maddy, my girl, shame on you! Bad enough you deserted poor old Justin! Did you have to abscond with the family jewels, too?"

"Enough yapping. Let's go, Michael! We're

wasting precious time here," Effie urged. "Do it! Get it over with!"

Maddy felt Michael stiffen.

"Don't tell me what to do, Effie, *love*, or so help me, you'll join her," he threatened through clenched jaws. "Get along, Maddy. Move!

The lantern Latimer carried in his free hand splashed light in crazy arcs around them as he forced Madeleine ahead of him.

They had almost reached the graves of Lenore and William de Harcourt when her captor commanded her to halt, freezing Madeleine in her tracks.

Only inches before her, the ground dropped away, exposing a yawning black hole in the earth. 'Twas like a greedy, bottomless mouth, she thought with a shudder of revulsion. The air that rose from the pit was sour and ancient, rank with the stink of age, mouse and bat droppings.

"What are we doing here?" she demanded. "What is this place? A mine shaft?"

Latimer shook his head, an eerie smile playing about his lips. "An old stone staircase. I discovered it quite by accident, in my misspent youth, buried under heaps of rubble. It was my secret hiding place when Father was after my hide. It leads down to the priory's undercrofts, where the wool was once stored. I've never shown it to anyone before, until now. Not even Justin. Consider yourself honored, Maddy, love."

He laughed. It was an ugly, gloating sound. That and the hard glitter in his eyes terrified her. It was not an effect of the lantern light, she realized with a shudder, but his true character, stripped of its charming patina to expose the ugliness, the evil, beneath the smile. He was not merely a pathetic thief—he was deadly dangerous.

She swallowed. He must have spent hours, months—perhaps even years—down there, planning Justin's ruin, clearing away seven centuries of fallen stone and overgrown vegetation to expose this ancient staircase. But why?

"In case you're wondering, it's your grave, Maddy," he answered her silent question.

His first blow struck her between the shoulder blades and slammed the breath from her in a sickening rush. His second blow pitched her forward.

She flung out her arms to regain her balance. But it was not to be. Not this time.

Lurching and off balance, she toppled head first into the yawning blackness at her feet. A high-pitched scream followed her down. A scream that was her own.

The thought flashed through her mind that she was going to die, and that her poor little baby would never draw breath. She would never see Justin again, to tell him how she loved him, or warn him that Michael intended to kill him.

Cold damp air kissed her cheeks. Pain jolted through her skull. There was a glare of white light, a jarring explosion of pain, then the moon was snuffed out like a penny candle.

Chapter Nineteen

Steyning Forest
The Year of Our Lord, July 1067

Hal stiffened, one hand clamped over the hilt of his dagger, his sharp ears cocked like a hound's for the sound of its quarry.

Since the lady Lenore's sharp admonition some days past to tend to his duties as lookout, Hal Miller had taken his turn as sentry very seriously.

For that reason, he decided to investigate the cause of that sharp snapping sound. Better safe than sorry, aye? It could have been nothing—or it could have been a dry twig snapping under a Norman boot heel. Hal intended to find out which. . . .

Treading softly, he crept between the trees and

bushes, moving as silently as one of the creatures who made the forest their home.

He never saw the man standing between the trees, nor the arm that hooked around his throat from behind. The dagger in his assailant's fist winked silver in the moonlight as he drew it across Hal's throat. It was the last sight he saw in this world.

The sharp blade severed his windpipe, then his spine, and splashed great gouts of warm blood over the shadowed earth.

Like the other two sentinels who had stood their posts across the clearing, Hal died silently, without sounding a cry of alarm to warn his fellows of their enemies' approach.

When the Norman soldiers entered the clearing, on foot with their long swords drawn, Eydmond thought at first it was Hal and the other sentinels. His question died on his lips as he saw the ring of men with pointed helmets, noseguards, and chainmail. They were surrounded on all sides.

"In the name of Giles, lord of Steyning, lay down your weapons and come with us peacefully," ordered the sergeant at arms. "Or else!"

"Or else what, Francois d'Anjou," scoffed Alan, Eydmond's right-hand man, who obviously recognized the Norman and addressed him by name. "Will ye wallop our Saxon arses with your pretty swords, aye?"

"*Non.* I shall skewer you upon them like the Saxon hogs you are," Francois promised softly, wearing a gloating smile. "And then, when you are all dead, I shall use your wives and your daughters as my whores. The meat of the youngest chickens is always the sweetest, *n'est ce pas?* Especially Saxon chicken."

"Why, you bloody bastard! I'll kill you before I ev—!"

"Hold!" barked Eydmond, cutting Alan off. He physically restrained his friend with a hand clamped heavily over his shoulder. "Hear him out. Go on, Francois d'Anjou. State your business with us."

"My lord de Harcourt seeks your arrest, Eydmond of Lewes, by order of William, king of England."

"Does he, indeed? Upon what charge, sergeant?" Eydmond asked calmly.

"The charge is treason. Plotting an insurrection against your government and king."

"But how can that be?" Eydmond asked softly, a faint smile playing about his lips. "When the only king I recognise is Harold Godwinson—and he is dead, may God assoil him. I acknowledge no other man as rightful sovereign of this isle."

"King William, duke of Normandy, was crowned king of England last Christmastide, and well you do know it. You would be well advised to surrender to my lord, de Harcourt, sir. You are, after all, a known rebel leader. Furthermore, my lord bade me tell you that he has taken into his safe-keeping a certain beauteous lady who is, by all accounts, most dear to thee. The lady Lenore's continued . . . good health is in your hands, milord Lewes. Surrender, and she shall go free. Resist, and? . . ." Francios shrugged eloquently. It was his turn to smile now. "Well, I am sure you can imagine. . . . It would not be pleasant for the lovely damosel, *oui*?"

"*Bastard!*" Eydmond ground out, his fists clenched at his sides. His blue eyes blazed with loathing and murderous fury in his ashen face. "Harm a single hair upon her head, and by God, I . . . I'll—!"

"Decide! We do not have all night, my lord Lewes!" Francois barked impatiently. Insolently.

"If I surrender to de Harcourt, will you release my fellows, as well as my betrothed?"

"Do not do this, Eydmond. Normans are without honor. You cannot trust them to keep any promise they make you," Godfrey said in a low voice intended for Eydmond's ears alone. "I would rather take my chances and fight them here, to the death, if need be."

"And I, my friend . . . were it not for Lenore," Eydmond replied with a sigh, his expression bleak, his eyes tortured. "She carries my child, friend Godfrey!" he added in a low murmur.

"Dear God in Heaven!"

"For their sakes, I must do exactly as he asks—and pray."

"We are waiting, milord Lewes," the Norman reminded him. His horse, impatient to be on the move again, tossed its head, so that its bit jingled.

"As am I, Francois. I asked you a question, but I have yet to be given an answer. What is to become of my men, should I surrender?"

"His lordship gave me leave to make you certain promises. If you surrender your sword and accompany me peacefully, your men will be put in chains and marched to London. There, they will be asked to swear fealty to King William. If they swear, they will be freed. Should they refuse to do so, however, they will be imprisoned as outlaws and poachers."

"The lady Lenore will be removed to a distant convent, and cloistered within its confines for the remainder of her days. Resist, and she and your fellows will be killed, to the last man among them."

Eydmond snorted. "Your choice is no choice at all, master d'Anjou."

D'Anjou inclined his head. "I am but following my master's orders, milord."

"As do all dogs," Eydmond agreed with a contemptuous smile. "And those cowards that make war on gentle women."

"Your answer, damn thee!" spat Francois, visibly nettled.

"Very well. But I may speak only for myself. My men have their own minds and will make their own choices. For my part, I will surrender my sword and accompany you peacefully to your lord. What say you, my friends?"

"We shall likewise surrender," Godfrey said softly, after conferring with the other Saxons. He spoke for them all. There was a chance, albeit a poor one, that the Normans would keep their promise. It was their only chance, slim as it was. The clearing was surrounded by well-fed enemy men-at-arms, bristling with weapons, robust with good health—unlike their own ragged, half-starved band of poorly armed rebels. The good Lord knew, they had no hope of escaping with their lives in the event of a pitched battle!

"Are you agreed?" Francois demanded, his eyes narrowed in the firelight.

"We are," Eydmond said.

"Very well. All of you. Throw down your arms!"

The Saxons drew their swords, their daggers—even their wooden staffs—and tossed them into a heap.

"My lord Lewes. Your weapon, if you please," the sergeant urged him.

Tight-lipped, Eydmond shot him a disdainful glare and drew his own sword.

It had been in his family for three generations, a relic of the great viking *jarl*, Sven of Jutland,

Sven Golden Blade, who had been his ancestor. He turned the damascened weapon about and, holding it by the point, passed it to Francois d'Anjou, as was proper for a man of honor, surrendering his weapon to another man of honor. The design of viking longships and sea serpents worked into the polished blade flashed in the moonlight.

D'Anjou took it and carelessly tossed it onto the heap of weapons, adding it to the rest as if it were of little consequence. His actions demonstrated his utter contempt for his prisoner as nothing else could.

"Why, that dog!" Godfrey growled.

"Hold hard. It matters not, friend Godfrey," Eydmond murmured. "Leash your anger, and you may yet escape from this with your life."

"And you, sir."

"Nay, I fear not, my friend," Eydmond said heavily. "Tell my Lenore that I loved her, would you, Godfrey? Tell her that I never stopped loving her. That I'll always love her."

"You shall tell her yourself, my lord Lewes. You shall see," Godfrey insisted, tears in his eyes.

"Go with God, my old friend," Eydmond said, squeezing his shoulder.

"And you," Godfrey murmured as one of the men-at-arms bound his wrists together, and linked him to three other captives with a rope.

"Move out!" came the sergeant's low orders.

305

Four of the Normans urged their horses out of the clearing. The Saxon captives, numbering twenty or so, were linked together by ropes in groups of five. They had little choice but to follow the horses, or be dragged along after the trotting mounts.

"What are your orders concerning the prisoners, sergeant?" asked the second-in-command when they were alone and the clearing was empty, save for the Saxon thane and the rest of the Normans.

"March them along the coast road for an hour or two. When you are quite certain that a high tide will not wash their corpses ashore, kill them all. Throw them into the sea. And Julien?"

"Oui, monsieur?"

"Leave no trace of what you have done. That part of it is of the utmost importance to Lord Giles, you understand? You, Boulanger, and you, Foret, at first light, you and your men are to remove all evidence that these Saxon upstarts ever made their camp here! His lordship wants every trace of their existence removed—right down to the ashes of their fire. Dispose of the sentinels' bodies, too."

"You bastard!" Eydmond exploded. Bringing up his booted foot, he kicked d'Anjou squarely in the groin. The Norman uttered an unearthly shriek and doubled over as a man-at-arms clubbed Eydmond across the temple with the heavy hilt of his sword.

Later, when he came to—how much later, Eydmond did not know—he was huddled on the cold stone floor of a dungeon cell, cold water streaming from his face.

Blood had dried on his temple and his head was throbbing. Beside him was a pair of soft kid boots. Fighting a wave of nausea and pain, he turned his head, inch by inch, and found himself flat on his back, looking up into de Harcourt's face.

"Well, well. So this is the rebel Lord of Lewes!" The Norman gestured to a bucket of foul-smelling night slops. "Douse him again, Henri."

"But . . . but he is awake, my lord."

"I know," de Harcourt said, delicately holding a kerchief to his nose. "Douse him anyway. I want our Saxon friend here to be wide awake when I tell him what plans I have for him, and for the lovely lady Lenore and myself. Did I mention that she has gone on a pilgrimage to Canterbury?"

"Devil take thee, de Harcourt," Eydmond hissed. Despite his wound, his voice vibrated with hatred.

Giles de Harcourt chuckled. "I wager there is a greater chance of the Devil taking *you* today, my lord Lewes, than there is of him taking me. Henri?"

"*Oui, monsieur?*"

"Send a man to the village. Bid him bring one of the laborers here."

"Tonight, my lord?"

"*Oui*. Immediately. There is a gold coin in it for the man, provided he comes to me straightway, and tells no one."

Henri nodded eagerly. He had been sweet on the sister of one of the masons from the village for quite some time now. She was a full-breasted beauty with red hair, who shot a bold smile in his direction whenever they happened to meet.

He dreamed of marrying her some day, although he knew she made her money on her back. He was not one to hold it against her. Born a bastard himself, he knew that life for a woman on her own was not easy—especially a pretty woman like Eartha, who had been ravished by his fellows when they attacked Steyning village last year.

He would rise in her favor, should he be the means that put a gold coin in her brother's purse!

"I know just the fellow, my lord," Henri promised eagerly.

Chapter Twenty

There was dirt in her mouth. She could taste it. It was the dirt of the cellars. The dirt of the undercrofts, where wool and other goods had once been stored by the sisters of the priory's order. There was nothing to fear here, she told herself. It was as Mother Lee had said. She had nothing to fear from those of the spirit world. They—he— had tried to warn, not harm her. No. she had nothing to fear from ghosts. It was the living that had brought her to this pass.

Michael Latimer.

And as for the darkness . . . well, darkness was no more than an utter absence of light, was it not? Of itself, it was nothing to be afraid of. Nothing at all! It was what came forth from the darkness that was so very frightening. . . .

Things . . . creatures . . . those unnamed beings that could not exist in light, much as fishes could not live out of water. Those beings were born to darkness, thrived upon it, and so to darkness they returned.

Ashes to ashes . . .

Dust to dust . . .

Cradle to grave. . . .

She wanted to live, she thought, her lower lip wobbling. And she wanted her baby to live, too. She wanted to see Justin again. She wanted to escape this . . . this cold dark grave to warn him about Michael, before it was too late.

Oh, God, how long had she been down here? Was it already too late? Had Justin come home from France, only to be told that she had left him? Had run off, and taken the de Harcourt diamonds with her? She had to find a way out! She couldn't breathe down here. There wasn't enough air. The walls were closing in. Suffocating her. Darkness pressed close all around her like a . . . a velvet bag. A suffocating velvet bag.

Her thoughts drifted aimlessly, idly, spinning slowly, around and around, as she lay there at the foot of the stairs, like a shattered porcelain doll.

If she gingerly put out her left arm, she could feel the two bottom steps. Hewn from slabs of rough stone, they were solid. Icy. Steep. It was a wonder she had not broken her neck.

If she could crawl up those stairs, perhaps she

could climb out, into the light and air?

She managed to do so, slowly, one excruciating, painful step at a time, hitching herself up the stairs by an arm—her right arm—then dragging herself after it. She could hardly use her left arm at all. She thought her left wrist and possibly her left ankle were broken. They were swollen and stiff and they hurt, oh, lord, how they hurt.

When, at last she reached the top of the staircase, she was sobbing with relief and exhaustion. But her joy—and her hope—were miserably short-lived. Latimer had replaced the slabs of stone and rubble that concealed the stairs. The opening was blocked again, hidden beneath rubble from the ruins. His secret would remain a secret.

There was an enormous lump on her left temple. Her entire head ached. The waves of pain that washed over her left her weak, made her faint and dizzy. How long she had been unconscious, she had no idea. There was no sky to tell her whether it was day or night, or somewhere between the two.

Time stretched. Time shrank, as malleable as clay, as fluid as mercury. How much of it passed, or how little, she could not begin to guess. She woke and slept, woke and slept, feeling sweaty and hot, or shivering with a bone-deep chill by turns. Whether it was hours, minutes or even days between waking and sleeping, she could not have said had her life depended upon it.

Her mind felt as if it was packed with spider webs; a mesh of gossamer-fine, insubstantial threads that did not snare her thoughts, but instead let them float between their sticky filaments to freedom like wisps of smoke. Let them flit away like butterflies. . . .

Again, she slept. And once again, the dreams came.

"Three days, without a trace of her!" Justin exploded. His voice was like the crack of a whip. His fists pounded the desktop. "Damn it, where is she? My wife cannot have simply vanished into thin air, I tell you! She must be *somewhere*—if not at her father's home in Whitchurch, then somewhere else. We shall find her, or I'll know the bloody reason why!"

Trevor Fox nodded. For once, he was not smiling his cocksure grin. On the contrary, his swarthy face was drawn and tired-looking, as if he had not slept in several nights. His master appeared in even worse shape.

"Aye, that we will, sir. That we will. If there's nothing else ye need me for, I'd like to go now, sir. I thought I'd take a couple of the lads and comb the woods again, then go down by the . . . er . . . the weir, sir." He could have kicked himself the moment he said it.

His eyes met Justin's anguished ones. Justin nodded. "Right. Go on, then."

Trevor cleared his throat. "Sir. I . . . er . . . I take full responsibility for her ladyship's disappearance," he said huskily.

"I know you do, Fox." Justin sighed heavily. "But it wasn't your fault. Neither of us expected any trouble during the night."

He had instructed the gamekeeper to keep an eye on his wife when she went out during the day. But Madeleine had proven a difficult woman to keep track of, inclined to making impulsive decisions to take walks and so forth at odd moments. Trevor had done the best he could, short of mounting a twenty-four-hour guard on his mistress and frightening her. At the time, neither of them had thought that was necessary.

"Trouble?" Michael Latimer asked after the gamekeeper left the study. He was sprawled in Justin's wing chair of ox-blood leather, his booted feet propped up on the matching leather-topped desk. "What sort of trouble were you talking about?"

Justin frowned. "Odd things have been happening at the Hall over the past few weeks. Fox thinks a poacher or a tramp has been getting into the house at night, filching my liquor, stealing odds and ends. We're wondering if the petty thefts are connected to Madeleine's disappearance. Perhaps she awoke and surprised him?"

Michael snorted, obviously disgusted. "If Five Gables was missing liquor and so on, the first thing I'd do is have that gamekeeper's cottage searched. I never liked the fellow, myself, not even when we were children."

"You didn't like him because he treated you as an equal. Be honest. You expected him to tug his forelock to you and call you sir. You did then— you do now."

"That has nothing to do with it. There's a . . . a look about him. Oh, I know you think otherwise, Jus, but I doubt he's the innocent you'd like to think he is."

"So you've said before. Michael, what about Five Gables?"

"What about it?"

"Have you had your people search the estate? The storerooms?"

"Um, no. Not really."

"Would you? Just in case?"

"Of course. You're quite right. We should leave no possible stone unturned, however unlikely. I'll get a search underway immediately." He sprang to his feet. "Chin up, Jus. We'll find her. You'll see."

"I hope to God you're right."

"Have you been to London yet? I thought you said Chalmers's wife saw a woman in a blue gown board the mail coach?"

Mistress Chalmers was the wife of Sidney

Chalmers, the innkeeper of the Steyning Arms.

"I said she reported seeing a lady in a hooded velvet cloak board the post coach. There is no guarantee that the woman in question was Madeleine."

"Of course not. But, when was that?"

"Three mornings ago. The woman was on foot, without attendants, and carrying two bulging carpet bags. Madeleine's maid, Tabby Lee, says similar items of clothing and two carpet bags are missing from her mistress's armoire. One of the maids—Effie—is missing, too."

What he did not add was that Tabitha had also insisted, loyally—and quite hotly—that her ladyship had not run home to her papa, regardless of what the circumstances might imply.

"Milady's in trouble, sir. I feel it here," she had told Justin urgently, touching her breast. "We must find her, before it's too late."

He had hidden it well, but Tabby's statement had shaken him—even as it chilled him to the bone.

The girl's uncanny intuition was legendary in the area. Her opinions were not things those who knew her, or of her, took lightly. If Tabby was scared for Madeleine's safety, then he was terrified.

Besides, he had to admit he agreed with the girl. He and Madeleine had parted on loving terms, their quarrel mended, her fears for his safety on her lips, along with her loving good-byes. There was no reason for her to have run off home to her father. Or at least, none that he was aware of.

Nevertheless, after speaking with Mistress Chalmers, he had ridden post haste to Whit-church to inquire after his wife, only to learn from her concerned father, that if his daughter had ever intended to return to Rose Arbor, she'd never arrived.

"We must find her, my boy! I know my daughter. She loved you very dearly and was looking forward to having your child. Her letters were lively, sunny things, full of her life with you. She would never have left you, not of her own free will. I fear there has been some foul play here," he had finished, looking suddenly far older and more stooped than his years.

From Whitchurch, Justin had ridden into the city of London. There, he had managed to locate the coachman who had driven the mail coach down the king's highway to Dover the morning Mistress Chalmers had spotted that well-dressed young woman boarding the coach in the innyard of her establishment.

"Rode with us all the way ter the city she did, sir," the coachman had told him.

"You're sure of that?"

"As I am of my own name, sir."

"I see. And do you halt to water the team at

Whitchurch?" The village was in the Thames Valley and still some distance from the city proper.

"That we do, m'lord. But all me passengers climbed back aboard after that, aye? The young leddy never got down until we reached the Plough and Four, sir—that's a rowdy tavern on the outskirts of the city, much frequented by highwaymen, cutpurses and other ne'er do wells, aye? She were met there, it looked ter me, by a handful of rowdies, lads as well as lassies."

"Met, you say? And did she state her name, at any point, driver?" he had asked.

"Well, I wouldn't like to ha' sworn to it on the Good Book, but . . . I believe they hailed 'er as 'Madeleine.' "

"I know what you're thinking, Jus, but I don't believe it. Not for a minute. And nor should you!" Michael Latimer insisted after Justin had recounted the coachman's story. Latimer tossed back the last of his glass of Canary. "Madeleine, she's a—well, she's an extraordinary woman. What's more, she loved you very dearly. I know she did. She would never have left you, and run off to London. Not in a million years!"

"I agree completely," Justin acknowledged. His emphatic response drew raised brows from his friend. "Besides, there was no reason for her to do so."

"Let's hope not." Michael's tone was doubtful.

"Then again, you know how women are, hmm?"

"Not really." Justin allowed himself a tight-lipped grin. Michael always tried to appear so worldly wise. So all-knowing. "How are they, Latimer?"

"Emotional. Easily slighted. Fickle as the winds that blow." Michael grinned. "One silly little tiff, and they take it to extremes. Turn it into some . . . some enormous quarrel! I . . . er . . . I understand you and Madeleine were on cool terms before you went to France? Is it possible she read more into your quarrel than you did? Took it more seriously?"

Justin considered Michael's question for all of two seconds. The delightful recollection of his and Madeleine's passionate farewell the night of the fire flashed across his memory. "Not a chance," he said with crisp conviction. "By the way, how did you know we had quarreled?"

Michael grinned. "Oh, come on, Justin! It was more than obvious that day at the churchyard! A man can tell when a woman is . . . well, in need of consolation. At least, I can. I mean to say, not that your wife would ever . . . or that I . . . well, you know what I'm trying to say! But . . . perhaps a sympathetic ear? . . . A friendly shoulder to cry on? . . . I am happy to say that Maddy . . . Madeleine . . . was coming to consider me a friend these last few weeks, although our friendship got off to a bad start."

318

"Lucky you," Justin ground out, remembering the way Madeleine's hand had lain in Michael's when he rode up to the churchyard that day.

Fortunately, he trusted his wife, even if he wasn't nearly so sanguine about Latimer. His tone was almost a snarl as he added, "Now, if you'll excuse me, I must resume the search for my wife."

Madeleine was growing steadily weaker with every hour, every day, that passed, yet she continued to explore her dark prison, inch by inch, to the best of her ability, desperately seeking a way out.

Clenching her teeth to control the pain, she edged her way along, using her uninjured arm and leg to propel herself, like a baby who has not yet learned to walk, who creeps along on its side.

Her damaged wrist and ankle were hugely swollen now. The gnawing, throbbing pain of them made her sick to her stomach. She would have given up, if the baby's fluttering movements had not served to rally her flagging spirits and comfort her. As long as she could still feel her baby, she was not alone.

Her determination that her child would live, coupled with her love for Justin, fueled her determination to survive. Somehow, *somehow*, she would get free, she told herself. Then she would warn Justin against the viper he called friend!

At some point during those long, suffocating hours of darkness, she heard faint chirruping sounds, heavily muffled by stone and other debris, as if they were in another room.

The chirps and squeaks grew louder, building to a twittering crescendo of sound.

What on earth were those sounds? *Birds*, she decided. She could think of no other creature that made such sounds. Her heartbeat quickened. There were birds down here, somewhere. She had heard their twittering! And if there were birds, then surely there was a way out, other than the one that was blocked!

Eagerly now, she crawled along, dragging her bad leg after her, her strong arm clawing at the darkness ahead of her, searching, searching blindly for something, anything, to hang onto, some means to haul herself another inch, another foot, another yard.

She was close to the end of her tether, her body exhausted, her emotions at a dangerously low ebb, thirsty, hungry, feverish and hurting, when the twittering sounds abruptly ceased.

"No! Don't stop. Come back, come back!" she muttered, frantically trying to push herself faster toward the source of those sounds. "Please. Oh, please don't leave me. Don't."

It was in that moment that her fingertips brushed a small object, knocking it away. Drawing a deep breath, she reached for it again. But for the second time, she succeeded only in pushing it farther from her. She was now a much greater distance from the ancient staircase than she had ever dared to venture before. At last, her reaching fingers snagged the elusive object.

Fine hairs prickled on the back of her neck. A chill of recognition tingled in her fingertips, shimmied up her arm. She needed neither light nor sight to tell her what she had found.

As her fingers closed around it, she could see it clearly in her mind's eye, exactly as she had seen it in her dreams. The lovely lavender *cabuchon* amethyst; the smooth bumps of the pink freshwater pearls that surrounded it, the slim gold band, bathed in a single ray of sunshine— although now, of course, the bauble was encrusted with the dust of ages, lost in the darkness of the priory's undercrofts. The coarseness of corrosion blurred the edges of the jewels, tarnished the gold.

Giles de Harcourt's ring. The pretty bauble the Norman had given the lady Lenore in the priory gardens as a token of his love. The ring that Lenore, in turn, had given to her betrothed, to fund an uprising against the hated Norman invaders.

Struggling with one hand, Madeleine drew the narrow ribbon drawstring of her nightgown free of its casing. She threaded the ring upon it, before clumsily looping it around her neck, like a talisman on a chain.

Breathing unsteadily, every breath loud and rasping in the stifling darkness of her close confines—feeling a mixture of excitement and terror—she clawed about her in the darkness. Nothing. Inching her way along wormlike, she grasped handfuls of air, or crumbling lumps of ancient mortar, groping around her in a full circle.

Both broken stone blocks and intact bricks revealed the original placement of eleventh-century walls to her touch, although the ground had subsided in some places, over the years, perhaps because of the priory's proximity to the sea. The first few courses of stone blocks remained, to show where the original walls had once been.

Inch by careful, painful inch, terrified that any sudden, too-vigorous movement on her part might bring more stone and rubble crashing down upon her head, she reached farther, wider, brushing aside clinging cobwebs.

Her careful fingertips told the tale her eyes could not make out in the gloom.

Four walls. Four walls that had no door? Yes. Four walls without any opening whatsoever, enclosing a space the size of a small cupboard, just big enough for a man to stand upright. Four suffocating walls. A secret room—or a chamber of death?

"Help me. . . . I can't breathe . . ." she had told Justin that day, the bitter reek of lime and

mortar burning her nostrils. *"I can't breathe!"*

As Eydmond had been unable to breathe, all those centuries ago? Had he tried, in the only way he knew how, to tell her what had befallen him?

Oh, God. *No!*

She was scrabbling now, scrabbling frantically at the fragments of stone and rubble, knowing, deep in her heart, what she would find, if she was right. What she had known, in her heart, she *must* find, from the instant her fingers closed over the ancient ring.

The object was larger than she expected, its surface cold, smooth and rounded beneath her trembling fingertips. She ran her shaking hand down, over the smooth cranium, then around, shuddering as her thumb slipped deep into an empty socket, before moving on, over maxilla and mandible in turn.

As she feared, everything was exactly where she, a physician's daughter, expected it to be. *Familiar territory*. She had spent many long hours in her father's study as a little girl, playing with his anatomical models, learning the Greek and Latin names for the organs and structures they represented,

Even so, it was not until she was certain beyond all shadow of a doubt that she began to tremble violently in reaction. Hot tears trickled, then flooded freely down her cheeks. And, once they had started, she could not staunch the deluge of sobs that wracked her.

For what she was holding was a skull—a human skull. The cranium, maxilla and mandible of Eydmond, thane of Lewes, who had vanished in the Year of Our Lord 1067, never to be seen again.

She had found Eydmond, after he had been missing for seven centuries! He had reached out from the grave to tell her his story. At last, she knew to what cruel fate de Harcourt had condemned his rival for Lenore's heart.

He had walled him up alive!

Chapter Twenty-one

She must have cried herself into an exhausted sleep after finding Eydmond's bones, because she remembered nothing more until she awoke again with a jolt, her heart racing.

She could not have sworn to it—it could have been wishful thinking—but she thought she felt a faint chill breath, a sweet breath, upon her burning cheek.

But those few seconds of fresh air were abruptly—horribly, rudely—replaced by the eye-watering reek of ammonia, wafting in her direction. The foul, caustic smell was so powerful it stole her breath away, made her gag—yet perversely, she had never been as glad to smell such a noxious odor in her life.

Coughing, eyes watering, she turned her head aside. She hoped to get a small respite from the burning odor that flayed her nostrils and throat, and left her eyes tearing—yet knew, if she was ever to escape her cellar prison, she had to press forward. She had to move *toward* that loathsome odor, not away from it. Through that way, beyond it, lay the possibility of escape.

Justin was relying on her, after all. Hadn't he said she brought the light and laughter back into his life after his parents were killed? Hadn't they planned to turn Steyning Hall into a happy place, for the two of them and for their children? She owed it to Justin to do everything in her power to survive, to save herself and their baby. No matter how difficult it was, she must never give up. Never! As long as she drew breath, she would grit her teeth and keep trying.

The ammonia odor was urine, she was almost certain. *Bird urine.* And if so many birds made their roost in this tunnel, it was possible she could get out the same way they did. There had to be an opening of some kind.

There was.

When next she opened her eyes, she could see it. Several feet above her, an irregular wedge of gray daylight had appeared in the pitch darkness. She blinked back stinging tears. Outside her prison, the world was awakening, she realized. It was the beginning of yet another precious, glorious day. Fresh tears clogged her throat. Rage, grief, disappointment, despair overwhelmed her by turns.

The opening was about twenty inches long and six inches wide—too narrow for her to squirm through. Too narrow, she would have thought, for most birds. Was it owls that roosted here, in this cavelike tunnel, in almost complete darkness, she wondered, forcing herself to consider the question, but not really caring about the answer. Not now. Not anymore. Not when all those hours of clawing and crawling and hitching herself along, despite the gnawing pain, the cold, had ended in this: a stinking hole in the ground that was too small to offer any hope of escape.

"Help!" she cried weakly, her voice hoarse from fever and lack of fluid. "Down here! *Help!*"

She called until she had no voice left to call with. It was then, when the sky framed by the opening had grown lighter, was flushed pink and lemon with the dawn, that Madeleine discovered the true source of the ammonia-smell—and with it, the identity of her fellow cave dwellers.

They returned from the night's hunt with the first light of dawn, pouring in through the opening in a seemingly endless tide, twittering, twittering, chirruping in their tiny voices. There they hung, above her, suspended upside down, their leathery wings folded, their demon faces hideous miniature gargoyles, until the dark cloak of night settled across the world once again.

They were, she saw with a shudder of horror, as thousand upon thousand of them flapped, squeaking, to their cave roosts, not birds at all, but . . . *bats*.

"Here, 'Pie! T'me, girl," Trevor called, alerted by his small collie's erratic behavior. The little black and white beast had, in his opinion, more common sense than most humans. He preferred her company to that of people. Today, she kept wandering off, rooting around after rabbits and rats like a terrier that must have its muzzle and nose down every hole and burrow; more like a terrier than a collie.

Trevor whistled her up, noting that Magpie turned her head and stared at him long and hard, but for once, made no move to obey his command to come. Rather, the dog's bright eyes met his, sending some silent, urgent message that Trevor would be damned if he understood, for all that he knew animals better than most gamekeepers. The dog whined and seemed agitated. What had it heard, that its master had not, he wondered, cocking his head to listen? Nothing that he could hear.

"Here, 'Pie!" he tried again. "Come on, girl." He and the dog had been out all night, wandering familiar haunts, keeping a weather eye out for the missing lady of Steyning, rather than any poachers.

He had run into Five Gables' head groom, headed home from the Steyning Arms, while he was out and about last night. He had discovered from talking with the man that Michael Latimer had given no instructions for his servants to search the estate for their neighbor's wife.

Why not? he had wondered. Was it possible Latimer had launched no search because he knew such an effort would be a waste of both time and manpower? If that were true, he either had to know where Lady Madeleine really was—or not give a damn about her being found! Either way, Lord Justin needed to know about it. He intended to tell him, the moment he reached the Hall.

The obedient collie took two or three more steps then dropped low to the ground and crawled toward him on her belly, as if reluctant to obey his order. Her tail wagged vigorously as he turned and started striding back toward her.

Had the dog been hurt, somehow? Did that explain her odd behavior? Or . . . was she sick? She was no longer a young dog, after all. They had been together for some time—ever since he'd abandoned the sea-faring life to take over his father's job, keeping Lord Justin's estates free of poachers. The possibility of losing a loyal companion like Pie saddened him.

He frowned. Speaking of 'Pie, where was she? She had been crouched on all fours, only a few feet from him, when she'd suddenly vanished!

He reached the low mound where she had been only moments before. There was no sign of her. Where the devil had she disappeared to?

There were a few pieces of stone, a short length of wall, left from the ruins of Steyning Keep, or perhaps the priory, scattered about between the tall grasses, and some purple and yellow flowering weeds—and there, between them, was a narrow dark opening. It was hardly more than a slit, like a wound in the ground.

"'Pie, ye bloody fool! Come on out of there!" he called, bending low to the opening. The odor of bats that filled his nostrils was overpowering and made his eyes water.

It was the only bloody place the dog could have gone, though. He shook his head. Large rabbit holes or abandoned burrows like this one were favorites with badgers. Their powerful claws could easily kill a small dog like Pie, tear her to ribbons.

"Here, girl!" he called sternly. "'Pie! Come out here, I say!"

But although he waited for some time, 'Pie did not reappear. Bloody dog had probably gotten herself stuck in the burrow, he decided. He would need a spade to dig her out. He went through the rusted gate, into the spice gardens. The gardeners' toolshed was closer than his own cottage.

He looked up at the sky, rubbing cold hands together as he went. It looked like another crisp cold November day—the fifth day since Lady Madeleine had disappeared.

His lordship insisted he would not give up the search for her until she was found, alive and well—or he had some tangible proof that she was dead, and so beyond help—and who could blame him? He loved her. Any fool could see that. He'd do the same, were it his Tabitha they were hunting for. But Trevor knew Justin was beginning to fear the worst. They all were. The only person who did not secretly believe her ladyship was already dead was Tabby, God bless her.

"Don't ye give up on her, Trev," she urged, "even if everyone else does. She's alive, and she's trying to hang on until ye find her, I know she is! I feel it here, in my heart. Tell his lordship the same. We owe it to her t'keep looking."

St. Mary's Priory
The Cellars, 1067

The priest was terrified. His hands shook as he draped the stole about his shoulders and opened his missal to begin the prayers for Extreme Unction, the Last Rites of the Holy Roman Catholic Church that would send the soul of Eydmond of Lewes to Heaven.

"Bless me, Father, for I have sinned," murmured the Saxon lord. He stood with his back pressed to the wall, his fair head bowed, his manacled wrists clasped in prayer. Despite his ragged mantle, he had a king-like dignity, a serenity granted few men soon to die.

"I beg thee, forgive my part in this, my son."

"I do, in truth, Father Clarence," Eydmond murmured softly. "Take heart, I pray thee, for I am not afraid to die. Though I have lived no saintly life, I trust that my Lord will not deal harshly with His obedient servant. Nor do I hold you in any way to blame for my murder, Rufus," he added for the benefit of the mason, who knelt at his feet.

"Thank ye, milord," the red-haired mason mumured. Tears streamed down his cheeks, unchecked. Had he known what duty he was to perform for the Norman lord's blasted gold piece, he would have run when the homely man-at-arms, Henri, came to his cottage and bade him accompany him to the keep. Devil take the wretched coin! He would rather be poor and alive, than rich but dead. Better he had fled into the forest—become an outlaw—than be a party to this . . . this murder!

As it was, he found himself in an impossible position: damned if he did Lord Giles's bidding, and damned if he didn't.

Dread lay like a cold weight in his belly, for unless he missed his mark, secrecy was all in this dark deed. That being so, why would the Norman let any who witnessed it live?

Why, indeed!

In truth, he was already dead. Nor would his widow, his fatherless children, his sister and mother ever know what truly befell him. The Norman would see to that.

"Make haste, priest!" Giles said thickly, sipping red wine from a jeweled goblet. Fleshy lips glistened in the torchlight, as if it were blood, not wine, he sipped. "Anoint him and have done! You men of God, you are all slower than little snails. And you, mason! What the Devil are you gaping at? Keep working, damn ye!"

As the priest anointed Eydmond's brow with holy oil, Rufus squatted down. He hastily troweled a clump of mortar onto the first course of bricks. After smoothing it out, he placed a second row of bricks upon the first. After spreading them with mortar, he tapped them firmly in place, then trimmed the extra mortar neatly to fit. Brick by brick, trowel by trowel, Eydmond of Lewes disappeared, entombed alive within the walls of the priory's cellars.

Giles bent his dark head to rasp in Henri's ear, "When you leave here, take the mason to the weir and kill him."

"Please, *monsieur, non!*" Henri whispered. "Do not ask this of me, I beg you!" His face was whiter than a shroud. "Rufus is a good man! A fine father and husband!"

"What he is, you fool, is a *witness!* Do as I command. And Henri?"

"Sir?"

"You will make it look like an accident, yes?"

"Oui, monsieur," Henri said in a voice so faint, it was more like a hopeless sigh. *Mon dieu,* where would it end, he wondered? How many more innocent men must die to keep de Harcourt's terrible secret? And what would prevent the Norman from ordering Henri's own murder, once he had silenced the mason?

Nothing. Nothing at all.

Henri decided he would follow his lord's final command, then flee Steyning, never to return. He would change his name, start a new life somewhere else—if he could live with himself after this.

Unlike Giles de Harcourt, Henri was a man of conscience. His lordship might have his victims blessed, their tombs consecrated, before he murdered them, to keep their ghosts from coming back to haunt him. But for Henri, what he had seen and done this night would remain with him forever. . . .

Madeleine awoke to feel 'Pie's warm wet tongue licking her face. Weakly she managed to stick her hand through the little animal's collar and hang on.

Scalding tears spilled down her cheeks. The salt stung as it washed the countless small abrasions and scratches on her face. She couldn't bear to let the little dog go! She desperately needed contact with this small, warm living creature from the world above—the world denied her. She feared for her sanity if she let 'Pie go. She needed to hold on to her, just for a little while, just until she had found the courage buried deep within her to go on a little longer.

Afraid she would fall asleep and that 'Pie would abandon her, she drew the ribbon on which hung Eydmond's ring from about her own neck, and managed to fasten it securely to 'Pie's collar. She would have liked to add her own wedding ring to it, so that Trevor Fox would know it came from her, but her finger was too swollen. Try as she might, she could not get it off.

For the collie's part, 'Pie seemed in no hurry to abandon her. She licked Madeleine's face, her swollen ankle, her hurt wrist, as if somehow, she knew that they were injured. Afterwards, she curled up as close to Madeleine as she could get, her little white chin resting on Madeleine's arm, her bright eyes watching her protectively, sharing the softness, comfort and warmth of her body with the injured woman.

Her arms wrapped around the dog, Madeleine fell deeply asleep.

When she woke again, it was to the harsh glare of wintry light and to the pale gray skies of a November afternoon. The light was so bright, after days of darkness, it hurt her eyes. Was she dreaming again? How odd! In this dream, instead of grinning, as he usually did, Trevor was weeping unashamedly. He and several other men were standing around her in a circle, all of them leaning on their spades while they looked down at her as if unable to believe their eyes.

'Pie was barking and dancing about, pink tongue lolling, her black-feathered tail whisking madly to and fro. Tabby was kneeling beside her head, her apron covered in streaks of dirt, beside Mrs. Fox. The housekeeper was holding a stack of woolen blankets.

"Ye did it, mum. You're safe now, you are, God bless ye!" Tabby exclaimed. Her gray eyes sparkled. "Oh, mum, I'm right glad to see you again!"

"We all are, my lady. We've been so worried about ye, aye, Trevor?" Mrs. Fox murmured, tucking thick warm blankets over her.

"Aye. Thank the good Lord," her son managed through his tears. "All together now, lads. Up, up—and easy as you go, mind!"

They lifted her onto a door. She was blue with cold, battered and bruised, covered in dirt and blood, her ankle and wrist still painful, but she had survived, thank God. Both she and her baby would live! She closed her eyes and let tears of gratitude to God, to Pie, to Trevor—to all of them—trickle down her cheeks.

"Latimer. Justin. Must . . . be . . . careful," she croaked. "He's . . . next."

Trevor met Tabby's eyes. Neither of them wanted to be the one to tell her ladyship that her warning had come just a few hours too late.

Justin had left for the Tudor farmhouse soon after luncheon, to see if his wife could possibly have gone back to the scene of their honeymoon. Michael had offered to go with him. And, although the place was little more than an hour's ride away, his lordship had not yet returned.

Chapter Twenty-two

"Where will you look for your lady now?" Michael Latimer asked casually, his expression concerned as he stacked logs on the hearth. Taking the tinderbox down from the fieldstone mantle, he lit the fire, coaxing the tiny flame to catch the dried woodshavings.

A fire would be welcome. It was a cold, damp evening. This close to the shore, the wind that blew off the Channel cut deep into a man's lungs, like a clammy blade.

"Nowhere," Justin said simply. "You see, I've had enough of this wild-goose chase. I thought I'd let you tell me where she is."

A crackling silence followed in the wake of his words.

"Me?" Michael echoed shakily, his tone incredulous. "You think I did something to Madeleine? That I know her whereabouts?"

He looked taken aback, the consummate actor. Those who trod the boards of Drury Lane would have envied his performance.

"Don't be ridiculous, man! Why would I hurt your wife? What had I to gain from it? And what on earth would make you think me capable of such a . . . a terrible thing, after the friendship we've shared? After the friendship that good lady and myself had but recently embarked upon? Clearly, grief has addled your wits, sir!"

Michael Latimer's back was to Justin. He had grown very still now, Justin saw.

In that moment's stillness, Justin could hear the restless booming of the breakers against the rocks across the king's highway, only a little louder than the beating of his heart. *His shattered, empty heart, if there was to be no Madeleine to mend it, no Madeleine to fill it.*

"It was the blue gown," he said heavily. "I could not think what it was about our conversation that disturbed me. It nagged at me for the remainder of yesterday, like a pup worrying a bone. And then this morning, it came to me. You mentioned that the young woman who boarded the mail coach was wearing a blue gown. But how could you possibly have known that, unless you had seen her? Or knew that someone wearing a blue gown had boarded the coach, pretending to be my wife? Mistress Chalmers never said so, nor did anyone else, to my knowledge."

"That's preposterous!" Michael sputtered, still with his back to Justin, as if he was preoccupied with the fire he had built and lit. "You told me yourself that the innkeeper's wife described her!"

"I beg to disagree. I said Mistress Chalmers described a woman in a hooded velvet cloak. She said nothing about any gown, blue or otherwise. That was your own addition. So. Why don't you tell me the truth, Michael? It was you, wasn't it? You and our serving girl, Effie. You used her to help you steal the de Harcourt diamonds. Madeleine surprised you. She tried to keep you from taking them. Is that how it went?"

"Diamonds?" Michael spun about to face Justin. He was holding a pistol, leveled at Justin's gut. "*Do you really* think that's what this was all about? A fortune in bloody diamonds? No, Jus. It was about much more than that. The diamonds are a delightful . . . windfall, shall we say? 'Twas all about you and me—and about a lifetime of being second-best."

"I don't give a tinker's damn about your reasons why," Justin ground out through a jaw like iron. "Where is she, Latimer? Tell me what you did to her. Where I can find her. Tell me, or so help me, I'll tear you apart, limb by limb."

"Finding her won't do you any good. She's dead by now. Poor, frightened little Maddy. All alone in the dark of the priory's cellars. She hated t'be shut up in the dark—did you know that, Jus? I locked her down in St. Nicholas's vaults once—and she thanked me for letting her out!" He laughed, pleased with himself. "Thanked me, after I locked her in!"

"You bastard!" Justin's sapphire eyes blazed. His complexion was dark with fury. "You cowardly, dirty, murdering scoundrel! And you call yourself a man?"

"Go to Hell, de Harcourt!" Swinging around, Latimer raised his arm, leveling the muzzle of the pistol directly at Justin's heart. There was a loud "click" as he squeezed back on the flintlock's trigger, but no answering report.

In that same moment, Justin went for Latimer's throat.

The pistol skittered across the farmhouse floor, knocked out of Michael's hands as Justin slammed him backwards to the flagstones. His fingers clamped around Michael's throat and squeezed.

"It wasn't loaded, you son of a bitch!" Justin seethed, his face thrust full into Michael's as he shook him, like a mastiff shaking a rabbit in its jaws. "What did you take me for? A fool, like you? I took the liberty of removing the ball hours ago. You should have made sure it was loaded before you aimed it at me, Latimer. But then, you were never any good at following through, were you? Not even when it came to murder."

"No? I fancy I did well enough with your mother and father, don't y—aagh!"

He cried out as Justin grasped a handful of his hair and bashed his head against the stone floor.

"That's for my mother. And this one's for my father," he added as Latimer's teeth snapped together, slicing his tongue. Bright blood spurted from the corner of his mouth.

"Aren't you . . . aren't going to summon the authorities?" Michael managed to gurgle.

"The authorities be damned!" Justin rasped, his chest heaving. "That's only a taste of what I've got in store for you, my old friend. I'm going to tear you apart with my bare hands—and I'm going to enjoy every bloody minute of it!"

There was apprehension—fear—in Latimer's eyes now. Justin could smell it on him, like rank perfume.

"Do it! Kill me—and you will never find your precious wife," Michael choked out. Blood and pink spittle ran down his chin as he managed a strangled laugh. "You always had the Devil's own luck—until now. I do believe your good fortune has played out, Jus, my friend."

Justin gave a thin disparaging smile as he dragged Michael upright by his collar. He held him there, against the whitewashed brick, dangling by the throat. "And as I told you before, you son of a bitch, it's not luck," he rasped.

"Now, talk, you bastard. Tell me where she is, while I'm still in a generous mood."

"Feel free t'take your time and enjoy yourself, just for the fun of it, milord," drawled a voice behind him. "There's no need t'hurry, aye? Ye see, your lady's been found. She's safe and well, in her own bed at the Hall. No thanks to him!" Trevor's height and size filled the doorway. "That bastard threw her into a cold dirty hole in the ground, then he left her there to die, poor little lady. You don't need him anymore, sir. Finish the bastard off. Or better yet, let me do it for ye. Learned some special tricks in the Orient, I did. He killed His Lordship and Lady Emilie. He almost killed our new Lady Harcourt. He was going to kill you." Trevor shook his head. "It could take him days t'die. A week, if I'm extra careful. . . ."

They both heard it as Latimer's courage gave out.

"Well, I'll be! Pissed yourself have ye, Sir Michael?" Trevor asked. "Here, milord. Let me have 'im."

With a desperate scream, Latimer wrenched himself free of Justin's grip. With a great leap, he ran and hurled himself through the narrow window across the farmhouse's great room, shattering glass and lead mullions as he did so.

Outside, he crawled to his feet and sprang astride Trevor's waiting horse before they could get out of the farmhouse. Slashing the reins across its poor head, he galloped away.

Both Justin and Trevor ran outside, pistols raised and leveled at his back. They took aim and fired in almost the same instant, both muzzles spurting tongues of yellow flame and wisps of thick smoke. Latimer seemed to twist momentarily in the saddle, but recovered and rode furiously on.

"Damn him!" When the two men reached the spot where he had faltered, they saw blood, glistening in the pale moonlight as it dripped off a hedgerow. The drops were still warm as Trevor rubbed the moisture between his fingers.

"He's hit, sir. But not badly enough, I'm thinking."

"I agree. Some sawbones will patch him up, for a price. The bastard got away, damn him!" He was furious.

"Do we go after him, sir?" Trevor asked hopefully.

"No," Justin decided reluctantly, shaking his head. "One of us winged him. That's good enough to slow him down. This is the beginning of the end for him, Fox—and he knows it."

"How so, sir?" Trevor looked disappointed and decidedly sulky. He wanted to ride Latimer into the ground and finish him off.

In that moment, Justin wanted nothing so badly as he wanted to go home to Madeleine.

Once he had seen for himself that she was safe at home, and would recover fully from her injuries with no harm done to their child, he would go after Latimer. For the time being, his need to avenge his parents' deaths had been satisfied by anchoring his hands about the man's throat and bashing his head on the stone floor.

"I'll notify the authorities. He'll never be able to return to Five Gables, or his family. Nor can he go about in public, without fear of being placed under arrest. His only hope now is to escape to the Continent, or perhaps the Americas, and start over there, alone and penniless. Unless I'm way off the mark, he's bound for London, even as we speak. He'll want to find Effie and try to get back the diamonds. I seriously doubt he'll give me or my family much thought, from here on."

Trevor snorted as they strode back to the farmhouse side by side. "If ye ask me, that's still more than he deserves. To get away with his life, I mean."

"I agree," Justin said with feeling. "And no one would like to see him dance at the end of a noose more than I would. But I've see enough killing to last me a lifetime in the past two years. Enough, Trevor. 'Tis enough. You have your Tabitha, and I, my Madeleine. Two likely lassies, aye? I suggest we throw ourselves wholeheartedly into the business of life, instead."

Leading the way inside, he splashed a healthy measure of brandy from the decanter he kept on the fieldstone mantle into a snifter for Fox, then poured another for himself. "Drink it down, man. It'll warm you. Your very good health, sir—and my thanks."

"Thank you, milord. And yours. To our ladies!" Trevor took a generous swig.

"Our ladies. Now. When you're finished guzzling my brandy, let's go home. I am most anxious to see my wife."

Trevor grabbed the decanter and tucked it snugly under his arm as if he was carrying a chicken. He winked at his master. "We'll take this along for the road, sir, by way of celebration. I'm ready when you are, sir."

"Lead on, Fox. Lead on! By the way, did I mention that I've been looking for a good man to replace my steward? The position comes with a cottage and seven guineas a year. Interested?"

"I might be—if it were eight guineas, and a horse. A man about to be married has to think ahead, aye, sir?"

"He does, indeed. All right. Eight it is."

"You're a good man, sir.

"Dammit, man, don't push your luck!" Justin retorted with a grin.

Smythe was just leaving when Justin met him on the stairs, which he was climbing two at a time.

"How is she? How is the baby?"

"Both mother and child appear to be doing remarkably well, all things considered. What they both need now is rest and good food, in loving and familiar surroundings."

"And her emotional state?"

"Much calmer than the last time I saw her. She seems to believe that someone named Eydmond has been found. Does the name mean anything to you? Apparently, some bones were uncovered—and a ring of some antiquity. Your wife seems to think someone was walled up alive in the priory cellars, centuries ago. Odd, the fantasies that women in a delicate condition come up with, don't you think?"

"Amazing," Justin agreed. "Thank you, doctor."

She was asleep when he went in. The room was cozy and warm, with no trace of the cold spots he'd noticed before.

Frowning, he went across to the tester and stood, looking down at her.

Tears burned behind his eyes. Even in the chamber's half-light, he could see the bruises and scrapes that blotched her complexion, and the lumpy shape of the bandages in which her left hand was swathed. Yet she had never been more precious to him, nor looked more beautiful, than she did in that moment.

He should have listened to what she was telling him. He should never have dismissed her dreams as idle fantasies, caused by her pregnancy. Thank God she was all right. He had come so very close to losing her. . . .

Her eyelids fluttered. She smiled sleepily as she woke up, to see him standing there.

"We had planned a rendezvous, had we not, *chérie?*" he murmured, pretending to be stern. "I was here, as promised, but where were you?"

"I regret I was unavoidably detained, *monsieur,*" she apologized. "You won't tell my husband?"

He grinned. "Never."

"Good. Then give me your hand. Quickly."

"Would you like my heart with it?"

"I already have your heart, thank you. It is here, beating inside me. Do you feel it?"

She placed his hand over her belly, which was harder, rounder than he remembered. At first, there was stillness, and then, he felt wonder fill him. There was a distinct flutter beneath his hand as his child moved inside its mother's body. To feel that life, small but tenacious, filled him with enormous joy.

"Soon," Madeleine whispered. "Come spring we three will all be together."

"Yes," he whispered. He was so moved, the words stuck in his throat. "I love you, Madeleine."

"And I love you. You and the baby are all that

349

kept me going down there. You . . . and . . . and Eydmond."

"Ah. Eydmond. Should I be jealous?"

"Yes. Very," she teased. "Look at this. 'Tis a gift he gave me. I wanted to show you."

She opened her hand, and in the lamplight he saw a ring. It appeared very old, indeed. The band was of plaited gold; its center a lavender *cabuchon* amethyst surrounded by freshwater pearls. Mr. Digby had cleaned and polished it for her, she explained, so that it shone like the finest de Harcourt silverware.

"It's beautiful. Where did it come from?"

"Lie down with me, and I'll tell you. . . ."

Chapter Twenty-three

Justin and Madeleine's first child was, as Peg Lee had teasingly hinted to Madeleine several months earlier, a lusty boy. He was born in the wee hours of March 15, after one of the worst winters in local memory, following a surprisingly short and uncomplicated labor.

Justin remarked that if all his brood mares dropped their foals as easily as Madeleine had presented him with his first child—and heir—Steyning Thoroughbred Stables would do splendidly.

At the time, Madeleine had not been amused.

"Here you go. You first grandson, sir!" Justin said proudly, lifting the baby from the rocking cradle they had brought down from the attic. He placed his newborn son in his grandfather's arms for the very first time.

The physician had driven down from Whitchurch, hoping to be there for the birth, but arrived just a few hours too late to deliver his grandchild, who had been born in the early hours of the morning.

"So he is," William Lewis murmured, his expression delighted and rapt as he looked down at the infant. "So he is! Has my boy a name yet?"

"He has." Justin exchanged a quick glance with Madeleine, who gave a slight nod. "We thought we'd call him Jonathan Edmond, after my father and . . . an earlier ancestor."

Madeleine smiled drowsily and mouthed, "Thank you."

"Splendid names, both of them, aren't they, little Jonno?" William murmured to his grandson, kissing the sleeping baby on the brow.

In that moment, the thirteenth earl of Steyning received the nickname he would carry all his life. *Jonno.* He was barely twelve hours old.

Jonno's tiny face puckered in protest at his grandfather's kiss. His entire head turned bright red beneath soft wisps of gold hair that lay close to his scalp, like a cap of feathers. His miniature fists, the tiny pink thumbs tucked in, flailed as he stirred. Sturdy little legs kicked vigorously within the folds of lace and swaddling. After hiccuping and whimpering for a few moments, perhaps to see if anyone would come to rescue him, he began bawling in earnest, turning beet-red.

"Tsk. What have those horrid men done to my poor little son?" Madeleine teased. Her breasts had immediately engorged at the sound of his cry. Milk leaked from her nipples. It dampened the clean linen cloths with which she had covered her breasts to protect her nightgown. "Come. Give him back to his mama, immediately!"

"Here you go." William Lewis bent to kiss his daughter. "Congratulations, my darling girl. You've given us both a handsome boy, hasn't she, Justin?"

"Indeed she has, sir," Justin seconded, bending down to kiss his wife again. "And she's a wonderful mother. Thank you, *chérie*."

"Thank you," she murmured, love in her eyes as she looked up at him. "And how is little Elizabeth?" she asked her father. Her sister Felicity's daughter was already nine months old and, according to Felicity's letters, showed every evidence of trying to toddle about.

"My darling little Lizzie—Busy Lizzie, I call her—is blooming, like her namesake! I call her Busy Lizzie because she is never content simply to dandle upon her grandfather's knees, but must forever be moving about and getting into everything. She reminds me of your mother in more than her name, Madeleine. Always busy, always doing something. I believe your Jonno's temperament will be quite different—more like his mama's."

"Or perhaps like a little suckling piglet's rooting about!" Madeleine said ruefully, gritting her teeth as the baby nursed with lip-smacking gusto. Her breasts were not yet hardened to her little son's surprisingly powerful lips, gums and jaws. When the baby nursed on her still-tender breasts, it was a little like being eaten alive.

Jonathan chose that moment to surface for air by turning his head slightly. He looked blissfully drunk! A dribble of milk leaked from the corner of his mouth and ran down his chubby little cheek, before he greedily latched back on to her nipple.

"I cannot believe he has no teeth!" she added, gritting her own.

"My son, the cannibal," Justin murmured, dark blue eyes twinkling.

Madeleine smiled fondly. The dear man! He had spent the night awake, waiting for her to deliver their child, worrying, wondering, pacing and praying for a safe outcome for both her and their baby. Yet to look at him, he appeared not only wide awake, but well-rested and happy, she decided. *Very happy*. Her husband's smiles were no longer a rarity, but blessedly commonplace.

"*Chérie*, I'm going to take your father downstairs for a drink to wet the baby's head."

"Good idea. Go ahead. You should show him the horses, too."

"Will you be all right? Shall I send someone to sit with you?"

"There's no need for that. I'll ring if I need something. I think I'll go back to sleep when this little glutton is full." She leaned down and kissed her tiny son's flushed cheek. "Hmm, you smell so sweet, Jonno. Mama loves you so much, you darling boy. Oh, yes, she does. . . ."

"I'll look in on you two later."

She smiled. "Don't worry. We'll be here."

"Any word on that Latimer fellow?" William Lewis asked in Justin's study, after they'd toasted the health of the new arrival.

"Yes, there is. According to my contact in London, he's dead and buried, thank God. He died of blood-poisoning in some wretched flea-bitten lodging a week or two after his escape from us. We thought we'd missed him, but my pistol—or my gamekeeper's—must have found its mark, after all. He should have found somebody to remove that ball, before the wound festered."

"And you had no idea he hated you all those years?"

"Not really, no. I knew he'd always been jealous of me—he always claimed I had 'luck,' whereas he didn't. I knew he must resent me, at times, when his fortunes took a downward turn. But I certainly never dreamed he hated me enough to kill my wife and child—or my parents. Or, for that matter, me!"

"Dreadful business, that. You have my deepest sympathies, Justin. I hope that goes without saying."

"It does, indeed. Thank you, sir.

"And what of the diamonds Latimer stole to recoup his fortunes?"

"Good news! They have recently been returned to us, sir. The maid who helped Latimer was apprehended in London, trying to sell the set to a crooked jeweler. She claimed she was a lady who had come down in the world and was selling her jewelry to live.

"That rogue of a jeweler would have taken the necklaces and the bracelet apart and sold both sapphire and diamonds separately. Fortunately for us, he didn't have time. One of his apprentices turned him in to the authorities and claimed the reward I offered. I have no doubt that within the year, Latimer's accomplice will find herself aboard a transport ship, bound for Botany Bay along with other convicts."

"I'll drink to that!" William declared. He told his son-in-law, "Another, if you will, my boy."

"My pleasure, sir." Justin poured.

"I'm called 'William' by my friends, my boy. Please, call me, William."

"There you go, William. When you've finished your drink, would you care to see the horses?

"We have a total of six Thoroughbred mares here, all descended from the three great founding stallions. Their names are Moondancer, Queen Luna, Salome, Zerdali, Barrakah and Crescent Moon. Also, three stud stallions from different Thoroughbred lines. Satan, Saracen and Scirocco. Once Nowles, my head groom, feels the mares are in top condition, we're going to . . ."

Madeleine lay with her small son nestled in the crook of her arm, still exhausted from his birth, but filled with the glowing warmth and contentment that comes following any great accomplishment.

Jonathan's birth had begun with a nagging backache the afternoon previous which she had at first blamed on overdoing things that day.

From the moment she awoke, she had been restless and itching to be up and about, and doing things. She had shooed Mrs. Beaton from the kitchen, insisting on baking the day's bread herself, kneading and pounding the dough just as she had often done at Rose Arbor.

From bread baking, she had moved on to sewing, putting the finishing touches to the little gowns and blankets she had sewn in readiness for the baby's arrival. She added those to the layette of exquisite items, daintily embroidered, hemmed, crocheted or knitted by her sister, Felicity, Mrs. Fox, Tabby, Mother Lee or Althea

Cargill. After that, she had polished all the brass and silver candlesticks.

Exasperated by her mistress's energetic antics, Mrs. Fox had urged Tabby to accompany Madeleine on a short but brisk walk.

"Mark my words, that baby will be here before tomorrow night, else I'm a Dutchman!" she overheard the housekeeper tell the cook. "A brisk walk will help it along."

Madeleine and Tabby had donned cloaks, hoods and boots and gone tramping out into the windy March weather.

The gray skies had streamers of cloud that sailors called "mares tails." Yet tiny points of green leaf here and there showed where spring crocuses and snowdrops waited to put forth their shoots, provided a late frost did not nip them in the bud.

Without any definite destination in mind, they had walked as far as the weir, with Tabby excitedly confiding as they went that she and Trevor had set a date, and were to be married at Christmas. Mr. Digby had gallantly offered to give the bride away, in her father's place.

They had come back to the house by way of the graves. There were three of the low mounds now, rather than two. The third bore an effigy in stone, exactly like the others, except that it was newly hewn stone, and unweathered, lacking the mosses and lichens of the original two.

Below the effigy, in a casket of stone, were buried the remains of Eydmond, thane of Lewes, properly blessed and reconsecrated. His spirit would, God willing, be at peace, now that he was with his "lady fayre" for all eternity.

The inscription Madeleine had asked the stone mason to etch at the foot of his effigy was, she thought, a fitting one:

> *EYDMOND*
> *THANE OF LEWES*
> *d.1067*
> *Men live. Men die.*
> *Kings rise and fall.*
> *There is but one thing*
> *Conquers all.*
> *'Tis*
> *LOVE*

Her waters had broken just after they returned to the house. She had passed the remainder of that day and evening tucked up on the sofa in the drawing room, with carriage rugs covering her and a pot of tea and a bowl of beef-barley broth to sustain her.

A few uncomfortable cramps had begun soon after supper, but her labor pains had not started in earnest until about nine. Doctor Smythe and Mother Lee, the village midwife, had been summoned by Trevor at around midnight, when her pains had increased in severity and length, and were much closer together.

Jonathan had entered the world three hours later, pink, bloody and squalling, yet so beautiful, he had brought tears to both his mama's and papa's eyes.

"This birthing business isn't nearly as bad as everyone implies, is it?" Madeleine murmured, tracing the perfect pink whorl of her baby's ear. It reminded her of a sea shell. "We'll have to talk to Papa about getting a baby sister for you, just as soon as we can, hmm?" she murmured as they both drifted off to sleep.

Chapter Twenty-four

Steyning Hall
1801

"Yes, Digby? What is it?" Justin asked, opening the bedchamber door a few inches.

"I apologize for waking you at this hour, milord," Digby murmured, "but according to the stableboy, you left explicit instructions on the matter. . . ."

"I did?" Justin asked, his voice thick with sleep. He rubbed a hand over his face, feeling the rasp of new bristles as he tried to clear the fog from his thoughts. "And on what matter was that?"

"The mare, sir. Moondancer, I believe the . . . um . . . animal's name is. Mr. Nowles's stable lad

Penelope Neri

asked me to tell you she is about to deliver her foal, sir."

Justin's sleepy eyes lit up. All traces of his former fatigue vanished instantly. "Is she, by jove! Well, for your information, this is not just any old foal, Digby! This is our *first* foal. The first Steyning Thoroughbred!

"Tonight, a new enterprise will begin—one that will place Steyning Hall's stables on the road to recognition as one of England's top Thoroughbred-breeding stables!"

"By Jove. Will it really, sir?" Obviously impressed, the usually impassive butler allowed himself a small, rare smile. His lordship's excitement and enthusiasm was contagious. "Then perhaps I shall join his lordship out at the stables for this momentous event, if I may be so bold, sir?"

"By all means, do. Have Nanny wake the children, too, would you?"

"Nanny and the children, sir?" Digby's white brows rose in surprise—and, Justin noted, with pleasure, too. "At this hour?"

"You heard me. I want everyone to be there. This unborn foal is our future—Steyning's future—after all."

"Very well, sir."

"Oh, and Digby?"

"Sir?"

"Before you join us, get rid of that striped nightgown and that ridiculous nightcap! I don't want the children seeing you like that. It'd scare the daylights out of them." He grinned. "And make Nanny Winterbottom laugh, to boot. We wouldn't want that, now, would we, Digby?"

He hoped his question might wrench a rare reaction from Old Dig, but it did not.

"Indeed, we would not, sir," Digby agreed, implacable as ever, much to Justin's disappointment. "May I also take the liberty of bringing a bottle of champagne up from the cellars, sir?"

"Splendid idea! But make that two or three bottles. And milk for the children. Bring enough glasses for everyone concerned."

Digby blinked, looking owlish in the light of the candlestick he was holding. "Everyone, sir? Am I understanding you to mean Nowles and his . . . er . . . underlings, too?"

"Down to the youngest stableboy, yes," Justin confirmed.

He hadn't reached this momentous occasion on his own. It had taken the hard work of everyone involved with the horses—and the love, understanding and patience of those others who, although perhaps not as involved in the day-to-day running of it all, offered their support, understanding, and patience, nonetheless.

In just a few minutes, Madeleine and the children were awake, dressed and ready to go down.

Warm coats or capes had been thrown on over their nightclothes and stout boots covered their feet.

Nanny Winterbottom was up and awake, too, yawning and wearing a mob cap over her braided brown hair. She looked like a sleepy dormouse that someone had dressed in human clothing. Not, he wouldn't have thought, the sort of woman to inspire unbridled passion in a confirmed misogynist like his butler, which just went to show that there was no accounting for taste, since Old Dig was clearly smitten with his Persephone.

"Papa?" Little Jonathan Edmond tucked his small hand inside his father's. "Where Jonfin going, Papa?"

"We're all going to the stables, to see Satan and Moondancer's new baby," Justin gently explained to his small son. These days, the little lad was all questions. Who? What? Where? When? Why? How?

"Will Jonfin's baby bruvver be there, too?"

"I dearly hope not, darling!" Madeleine said fervently, waddling across the bedchamber with their little daughter in her arms.

"Why not, Mama?" Jonno asked.

"Because it's not time for him . . . for her . . . for the new baby to be born yet."

"Oh. When will it be time, Mama?"

"Soon, darling. Very soon."

"But, when is soon?"

"Oh, perhaps two more Sundays."

"What's a Sunday?"

"That's the day we all go to church. Remember?" Justin reminded him with a grin, chucking him beneath the chin.

"Jonfin 'member that," Jonno declared triumphantly, beaming. "The puppy lady's there!"

"That's right. The lady that gave Jonathan his very own puppy. Her name is Mistress Cargill, can you remember that?" Madeleine was still unsure whether to thank or curse her friend, Althea for the gift of Puddles. Although a dear little creature with a gentle disposition, the ten-week old spaniel puppy had not been given his name without reason.

"Will you take Emily, my dear? She's cross about being woken up and doesn't want me or Nanny to carry her," Madeleine said, tousling her son's head with her free hand. Bless him. He was almost as fair as she was, whereas Emmy was her father's daughter in every way, with dark blue eyes, coal-black curls and a smoldering temper.

Justin laughed and kissed his wife's brow. "She doesn't, hmm, the minx! Very well then. Come to Papa, Princess."

With two-year-old Emily Jayne carried on his shoulder, her Mama following close behind, fastening the sash of her wrapper over her enormous belly as they went, the family made its way downstairs, through the darkened house, and out, into the frosty March air.

A few stars still shone above. The pale moon poked a fingernail crescent of light from the charcoal sky. The door to the stables stood ajar, making a wedge of welcoming light against the dark stableyard.

Nowles nodded in welcome as they all crowded into the tackroom, where bridles, lunging reins and other pieces of tack were stored.

" 'Mornin', milord." The head groom nodded cordially.

"Good morning, Nowles. Time, is it?"

Nowles grinned. "Aye, milord. Any moment now, an' the first of Satan's foals by 'Dancer will be here. As I told ye, she began baggin' up a week or so ago, but didn't start waxing till yesterday."

By waxing, Nowles meant that milk had begun appearing at the ends of the mare's teats, Justin recalled, nodding. Waxing was an indication that a mare would foal within the next day or so.

"Her parts started slackenin' this morning, and she got proper restless earlier this evening. Then about a quarter hour ago, she lay down. It won't be long now, unless something goes awry."

Justin could hear the excitement—and the nervousness—in Nowles's voice. Even so, the head groom winked at his pet, the little princess with the inky curls who peeped and waved sleepily at him from her Papa's shoulder. He also ruffled his little lordship's fair head.

Nowles's face and the faces of the grooms and stableboys looked very ruddy in the lanterns' light. And, although they spoke in low murmurs, nothing could quite disguise the pent-up excitement in their voices or the bright anticipation of their eyes. The shadows their figures cast on the walls of the boxes and stalls looked like giants.

Emily Jayne clung very tightly to her papa's neck. She was not sure yet if all of this was real, or what Mama called a "bad dream." Papa would keep her safe, whatever it was. Mama said Papa knew 'zackly how to chase bad dreams away.

The smell of horses, straw, horse liniment, manure and lamp oil was pungent yet not unpleasant. Moondancer lay on her side in the straw, whickering softly. Nowles removed his coat and went to kneel at her hindquarters, where his undergroom was already positioned.

"Easy, my lass. Easy, there," he crooned in the soothing tones his horses knew and responded to, stroking her side.

The moment came faster—and far easier—than anyone had dared to hope. Not ten minutes later, exactly three-hundred-and-forty-five days since Satan stood at stud to sire him, his foal slithered free of the maiden mare's body, still in its slippery sac of membranes. It entered the world two feet first.

At once, Andy Cox, the undergroom, eagerly reached out to help the foal, but Nowles stayed his hand with a shake of his head.

"Let 'em go, Andy, lad. Our lass knows what to do, aye, 'Dancer? Never interfere with a foaling mare, unless she or the little 'un are in trouble, or unless the mare's had troubles before. Mares—even maiden mares—are born to do this. It's instinct, lad. It's in their blood. Let 'em get on with it, aye?"

Cox nodded. "If you say so, Mr. Nowles."

"I do, lad. I do."

Moments later, an ebony colt struggled free of the membranes, aided by its mother's rough tongue. Within the quarter hour, it was standing on spindly legs in the clean straw, wobbling unsteadily as it looked up at its mother.

"Hurray! My bruvver!" Jonno cried, clapping his chubby little hands in delight.

Everyone roared with laughter.

Startled by the sudden burst of sound, the little colt lost its precarious balance. Its dainty legs folded beneath it.

"Not quite, Master Jonno," Digby corrected the little boy. "But close," he added with a wink for Nanny Persephone Winterbottom, who dimpled, turned pink and smiled. "Very close."

"Speak to your son, Justin. It would appear he's still quite confused about colts and babies and which comes from where," Madeleine implored. "Now he probably thinks his mama will give birth to a little horse, too!"

Justin chuckled as he eased the cork from the first bottle of champagne. It opened with a dull "pop" and a breathy sigh.

"You mean a foal, *chérie*. Or—in this case—a colt!" He splashed sparkling wine into each glass in turn, handing them to Digby and Nanny to pass out. The stablelads grinned and held their glasses awkwardly, yet looked enormously pleased with themselves, nonetheless.

"Gentleman, ladies, children," Justin began with a proud grin. "Let us all raise our glasses to welcome the first colt born here at Steyning's Thoroughbred Stables, sired by our own founding stallion, Satan, standing at stud for one of our own mares. Have you a name for our first colt, *chérie?*" he asked his wife.

"You want me to name him?" she asked in surprise.

"Please." He handed her a glass of champagne.

"All right." She smiled with pleasure. "I suppose it's only fair, since I wasn't allowed to name my own children. . . ."

"God forbid. We couldn't have that!" Justin teased her. "We might have ended up with names like . . . Hypatia Maud or Algernon Percy." He shuddered.

When she laughed, he noted the way her violet eyes sparkled in the lantern light. After almost four years of marriage, she looked lovelier than ever, with her pale blonde hair still disheveled from sleep, and her face flushed and radiant with his third child.

She drew a deep breath. "Very well. I have a name for the new colt. One that I hope you'll like. Since his mother is Moondancer, I think we should call him Moonshadow. He's as dark as any shadow, after all."

"*Moonshadow!* It's perfect. Did you hear that, everyone? The new colt's name is Moonshadow. Charge your glasses for the toast, everyone." He lifted his own glass. "To Moonshadow, and the future of Steyning Thoroughbreds!"

"To Moonshadow!" Their murmurs echoed his ringing toast.

Although exhausted, as soon as the afterbirth had been delivered, Moondancer whickered and began licking her son.

His short tail whisking about like a fly swatter, the colt nuzzled and butted at his dam's belly, hungry and eager to nurse. Finding her engorged udder, he latched onto the teat and started to suckle. Moondancer seemed surprised by this development. Her ears flicked up and Madeleine laughed as the mare craned her elegant head to stare back at her handsome son. However, she stood patiently, making no attempt to push Moonshadow away from her udder, or to bite her baby.

"I know exactly how you feel, Moondancer," Madeleine muttered, her hands clasped over her belly as she looked at the mare. As if in response, the baby moved beneath her palms, rolling like a dolphin. "I only hope my own delivery goes as quickly and easily as yours."

"I'll second that," Justin declared, slipping an arm around his wife's almost non-existent waist. "We should let mother and son get some rest now. Back to bed with you, *chérie*. Nanny Winterbottom? It's time the children returned to the nursery, I believe."

"Quite right, milord. Come along, now, Miss Emily. Master Jonathan, hold Nanny's hand and tell Mama and Papa goodnight."

After the children and Nanny had returned to the house, escorted—Justin could not help but note—by none other than Digby himself, Justin slipped his arm around his wife and led her outside, into the stableyard.

While they were witnessing the birth of the new colt, the sky above them had lightened from charcoal to gray streaked with glorious lemon and saffron and every shade of salmon and rose. Birds were beginning their morning chorus in the trees and hedgerows.

Justin halted. He stood, staring thoughtfully up at the house. His lower cheeks and jaw were dark and bristly with beard-shadow in the gray light of dawn, but to her, he looked just as handsome, just as striking, as he had that first day in his Cousin Charles's rose garden at Whitchurch.

"It doesn't look half bad anymore, does it?" he said with obvious satisfaction. He sounded a little surprised.

"The house, you mean?" She looked up at the Hall, as if seeing it for the very first time.

Nothing had changed—at least, not physically. The gray stone walls and mullioned windows, the chimneys and the gabled roofs of copper, turned verdigris by time and weather—looked just as they had the first time she'd seen them, on her wedding day, four years ago last June. But there were changes, nonetheless.

Some of the ancient gloomy trees that surrounded the house had been cut down to allow more light into the rooms of the old Hall. The priory's tangle of lawns had been cleared and wicker garden furniture set out there, making it a delightful spot to take tea on sunny summer afternoons.

As for the house itself . . . despite the early hour, many of Steyning's windows were already filled with light; warm, welcoming, amber light!

But the most important change by far was one that went far deeper than lights, lawns and pruned trees. The Hall's foundations and walls were no longer steeped in sadness and misery. The miasma of sorrow that once pervaded the place had been replaced with the warm memories that were the milestones of a family's happiness.

Steyning Hall was no longer just a heap of stones, a place of nightmares and sad, frightening memories. It had become, quite simply, a beloved and happy home. Her and Justin's home, and the home of their children.

"I was right," Justin murmured, brushing his lips over hers.

"About what?"

"I always knew having you at Steyning would change things for the better."

"Then I was right, too, because I always knew we'd be happy," she replied, laughing.

He caught her about the waist and drew her to him.

"Hmmm. I love you, Madeleine."

"And I love you, Justin."

Arm in arm, her head resting on his shoulder, they went inside.

Sweet dreams, my lady fayre.

"Did you hear that?" Justin asked, pausing on the kitchen threshold, his dark head cocked.

"The dawn chorus?"

"No." He frowned. "Not the birds. That . . . voice."

"No. Not a thing," Madeleine murmured blithely, the fingers crossed on both hands, so that her tiny lie would not count.

She would wager that henceforth, neither of

them would hear that voice again. Like the house, Eydmond, thane of Lewes was at peace now, beside his lady and his love.

She smiled. Her face shone, radiant as a light. "Not a blessed thing!"

Seduction By CHOCOLATE

Nina Bangs, ♥ Lisa Cach, Thea Devine, ♥ Penelope Neri

Sweet Anticipation . . . More alluring than Aphrodite, more irresistible than Romeo, the power of this sensuous seductress is renowned. It teases the senses, tempting even the most staid; it inspires wantonness, demanding surrender. Whether savored or devoured, one languishes under its tantalizing spell. To sample it is to crave it. To taste it is to yearn for it. Habit-forming, mouth-watering, sinfully decadent, what promises to sate the hungers of the flesh more? Four couples whet their appetites to discover that seduction by chocolate feeds a growing desire and leads to only one conclusion: Nothing is more delectable than love.

___4667-9 $5.50 US/$6.50 CAN

KEEPER OF MY Heart

PENELOPE NERI

Morgan St. James is by far the most virile man Miranda Tallant has ever seen and she realizes at once that this man is no ordinary lighthouse keeper. But while she does not know if he has come to investigate her family's smuggling or if he truly has been disinherited, one glance at his emerald-dark eyes promises her untold nights of desire. Bent on discovering the blackguards responsible for his friend's death, Morgan doesn't expect to be caught up in the stormy sea of Miranda Tallant's turquoise eyes. The lovely widow consumes his every waking thought and his every dream with an all-encompassing passion. For while he cannot abandon his duty to his friend and his family, he knows that he can not rest until Miranda's heart is his.

___4647-4 $5.99 US/$6.99 CAN

SCANDALS

PENELOPE NERI

Marked by unwarranted rumor, Victoria's dance card was blank but for one handsome suitor: Steede Warring, eighth earl of Blackstone. Known behind his back as the Brute, he vows to have Victoria for his bride. Little does she suspect that Steede will uncover her body's hidden pleasures, and show her that only faith and trust can cast aside the bitter pain of scandals.

___4470-6 $5.99 US/$6.99 CAN

A Passionate Magic

Flora Speer

Sent as an offering of peace between two feuding families, Lady Emma is prepared to perform her wifely duties. But when she first lifts her gaze to the turquoise eyes of her lord, she senses that he is the man she has seen in her most intimate visions. Dain of Penruan has lived an austere life in his Cornish castle on the cliffs, and he doesn't intend to cease doing so, regardless of this arranged marriage to the daughter of his father's hated rival. But though he attempts to disdain Lady Emma, the lusty lord can not ignore her lush curves, or the strange amethyst light sparkling from the depths of her chestnut eyes. Perched upon the precipice of a feeling as mysterious and poignant as silvery moonlight on the sea, Lady and Lord plunge into a love that can only have been conjured by . . . a passionate magic.

___52439-2 $5.50 US/$6.50 CAN

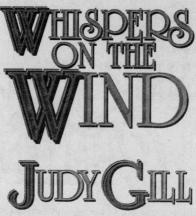

WHISPERS ON THE WIND

JUDY GILL

In a secluded cave amid the Canadian Rockies Lenore finds Jon: the lover of her dreams, a man quite literally from another world. In a desperate bid for survival he has sought her out telepathically. Injured and separated from his crew, Jon's success, the future of his planet, his very life depends on Lenore. She denies him nothing, sharing her home, her knowledge, her strength, and eventually her heart. Until what had begun as mere caresses of the consciousness progresses to a melding of not only bodies, but souls.

___52435-X $4.99 US/$5.99 CAN

Dorchester Publishing Co., Inc.
P.O. Box 6640
Wayne, PA 19087-8640

Please add $2.50 for shipping and handling for the first book and $.75 for each book thereafter. NY, NYC, and PA residents, please add appropriate sales tax. No cash, stamps, or C.O.D.s. All orders shipped within 6 weeks via postal service book rate. Canadian orders require $2.50 extra postage and must be paid in U.S. dollars through a U.S. banking facility.

Name _____
Address _____
City _____ State _____ Zip _____
I have enclosed $ _____ in payment for the checked book(s).
Payment <u>must</u> accompany all orders. ❏ Please send a free catalog.
CHECK OUT OUR WEBSITE! www.dorchesterpub.com

CHRISTINE FEEHAN DARK CHALLENGE

Julian Savage is golden. Powerful. But tormented. For the brooding hunter walks alone, always alone, far from his Carpathian kind. Like his name, his existence is savage. Until he meets the woman he has sworn to protect. . . .

When Julian hears Desari sing, emotions bombard his hardened heart. And a dark hunger to possess her floods his loins, blinding him to the danger stalking her, stalking him. And even as Desari enflames him, she dares to defy him—with mysterious, feminine powers. Is Desari more than his perfect mate? Julian has met his match in this woman, but will she drive him to madness . . . or save his soul?

___52409-0 $5.99 US/$6.99 CAN

He rides out of the Yorkshire mist, a dark figure on a dark horse. Is he a living man or a nightmare vision, conjured up by her fearful imagination and her uncertain future? Voices swirl in her head:

> They say he's more than human.
>
> A man's life is in danger when he's around . . .
>
> And a woman's virtue.

Repelled yet fascinated, Lucinda finds herself swept into a whirlwind courtship. Yet even as his lips set fire to her heart, she cannot forget his words of warning on the night they met:

> Tread softly. Heed little that you see and hear.
>
> Then leave.
>
> For God's sake, leave.

Whether he is the lover of her dreams or the embodiment of all she fears, she senses he will always be her . . . devil in the dark.

___52407-4 $5.99 US/$6.99 CAN

Dorchester Publishing Co., Inc.
P.O. Box 6640
Wayne, PA 19087-8640

Please add $2.50 for shipping and handling for the first book and $.75 for each book thereafter. NY, NYC, and PA residents, please add appropriate sales tax. No cash, stamps, or C.O.D.s. All orders shipped within 6 weeks via postal service book rate. Canadian orders require $2.50 extra postage and must be paid in U.S. dollars through a U.S. banking facility.

Name_____
Address_____
City_____ State_____ Zip_____
I have enclosed $ _____ in payment for the checked book(s).
Payment <u>must</u> accompany all orders. ❑ Please send a free catalog.
   CHECK OUT OUR WEBSITE! www.dorchesterpub.com

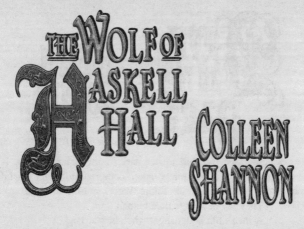

THE WOLF OF HASKELL HALL

COLLEEN SHANNON

With the coming of the moon, wild happenings disturb the seaswept peace of Haskell Hall. And for the newest heiress, deep longing mingles with still deeper fear. Never has she been so powerfully drawn to a man as she is to Ian Griffith, with his secretive amber eyes and tightly leashed sensuality. Awash in the seductive moonlight of his tower chamber, she bares herself to his fierce passions. But has she freed a tormented soul with her loving gift or loosed a demon who hunts unsuspecting women as his prey?

___52412-0 $5.99 US/$6.99 CAN

THE SCARLETTI CURSE
CHRISTINE FEEHAN

Strange, twisted carvings adorn the *palazzo* of the great Scarletti family. But a still more fearful secret lurks within its storm-tossed turrets. For every bride who enters its forbidding walls is doomed to leave in a casket. Mystical and unfettered, Nicoletta has no terror of ancient curses and no fear of marriage . . . until she looks into the dark, mesmerizing eyes of *Don* Scarletti. She has sworn no man will command her, thinks her gift of healing sets her apart, but his is the right to choose among his people. And he has chosen her. Compelled by duty, drawn by desire, she gives her body into his keeping, and prays the powerful, tormented *don* will be her heart's destiny, and not her soul's demise.

___52421-X $5.99 US/$6.99 CAN